A WOMAN SCORNED

A Novel

Darrin Lowery

iUniverse, Inc.
New York Lincoln Shanghai

A Woman Scorned

iUniverse books may be ordered through booksellers or by contacting:

iUniverse
2021 Pine Lake Road, Suite 100
Lincoln, NE 68512
www.iuniverse.com
1-800-Authors (1-800-288-4677)

This is a work of fiction. All of the characters, names, incidents, organizations, and dialogue in this novel are either the products of the author's imagination or are used fictitiously.

ISBN-13: 978-0-595-43687-3 (pbk)
ISBN-13: 978-0-595-88020-1 (ebk)
ISBN-10: 0-595-43687-0 (pbk)
ISBN-10: 0-595-88020-7 (ebk)

Printed in the United States of America

Special Thanks To the Following:

Knowing Books & Café

OOSA Online Book Club

Rawsistaz.com

Brenda Hampton and all of Saint Louis for your Support!

Tracy L. Foster

Infini Promoters

Ms. Toni

Waldenbooks in Calumet City

The Macro Publishing Group

Lissa Woodson

J.L. Woodson

Trista Russell {More Thanks at the end of the book}.

PART I

CHAPTER 1

▼

INTRUDING ON MY TIME

INTRODUCING, DEJA GAMBLE

It's 1:00 AM, and Mark isn't home. I lay in bed impatiently waiting and wondering when he will come home *this time*. I know he's *with her*. I can't prove that he is, but I know that he is. I know in my heart. If I call him now he'll lie. He'll speak some mistruth that will put further distance between us. I don't want any more distance between us because I love my husband. I love him dearly. The thing is, the longer he stays with her, the more I feel as if I've been disrespected. Not that this is not disrespectful anyway, but the longer he stays out, *the more I feel disrespected.*

When a man cheats, there are rules of etiquette. You know, things that he should do if he really respects his woman. My biggest fear is that he no longer wants to be with me and deep down, he wants to be with her.

If he wants to be with her, it's simply because she's new. He doesn't love her. He can't possibly love her. He might think that he does, but that's his body talking. His mind and his heart—belong to me. It may not seem like it right now, but that's the truth. No, I'm not looking at things through rose colored glasses. I'm looking at things as how they are. God, I want him home. I want him in my bed. Even if he doesn't make love to me tonight, I want him *here*.

Mark is a handsome man in his late twenties. He is a stock broker for Harrison, Buick and Lowery, a financial firm in beautiful downtown Chicago. He makes $65,000 a year and keeps me in a lifestyle that a woman could grow to love. We have a huge five bedroom bungalow home, no pets, no rug-rats and believe it or not, a healthy sex life. We have twin Toyota Camry's, a whirlpool on the deck in the back of the house that will fit six people, and an Olympic sized pool. We're living pretty large for what started out as a middle income couple from the south side of Chicago. I have an MBA from National Louis University and he has an MBA from USC.

Once upon a time, we were in love. Once upon a time, we were new. This was before *her*. This was when we were young ambitious and driven. These days we are old, bored with our respective routines, and for lack of a better word—tired.

I think we began to grow apart when I got my job at Third Metropolis Bank. I started work as an analyst on the 3-11 shift while Mark worked a 9-5. When I got in he would be sleep, and when I woke up, he would be gone. That might have been the beginning of the end. I liked my job and he liked his. We didn't get to spend the time with one another that we used to, but hey, we still had weekends, right?

Every weekend Mark and I used to go out. We went to clubs, museums, fine restaurants and three times a year, we flew out of town to vacation in some exotic spot. So how did we get here? It makes me wonder every time. He still treats me like I'm "his queen", as he used to call me. He still takes the time out to tell me that he loves me. He still buys me nice things and we make love every other night. That is starting to slowly drop off also.

I don't have the drama that most other women have whose husband has stepped out on them *or at least not yet*. I don't get harassing calls, hang ups on the phone where I pay the bill, and he seldom puts me off for anything. I get my time and its good time at that. But I know that Mark has a mistress. I simply don't know who she is or where she's at. It certainly isn't for lack of trying. So how do I know that my man is stepping out on me? The same way that all women know—his patterns of behavior have changed.

Mark is a handsome man. He always has been. He stands 5 feet 10 inches tall, he weighs 175 pounds of lean muscle and from a distance he looks like Gary Dourdan, the fine ass brother with the light eyes from the TV series *CSI*. His hair is in twists, but it is neatly cropped and lined up nicely. He has arms like Roy Jones Jr. and thighs like an Olympic swimmer. He has the looks, the intelligence and the heart of a man that is to be desired. He is also a smooth operator which is how he hooked me to begin with.

HOW WE MET

We used to catch the train together every morning to our respective jobs after we both finished college. He was making about $30, 000 then and so was I. He worked as a CPA in a small firm and I worked as a bank teller at First National. We both hated our jobs then because here we both were with Master's degrees and we both knew people with Bachelor's degrees or no degrees that made a lot more money than we did. What was worse is they didn't have student loans to pay off.

Anyway, we used to catch the Metra Train in together to downtown Chicago, from the station at 89th and Loomis. He would read his paper and I would read mine. After seeing each other regularly for a while, he would smile and I would exchange one with him as well. We knew each other in passing but for a long time, a year to be exact, we were just two people that happened to take the same train. It seemed in the beginning, as if that was the only way that we would know one another. Each day we rode the train, and each day we exchanged small pleasantries. We either talked about the weather, the bears, the bulls or today's gas prices which is why we were both on the train. Each day we got to the station at exactly 7:15 AM and waited on the 7:30 AM train. Each day we both grabbed a paper and a coffee (large extra extra) and a yellow cake donut.

One day I was running late as hell. My apartment sink flooded the night before, the dryer in my laundry room didn't dry a damn thing the night before when I did my laundry, and my hair, lord knows my hair was a mess. I remember it clearly. It was a rainy Thursday morning and I missed the 7:30 train and *just barely* made it to the train station in time for the 8:00 train. I had no time to get a paper, no time for a donut, and I still needed to do my makeup. I ran for the train as it was ready to pull off. I was glad that I had my gym shoes on. That's how a lot of sisters do in Chicago. We wear our gym shoes to and from work and our good shoes we keep with us to wear at the job. I caught the train as it was leaving and I thought that particular day was one where I should have just called off. Every now and then, a sister needs a mental day. You know, a day to just re-set and regroup. I quickly maneuvered between the doors and was upset at how my day was starting. I walked through the cars to the seat that I normally sit in on the earlier train, and sitting there with a smile, two coffees, two donuts and an umbrella, was Mark.

"I waited for you. I thought you were going to stand me up today."

I was thrown off, but it was a pleasant surprise.

"You waited for me?"

"Yeah, you missed the 7:30 train and my day just doesn't seem to be the same without seeing you first each morning."

"Really?"

I smiled a gentle smile. He was sweet. He had to be kidding though because my hair was barley done, my clothes could have used a second bout with the iron and I felt naked without my makeup.

"You're sweet, but you must also be partially blind." I said jokingly.

"Why do you say that?"

"Because I know that I look a hot mess."

"Actually, from where I'm standing, you look kinda fine."

"Really?" I said a second time with a hand on my hip like I was in third grade.

"Really". "Would you like a little something to warm you up?" He said with a smile.

I was thinking to myself, *"Only if you think you can hang."* I kept my dirty thoughts to myself.

"Sure, how thoughtful" I said.

"I find myself thinking about you a lot. Tell me, what's your name?"

"Deja."

"Deja? I like that. Well Deja, my name is Mark, Mark Gamble."

"Well Mark Gamble, my name is Deja Gamble … I mean Hawkins!"

I blushed and we both smiled at my error. I don't know what made me stumble like that, other than the fact that he was fine as hell. I don't know what it was about Mark but at that moment in that instant, I pictured myself as his wife. I thought we would make a beautiful couple and although I never want kids, if we ever had them, I think they would be beautiful. They would just be short.

Mark is 5, 10 but I'm 5, 2. Not only am I short, but all the men in my family are short. From the waist up people tell me that I look like Jada Pinkett Smith. From the waist down, everyone tells me that I look like I should be the spokeswoman for Nelly's clothing line *Applebottoms*. I guess that means that I have a big ass. Hell, I know I do, but I try to down play it as much as I can. That day, Mark and I shared coffee, donuts and the occasional smile. At the end of the ride that day, I went to work, he went to work, and neither of made an attempt at collecting the other's phone number. I thought about him all day at work. That night I thought about him as well.

That next day, we were both surprised to see each other even earlier than expected. We both arrived at the train station at 6:55 A.M., twenty minutes earlier than we normally arrived. I guess we were both anxious to see one another again. I smiled as I saw him and he smiled an equally precious smile to me.

I was looking at him to see if he had coffee and donuts for me today. That next day was when he gave me my first fix. He handed me coffee and *GHIRARDELLI* chocolates. I had my first taste of that chocolate and thought that I was in love (with the chocolate of course). Since we were both early, we decided to make use of the time by getting to know each other better. I told him how I grew up in a two parent household and how I went to school at NLU and he told me about growing up with his mother in a single parent household, and how she had to bust her ass all her life in order to send him off to school at USC.

In twenty minutes we talked about life goals, children (neither of us wanted any) and career goals. We were both in jobs that we hated, and we were both in agreement that we were no where near being paid what we were worth. We talked and talked and talked until the train came. We then got on the train and talked some more. This time, at the end of the ride we exchanged phone numbers. He was 25 at the time and so was I. We talked everyday and night on the phone for six months. Every day we chatted to one another via email from our jobs. Then in another six months we had both switched jobs and were we working hard at climbing the ladder of success. We discussed triumphs, failures and gossip from our respective workplaces.

A year later, we went out on our first date. We had dinner at the Olive Garden. We went dancing at the Wild Hare then dancing at *Secrets Nightclub* in Dolton Illinois, and a romantic car ride back to my south-side Roseland apartment. He didn't come in. Instead he gently gave me a light romantic peck on the lips. I made Mark wait for a taste of honey. He waited patiently for another two months. After waiting so long, I saw no reason why I shouldn't give him some and also commit to giving him some as often as he would like. In a rare moment of spontaneity and independence, I asked Mark to marry me. He said yes. That was four and a half years ago. In four and a half years we have traveled, bought property, bought time shares and seen all of the U.S and most of the world.

In the beginning we used to hold hands, send one another cute notes, go on private picnics, and make love anywhere there was a hard surface. These days, we make love consistently and we always talk, but it's just not the same anymore. He makes time for me, we communicate now as much as we ever did and like I said earlier, we still make love. These days though, he just seems somewhat … distracted; it's also like I said, some of his behavioral patterns have changed as well.

PRESENT DAY

Mark has started moisturizing his skin. He not only moisturizes, he uses some top shelf stuff on his face. I mean stuff like *Lancome* and *Elizabeth Arden*. He always went to the gym, but now he has begun to swim competitively at 30 years of age. He plays organized softball with his company in Grant Park, which is something that he vowed to never do because we both hate baseball. Now he says that he does it to stay in shape. He has recently given up pork and red meat, which isn't necessarily a bad thing. He also drinks water by the gallon. Over the years he had gained a few pounds. He was always handsome and had amazing arms, but he was just starting to get a bit of a stomach on him. In the past few months not only is the stomach gone, he is looking ripped like he did back in the day.

His skin is also smoother and even his style of clothing has changed. He had a nice beard and goatee, but he shaved all that off. Rather than sport suits like he used to, he wears a simple silk shirt to work, and dress slacks. I don't mind the new and improved Mark, but I can't help but to wonder if the change is for me or another woman.

I gave in to the temptation. I'm tired of waiting on him to come home. I phone him and his phone rings four times. Then his voice message comes on:

"Hi, this is Mark. I can't come to the phone right now, but if you leave a message as well as the time that you called, I will get back to you at my earliest possible convenience, thanks."

"To page this person, press 1 now, to leave a message press two or wait for the tone." Said the mechanical voice of a woman.

[BEEP].

"Mark, it's me. Where are you? I'm waiting up for you. Please call me back."

[CLICK].

I hope I didn't sound too desperate. I hope I didn't sound too suspicious. He may be working. He may be out with his boys. Aw, shit. Who am I fooling? It's after 1:00 and it's a weeknight. He is out there messing around. I sat up in bed, turned on the digital cable and ate GHIRARDELLI chocolate until a half hour later when I heard the click of the front door.

CHAPTER 2

▼

AN HOUR OR MORE EARLIER

MARK

I don't know why Mercedes waits until the last damned minute to want to have sex. We had dinner today after work, we talked, watched some videos, listened to some music and now at 11:30, when I am getting ready to go home, she pulls this shit. She knows I have a wife at home. She knows that Deja will be home at any minute. There is no way that I can explain being out this late on a work night—again.

I was getting ready to go and I went to the bathroom to relieve myself of all the wine that she and I drank. When I emerged from the bathroom she had on a red baby-doll silk teddy with red high heels. She had on no stockings and apparently had placed lotion on her bare and muscular legs. Mercedes had the body of a cheerleader. She had so much ass that you could see it from the front by just looking at her hips. She had a golden yet caramel complexion, ruby red suckable lips and long black hair. My wife, Deja used to have long hair, but like most black women, she got lazy and decided that she could no longer keep it up.

"It's my goddamned hair and you aren't the one that has to pay for it or keep it up!"

That's what my wife told me when she and I argued about her cutting her hair.

"What if I offer to pay to have your hair done, will you keep it long then?" I asked.

"What? No! I'm tired of the long hair. I want to try something new!"

She tried something new. Yes she's still pretty, but I hate the hell out of her short hair. So while she's trying something new, I'm trying something new. No, cutting her hair is not grounds for having an affair. In fact cutting her hair is just a small thing that is wrong in our marriage. My thing is this; we have a lot of small problems that have evolved into big problems in our marriage. One of the problems is yes, the length of her hair.

Sisters say that their hair is theirs to do what they want with it. They say that we don't know what it's like to maintain a hairstyle. They say that we are insensitive. Fuck that. The woman I dated had long hair. The woman I married had long hair and the woman that I plan on continuing to have sex with will have long hair. White girls cut their hair and the shit grows back in months. Most sisters I know cut their hair and the shit never comes back. Then, when they realize that they look like a cute ass boy rather than a woman, they want their hair back. Some sisters, can grow their hair back or so I've heard. Most, when they figure out that the Halle Berry or Jada Pinkett style doesn't work for them, they go and get a weave.

I didn't sign up for a weave.

Mercedes hair is long as hell.

It's all hers.

And right now, it's looking good as hell to me.

Mercedes gives me a devilish grin and takes me by the hand. She walks me over to the couch and sits me down. She kneels in front of me and smiles. She undid my belt buckle.

"Mercedes, what are you doing?"

"What does it look like I'm doing?"

"It's late. I have to get home. You know *she* will be looking for me."

I refer to my wife as *she*. I use her name as little as possible. I don't want to disrespect my wife any more than I have. I try to get home before her and I try to keep my visits to Mercedes' house to a minimum.

She ignores my statement and begins to undo my pants. I move my hands to stop her although I don't try very hard. She is 5,4 and 140 pounds of just ass and tits. She looks like the rap artist, Trina. You know, the baddest bitch? I could easily overpower her, but I know what time this is and she knows what time this is. She smiles at my act to try and stop her, and she uses the little strength that she has to force my hands down and overpower me. I play along like she's too strong as she places her head in my lap and begins to bob up and down on my thickness.

I protest for a second or two and then there is the warmth of her mouth.

I look down at her head and I can't see her face because of her hair; her long, strong and beautiful hair. She takes me deeper into her mouth. She moans as if she is the one getting off on the act. My chest and stomach rise and fall, as she takes me to a special place. I bite my bottom lip to help stifle my moans. I then allow passion to take over and I grab a fist full of her hair and help her up and down my shaft. The room is filled with slurping sounds, my moans and her moans. She reached out for a small pillow on the couch. She placed one pillow on my legs and grabbed a second pillow for her knees. She's getting comfortable and plans to make her home in my lap for some time. She licks me with abandon. She kisses the head and the shaft as if to pay homage to it. She strokes me up and down, slowly exposing pre-cum juices. She licks the head and gets every drop. She handles my manhood like a frozen popsicle on a warm day in the south in August. She licks, slurps, moans and savors my taste. I grab a fist full of hair and take her.

I'm ready to come. She knows this. She waits until my leg begins to tremble and rather than keep a rhythm going so I can explode, she slows down. She does so to keep me hard and also to stop my soldiers from abandoning the fort. She sucks me slowly. She uses one hand to firmly hold on to me. The other she uses to play with herself. The more she plays with herself, the louder she moans. The louder she moans, the more turned on I am. That's not what is going through my mind though. I am thinking what all men think when they are being given head. *She enjoys this. She loves this. She is getting off on sucking my dick. She loves this special muscle of mine that brings her so much pleasure. She not only loves this dick, she worships it. She must!* I watch her slowly take me in and go down far enough to choke. Her gagging turns me on as does the saliva running down my shaft. It flows down me like sap from a tree, but she is there to lick every drop. She fingers herself faster and faster and her moans become louder and louder. All that can be heard now is slurping and moaning, both coming from her. I'm now quiet because her sounds are turning me on, they are taking me there, she moans and purrs like a new car, a fast car, a Porsche, a Lamborghini or yes, a Mercedes.

She moans louder and louder and finally she comes.

She gets up and turns her back to me. She hikes up the teddy and exposes her juicy ass. Her sex is already wet and ready for me. Without asking, she tears open a condom, puts it on me and lowers her ass, her prize, onto my manhood.

Again, I feel warmth, sweet, wet warmth.

Her back is to me and she leans forward and places her hands palms down on the coffee table in front of the couch. Bent over like this her ass is just—perfect. She bounces up and down slowly. She flicks back her hair and looks back at me to make sure that I'm satisfied. I look at her as if to say she is insatiable. She smiles a devilish grin and looks forward. She bounces on my shaft and I'm loving her warmth while smacking her round juicy bottom over and over again. I smack her caramel cheeks until they turn red. With each slap she moans louder. I swear she's getting wetter by the minute.

She reaches out across the table and grabs the remote. She turns the TV on. I think that it's a porno being played on the screen until I realize **it's us**.

"What the fuck?"

She looks back at me and smiles again.

"You don't want to see yourself? You don't want to watch yourself banging this ass?"

I didn't know what to say. She began to pick up speed and make that ass clap.

"Do you want me to stop? Do you want me to slow down?"

"No, keep going." I responded.

"You like this shit?"

"I love it baby."

"Not as much as I love this dick!"

She began to roll back and forth allowing me to go deeper and deeper in her. With each stroke, she became more vocal.

"That's it. That's it, yeah! Hit that shit. Oh baby, that's your shit. That's your shit right there. Damn you got a big ass dick. Damn you are opening me up, Shit papi, shit papi, I might not be able to walk tomorrow! Damn this is some good dick. That's that good shit right there!"

Mercedes knew how to stroke my ego. I was now watching myself on TV and watching that ass. When she started talking shit, I got right into character.

"You like that dick? Then say that shit! Let a nigga know! Let loose up in this MF. Don't stop now [slap] move that ass [slap] get that shit. Go on, ride that dick [slap] handle that shit Mercedes. Do that shit, give that pussy to me, work that juicy wet MF."

Mercedes got up and turned that ass around so it would face the TV. I began to suck her breasts and play with her clit. She offered me one breast and then the other. She held both of them and made me take turns sucking them slowly and hard.

"Let me taste my pussy juices. Let's take this condom off for a minute."

"Mercedes ... no."

She pulled off the condom and straddled me. I expected her to give me more head but she didn't. The warmth of her pussy was overwhelming. I got a few strokes off but then tried to get her off me. I wasn't trying to have a baby or bring anything home.

"Mercedes, get up."

She kept rocking.

"I just want to ride a little while" she whispered in my ear. "I just want your bare dick wet with my pussy juice. You feel how wet it is? Just six more strokes and I will get up. Please baby? Just six more ... five more ... oh shit ... three more ... two more ... oh baby, oh baby just ... oh baby just one more ... one more ... stroke ... that's it. That's it, I'm cumming." She rocked and rocked and rocked and what was supposed to be six strokes came out to be about thirty. I was in control though. Her pussy was throbbing. I could feel her pulse. I could feel her vaginal and stomach muscles tighten. She came—hard. My dick was soppy wet with her juices. She then rested on top of me, kissing me deeply on the mouth. Minutes later she got up and as promised she began jagging me off and licking and sucking all her juices off my dick. That shit turned me on like a MF.

"I love the way my pussy tastes on your dick."

Just saying that shit almost made me explode in her mouth.

"Come in my mouth."

"What did you say?"

"Come in my mouth."

Generally I would climax in her, *in a condom*. Sometimes, if she gave me head, I would climax on her chest and she would rub it all in like a lotion. Today was new. Today's shit was extra. She said the one thing that most men want to hear.

"Mark baby, come in my mouth ... please?"

Who was I to argue with her? I began to jag myself off with my right hand and guide her head onto my dick with the other. Between the warmth of her mouth, the sight of her head bobbing up and down on my dick, and the sight of her naked ass on the TV screen, I was excited as hell. Just as I was about to cum, my cell phone started buzzing.

"Aw shit." I said.

"Fuck her, keep going."

"What did you say?"

"Fuck her."

I was about to stop. This bitch has obviously forgotten her place. She could tell that I was getting mad.

"Fuck ..." she started to say.

"Don't say that shit again." I said sternly.

"Fuck my mouth."

That softened my stance for a minute.

"Fuck my mouth Mark. Come in my mouth. Make me swallow your seed. I want your come in my mouth."

I stood up, grabbed a fist full of hair, moved the rest to the side, and began to fuck her mouth as ordered. I was jagging off faster with one hand and forcing Mercedes to take in as much of me as she could. Minutes later I was almost there.

"Oh shit, I'm gonna cum. Oh shit, I'm gonna cum. Oh shit … Oh shit … Oh … shiiiit!"

I exploded in her mouth. She closed her eyes and I made her take all of me. I made her lick every drop and lick me clean. She continued to jag me off and lick my balls and I swear that so much seed came out of me I was ready to re-populate the planet. I came so hard I thought I had burst a blood vessel in my brain.

"Oh shit." I said as I collapsed onto the couch.

Mercedes turned off the TV and went to clean herself up in the bathroom. As she did, I pulled up my pants, listened to my voicemail and tried to find the tape that was just made while I thought up a good lie to tell Deja when I got home. Minutes later after gargling and washing up, Mercedes emerged from the bathroom.

"Where's the video?" I asked.

"There isn't one. I figured you were too chicken shit for that, so I just turned a camera onto you to get you warmed up to the idea."

"So there is no tape?" I said in a concerned tone.

"No, look in the VCR and the DVD and the small camera on the TV set, there is no tape or video. There's nothing."

I looked at her suspiciously. I looked at the camera set up, and sure enough, there was no tape or DVD to speak of. I was feeling more comfortable now.

"So, what did wifey want?"

"Probably to know where I am."

"And what are you going to tell her?"

"I don't know."

"You could tell her that you have found someone younger, better looking and that will give you the sex that you really want."

"I could. Or I could just walk out of that door and never come back again."

"You would leave her?"

"I meant you. Look, Mercedes, you're fine as hell. You have no equal in bed, but I love my wife."

"If you love your wife, then why are you here?"

"Because you asked me to hook up with you, remember?"

"You didn't have to say yes."

"But I did."

"So again, you are here because?"

"Because I love the sex."

"And me?"

"Don't get it twisted. I like you. I love her. We're friends, that's all."

"You mean friends that fuck?"

"Yeah, I mean friends that fuck."

"Okay Mark, then I guess it's time that you went home to your wife."

"I guess so."

"Will I see you tomorrow?"

"I 'll probably stop at your job tomorrow."

"With Flowers?"

"With Flowers."

"For her?"

"For her."

"Can I get a goodnight kiss tonight?"

I kissed her.

"Can you kiss me like you aren't going to lay in another woman's bed tonight?"

I kissed her again the same way I first kissed her the first time.

"I'm going home to my bed, don't you forget that."

"So what am I supposed to do Mark?"

"About what?"

"You're the only man that I'm seeing right now."

"Start seeing someone else."

She gave me a look as if she couldn't believe what was coming out of my mouth. I didn't really want her to see anyone else. I wanted that ass all to myself. But I couldn't get caught up in the game. The struggle for control is always existent in husband-mistress relationships. Each are always vying for power. Each is always trying to hold on just enough to feel they are the one in control. I needed to keep Mercedes in check. She needed to stay in her place. The last thing in the world that I needed was to fall for her. Maybe seeing someone else would be good for us. It would help me to keep my distance from her. It would help me to keep my marriage. It would help me to not fuck up everything Deja and I have worked for over the years. This was an affair; it was just an affair, a fling that I could stop at any minute. At least that was the lie that I was telling myself.

I walked out of Mercedes condo, jumped in my car and sped off toward home.

I first had to stop at white castle and get a few burgers with extra onion.

CHAPTER 3

▼

TWENTY ONE QUESTIONS

DEJA

I heard the click of the door downstairs and Mark came in. I was expecting him to go to the bathroom and he didn't. That's usually a sign that a man is cheating. They will make a b-line for the bathroom. Instead, Mark came in with some white castle cheeseburgers, started eating, and turned on sports center on ESPN. I got up out of bed, walked downstairs in my bathrobe and had a conversation with my husband. It was going to be a conversation that I thought was long over-due.

"You're home late."

"Yeah, I had some work to do at the office and then I had some car trouble, and after that I went to some bar called the 9705 club to unwind for awhile."

"How is Adrienne?"

"Adrienne? Who is Adrienne?"

"She's the bartender at 9705."

"Really, are you sure?"

"Pretty Sure."

"Well she must not have been there tonight. The Bartender was some big black guy. I think his name is Tony."

"Oh?"

I wasn't buying the shit he was selling. He looked guilty the second that he found out I was familiar with the place that he mentioned. I knew the 9705 Bar well. I grew up on 93rd and Sangamon. 9705 is on 97th and Halsted. Adrienne was a good friend of mine and as long as I can remember she was always there. The 9705 bar had no male bartenders. Inside I was hurting. I knew in this moment that my husband was lying to me or at least I thought that he was. I hadn't been at the bar in a long time. Maybe I was wrong. Maybe, but my women's intuition told me otherwise. I decided to switch gears and change the conversation some.

"I called you." I said.

"Really, I didn't get the message."

"Really?"

"Really. Is there something on your mind babe?" He said innocently.

"Are you having an affair?"

"No, why? Are you?"

"Of course not."

"Then why do you ask?"

"Things have been different between us lately. Not only that, but you are up later and later these days, and you have to work in the morning. The other issue is that many of your behaviors have changed."

"Behaviors? What behaviors?"

"You're playing softball competitively now. You hate baseball."

"That's a networking opportunity."

"You're now moisturizing your skin."

"I should have done that years ago. I'm not getting any younger."

"What about your drastic change in attire? You seldom wear shirts and ties anymore."

"Sometimes I get tired of the same old shit! So let me get this straight, do I need to confer with you whenever I make a change in my routine?"

"No, but you have to admit, things look a bit out of place."

"Just because something looks a certain way doesn't mean it's that way. What is the problem here? We go out, we have a good time and as far as I can tell, everything is okay between us. Now if it's not, chances are it's on your end. If you aren't satisfied, then you need to speak up. So tell me, Deja are you seeing someone else? I mean really? Is that what is really on your mind? How do I know that you didn't just get in a few minutes before me?"

"I would never do that to you!"

"Oh, but I would do it to you is what you're saying."

"What I'm saying is, things are different between us."

"Different how?"

"I don't know how, but they are."

"Well, until you figure out what is so damned different, keep your accusations to yourself! They only put distance between us, or is that the plan?"

"Plan? What plan?"

"Who is it you're seeing behind my back Deja? What the fuck is really going on?"

"Mark, no one, I swear. If anything, it's you."

"Yeah, right … it's me. Goodnight Deja."

Mark got up and went into one of the guestrooms and went to sleep. I went back into the bedroom and I cried. Who did he think it was pulling that third grade-half reverse psychology bullshit on me? I have dated enough men to know that when they start accusing us, they are generally the ones messing around. I couldn't believe that he was trying to pull this shit. I expect that shit from most men, but not from my husband.

My husband.

A few minutes later the door to my bedroom opened up. In the doorway was Mark. He stood there silently for a few minutes before speaking. I turned my head away from him so that he would not see my tears. I closed my eyes and prayed for any other explanation as to why he was acting the way that he was. I prayed to God that I was wrong about Mark. Unfortunately, the devil answered.

"Baby, I'm sorry." He said.

I ignored him.

"D, baby, sit up, let's talk … it's me."

I closed my eyes tighter and let out a sigh. I searched inside me for the strength to deal with whatever it was that was about to walk out of his mouth.

I sat up slowly moving my hair out of my face, which was stuck to it because of the crying. I looked at him and he looked sad himself. He looked almost— guilty. Guilty or not, the look of sincerity on his face was enough to get me to at least listen to him.

"I'm not having an affair."

I looked into his eyes for some semblance of truth, some reassurance … but there was nothing. There was sincerity in his voice, but that's all. Sincerity, could be counterfeited, it was a gift men have mastered over the last two decades.

"I don't believe you."

He let out a gentle sigh.

"I've been having problems at work—financial problems. I have problems that may affect the both of us very soon. These are problems that I didn't want to burden you with."

"Go on."

"Baby, it's hard, hard for me to say."

The walls of my defenses were starting to go down. My anger slowly started to subside. His voice sounded almost fearful. I was starting to believe him but also getting scared myself.

"Go on." I said.

"I'd rather not."

"Mark, whatever it is, I need to know. I need to hear again that there isn't another woman."

Again he sighed. He came over to me, sat on the bed, exhaled yet again and told me something that I didn't want to hear, but something that put my heart at ease and in the same token made my mind race.

"We might be going through a merger soon at work. The word through the grapevine is that I, and others in my department might be losing our jobs. I've been talking with the competition, my boy Sean in Legal, and our financial planner. I have also talked with an attorney and my broker."

"Mark what are you saying?"

"I'm just planning things in the event that I lose my job. We can't maintain this house, the cars, and this lifestyle just on your salary."

"What about severance? We would be okay for a while. You should get severance and unemployment and we have a little money saved in the bank and then there is our vacation fund and ..."

"It's not enough." He said cutting me off.

"What do you mean?"

"There is talk of no severance, and the word from above is what is about to happen to us is almost as bad as the Enron scandal. My stocks, bonds and 401k are reportedly worth nothing. If the stock is bad, there is a chance that somehow the company has not been paying into unemployment insurance and even if they have, I'm sure with how many employees we have, there is still a danger of me coming out of this penniless."

The sincerity in his voice threw me off balance. I was no longer thinking that there may be another woman. I was no longer thinking with my heart. I was now focused on the new problem at hand.

"Mark, are you serious?"

"Yeah. It's been bad lately. Only a handful of us know or suspect this is what's going on. We have each been looking for jobs with the competition, looking for different careers entirely, and some of us are liquidating all of our assets in order to possibly start our own businesses."

"So why have you been out so late at night every now and then?" I asked needing additional confirmation that my marriage was still intact.

"Some days I can handle what's going on. Some days, I need a drink. Some days I need to drive. Tonight, I just couldn't face you. I needed to be away. I needed to get myself together. Then, when you started questioning me, I lost it. I figured you were cheating and if anything, you wanted out. I snapped like I did because all I could think of was that's one more thing in my life gone wrong. Seriously, I started to tell you if you have someone else, to move on to him."

I felt like shit. Here I was acting jealous and my husband was shouldering enough stress for the both of us. He was trying to protect me from worry. He was trying to keep me in the lifestyle that we have grown accustomed to.

"Mark, baby I don't give a damn about any of this shit. I don't care about this house, these cars, that pool ... baby if we need to go back to living in an apartment I'm okay with that as long as we have us. I can ask tomorrow if there are any openings at the bank. With your experience I'm sure that we can find something for you at a decent wage. I'll ask around. Baby you have to promise me something."

"What?"

"That if you are going through something you'll tell me."

"But ..."

"No buts. Listen, if you have a problem, we have a problem. Even if neither of us has the answer, the thing we need to do is see the thing through together. You hear me? We are in this together."

He smiled a soft smile at me.

Men are so proud. I wish they all understood that we women are a lot stronger than they give us credit for. I wish all black men out there knew that *the real black women have their back.* We can hold down the front too if need be.

I reached out to Mark and hugged him. It felt good to be in his arms again. It felt bad to know that we might be in financial trouble, but in the same token it felt good to know that I was the only one. My suspicions were wrong and rather than jump to conclusions, I should have asked before now. My man needed me and I wanted to be there for him. We hugged for a full minute before I started reaching for his package.

"Deja,. Do you think now is a good time for that?"

"I think so, why you don't?"

"No, I think it's a great time. It's just ... well I have been under so much stress, I don't want to disappoint you, that's all."

"How about I simply please you this evening to take your mind off things?"

"I don't know, I'm pretty stressed out."

"Then let me do all the work."

I helped him out of his pants and began to please him orally. It took a while to get him hard so he must have been stressed. His dick went from hard to soft to hard again. I was eventually able to get him consistently hard and within 20 minutes he came and went off to sleep. I placed the sheets over him and went back to sleep myself. In the morning I will see if there is any way that I can start working extra hours for overtime. He shouldn't be the only one planning for a rainy day. I can bring in some extra cash around here, that's what couples do. I kissed Mark on the cheek before drifting of to sleep. I said in a whisper, "Baby, Deja has got your back!"

CHAPTER 4

▼

THE CONSPIRACY

MERCEDES

Mark left and as soon as he did, I cut the TV back on to make sure that the recorder was still going. I then booted up my laptop which was on the desk next to the TV to make sure that I had all the footage of tonight's sex. I reviewed the DVD in the Laptop, and made an extra copy like I always do. I then put one copy in my video library and the other in my purse with all the others. Eventually, Mark will have to leave Deja. When he does, he is all mine. I just have to remember to keep him on a short leash.

I feel bad that I have to steal another woman's man but let's face it, there aren't a lot of good black men out there which means some of us have monogamy, some of us have to share, and some of us have to take what it is that we want. I want Mark. I know that shit is wrong but hey, if I can pull him, then he isn't Deja's man to begin with.

Men kill me with trying to say no to sex at the end of the evening. Mark had been trying to fuck me since I got home at 6:00 PM. I denied him then, not because I didn't want any, but because I knew what time *she got home.* What men and some women fail to realize is that mistresses know damn well what we are doing. When men get caught by their wives it's because either they wanted to get caught subconsciously, they are stupid to begin with, or the mistress is the one that set their ass up to get caught. That's why we wait until the end of the evening to try and get sexed. We want to plant seeds of doubt in the wife or girlfriend's mind. That helps put space between the two of you. We want the man to leave us smelling like fresh soap, fresh perfume, fresh cologne or **fresh sex.** That's all game. Men think they are the players. Now mistresses, we shouldn't even be called players or playettes. We should be called puppet-masters.

That's how I get down. Mark is a good man. He's a good man that went down the wrong path. Now that he's with me, I have to do my thing in order to get all my ducks in a row. Some women think that the man never leaves the wife for the mistress. That' bullshit. The man will leave the wife for the right mistress. That's why I'm the freak that I am. That's why I dress in lingerie. That's why I keep my hair long, stroke his ego and fuck him till his dick won't get hard anymore. I do all this shit because I'm the one.

Not all mistresses keep the man that they sometimes pursue. I just happen to want Mark. I've ruined quite a few marriages and near-marriages just to get the man that I wanted. Many times I will fuck a man until I get tired of him and then I send him on his way. Other times, I will play a player just because that nigga thinks he's the shit, and he needs to be brought down a peg or two. I plan to keep Mark. I plan to have him all to myself. Mark is going to be somebody. Mark already does okay financially, but he hasn't reached his full marketability yet. I plan to be there when he does, and at that time I plan to be Mrs. Mark Gamble. That is, unless he pisses me off. Then I will either divorce his ass and clean up financially or have his baby and clean up financially.

I have to break Mark in slowly. He's already up on some game and he keeps pretty good boundaries with me. He doesn't make some of the basic mistakes that men make when they take on a mistress. I call him on his cell phone or at work. He never calls me from his house phone. He never let's me know where he lives, and he and I basically go no where other than my apartment in Countryside Illinois. He lives in Chicago and if he and I go out, it's to neighboring suburb of my house like Hickory Hills, Justice and Matteson. Good boundaries are a key to having an affair. I think Mark understands that. The thing that he has to be worried most about is not getting pussy whipped, which is what I am working on with him now. They say that women can't differentiate between sex and love. Many women can't. Many women can't fuck a man without getting their feelings involved. I'm no different. I feel that I love him. The thing is, the same shit that affects women, affects men. Men sometimes get it twisted too. They sometimes will mistake good pussy for love and fall hard for a woman. That's not considered falling in love, so much as it is falling for the pussy.

I plan on having anal sex with him next week. I have been interviewing call girls that look clean, so we can possibly have a threesome. I'm not touching another woman or at least I don't plan to. But I have a whole host of plans for Mr. Gamble that will make him either leave his wife or fight with her. In either case it's just a matter of time before he leaves her. It's just a matter of time before, I win.

WHAT IT TAKES TO BE A GOOD MISTRESS

I keep my apartment stacked with lingerie, toys, videos, creams, wigs and costumes. The French Maid outfit is the shit! That, and the female cop uniform. I also have a laid apartment with top of the line everything, a $4000.00 laptop, plasma TV, and leather everything in my living room. I have Monet Prints on my walls, a double wide sleigh bed and unlike Mark, I drive a Lexus. You wouldn't believe that I roll like I do working part time as an Administrative Assistant. I work everyday from 11:00 AM-5:00 PM. My boss is a power broker named Justin Reynolds or JR. He thinks that I have a child which is why I work the hours that I do. I can't believe that with a body like mine that he would believe that I had anybody's baby. My shit is tight. I get up each day at 6:00 AM. I work out from 6:15-8:00 AM. I eat a light breakfast and then I go home and get in the shower. I then moisturize my entire body, stretch, do light yoga and get ready for work. I go in and work my six hours. Most days, my boss doesn't get there until noon. I get his daily reports done. I work on his itineraries, plan his travel dates, tell him how the market is doing and weed out all the knucklehead stuff that he doesn't want to see on his desk. From there, I walk around the other departments with him taking notes regarding the progress or lack thereof in each department and I keep him up on all the gossip in the office as well as who is rumored to make a run at his job.

When I get off work, I generally go to *Curves* for 30 minutes a day every other day to keep my body toned. On the weekends I date wealthy older men in Indiana and Evanston Illinois so I never make the mistake of running into Mark. The older men pay all my bills and I give them some once a month or so. My money is just that, my money. I make the older men give me money, t-bills, treasury bonds, jewelry and anything that they think is of value. I then take the shit that they give me and either have it appraised or sell it on EBay.

I put away the DVD of Mark and I having sex tonight and before turning into bed. I watched a DVD that he knows nothing about. I labeled it, "The beginning of the end." It's a 60 minute DVD where all Mark does is complain about Deja cutting her hair, complain about how he is bored with their routine, and bored with how they have sex. I plan to get some footage of us having anal sex, more oral sex, a ménage a trois and some role playing. If I can get all that footage and edit it right, that will be my trump card when it's time for Mark to leave Deja's ass.

He might think that he is with her until death do they part. But he will be with her until she is fed up with his antics. I call the DVD that I am watching the Beginning of the end because that's exactly what it is when a man starts complaining to another woman about his woman. That is a line that no man should ever cross if he's trying to hold on to a marriage.

CHAPTER 5

▼

FLOWERS, CANDY, A BIG BUTT AND A SMILE

MARK

I got up the next morning feeling guilty as hell about the lies that I told last night. Where did all of that shit come from? That shit just rolled off my tongue with no problem. I can't believe that I told Deja all that bullshit. Not only were we not in financial straits at my job, but I was damn close to making partner. In fact, I'm expecting a fat ass raise soon. Oh well, what's done is done. One thing is for sure though, I have a good woman at home and I need to respect that shit and set some clear boundaries with Mercedes.

I can never get caught cheating. A nigga is just too smooth for that. The reason I came in with the white castle cheeseburgers is to throw off her senses. I know all the secrets when it comes to cheating. Bring in food from a restaurant with a strong smell, take a players shower (which is where you wash up with just water so you are not smelling like fresh soap), make sure that you have on no lipstick, no perfume from another woman and no fresh sex smells. I know that this can be countered with the smell of food, coffee and a single spray of vanilla body spray to the genitals. Mercedes thinks that's she is slick by keeping me out late last night. That was indeed a mistake. I have to make it clear to her that I can only see her between 5:30-9:00 Monday–Friday. At 9:05, I am on the road home no matter what.

I walked into my job and jumped right into work. I phoned client's, looked at the market and worked on the Plato Program to tell me about upcoming spending trends and went to three meetings before noon. At 3:30 PM, I went downstairs, grabbed a dozen long stemmed roses from the florist on the first floor of my office building, and caught a cab to Madison and Dearborn to the upper offices of the bank to see my wife.

Deja was fine, but the women that she worked with were so tight that she sometimes looked average. The women in the bank were all fine and everyone there had a fat ass, including the white girls. I was starting to think that it was a damn pre-requisite at the bank that you had to be at least an 8 on a scale of 1-10 just to work here. I caught the elevator up to the 14th floor to the financial department and made a B-line for my wife's office.

Women in her department knew who I was. As I got closer and closer to Deja's office, women gave me all types of smiles. They thought it was sweet that I consistently brought my wife flowers. I didn't bring them because I was in the dog house (although sometimes I was). I brought them because I loved my wife. Each time that I brought her flowers, the card said the same thing, "Because I love you." The card was always dated and in all the time that we have dated, I brought her flowers maybe 100 times. This blew other women in the office away. I had the money set in my budget to consistently send my woman flowers because I'm the man that I am today because of her. Deja has always had a niggas back, and she always will. I try to bring flowers as often as I can. When I am too busy at work, I send them via messenger.

I walked up to the glass door and knocked. Without looking up, she ushered me to come in. She was on the phone with a client and filling out paperwork. She made about $20,000 less than I did, but you couldn't tell that by as hard as she was working. She looked up at me and smiled. I smiled back at her and thought to myself how beautiful my wife is. I just wish that she had never cut off her damned hair. Anyway, she still had a smile that could light up a room. I gave her the flowers and she cut the conversation with whomever she was speaking too short. She got up from her desk and hugged me. We then kissed like we were teenagers.

"You know, you have to stop with the flowers."

"Why? Is your other man is going to get jealous?" I said jokingly.

"No, I just figured that we needed to start watching our finances because, well you know?"

"No, what?" I had forgotten about my huge lie just that quickly.

"Because of our financial situation."

"What does bringing you flowers have to do with our finances?"

"I just don't want us to overextend ourselves if we don't have to."

Finally the light bulb went off over my head and I remembered what she was talking about.

"Oh, baby, no … No. I'm not going to let one thing influence the other. I plan to bring you flowers for the rest of your life, the rest of our lives."

"But Mark flowers can be costly and …"

"… And you are worth it. Now I don't want to hear another word about it. I love you Deja. I want to bring you flowers. Can I do that? Please?"

I gave her a huge smile and nuzzled a bit under her neck.

"Mark, stop. You had your shot at that last night." She said laughing.

"What, is there a limit now? Did my sex card expire? Do I need a coochie coupon or something?" I said laughing and still hugging her.

"No, but I started my cycle today. So I'm on strike for a few days." She said smiling.

"Well you know what they say? If there is blood on the front porch, go in through the *back door*." I said jokingly.

"Mark that's nasty."

"No it's not, it's just new."

"It won't be new with me."

"Never?" I asked.

"Never." She said confidently.

"Okay."

"Besides, comments like that make me worry about you."

"Worry? Why?"

"Because I think men that want anal sex, secretly want to sleep with other men."

"What?"

"You heard me. It's not unheard of with all these brothers out here on the down low."

J.L. King has no idea what he started with that book. It's a good book but damn!

"Baby, you can't mean that. Besides, you know I like pussy like I like oxygen."

"Boy you are silly. I just hope you aren't silly and Bi."

"What kinda shit is that to say?"

"It's just that every few months you are talking about fucking me in the ass. It's not happening. I hope that you don't think these flowers are going to soften my stance on that issue."

Now I was getting pissed off.

"I brought the flowers to say I love you."

"I love you too. I'm just tired of the anal innuendos. You have more important things to think about. We have more important things to think about."

"Like what?"

"Like our finances."

"Oh yeah, that. Well I'm working on that, don't trip. I got this."

"I know you do baby, but I'm going to help. I asked my boss for extra hours."

"You did what?"

"I am going to get here at Noon and stay until 3 a few nights a week. I already got the overtime authorized."

"Deja that's something you should have discussed with me."

"Our finances are something that you should have discussed with me."

"So when do you start this new schedule?"

"Tonight."

"Great." I said sarcastically.

"I know you're upset, but it will only be for a little while."

"I can take care of us Deja."

"I know that you can. All I'm asking is that you let me help."

I knew arguing with her was no good. She's a good woman. Because she is such a good woman, I felt like shit about cheating on her.

"Okay baby." I said reluctantly.

I hugged her tighter and kissed her on the cheek. She then spoke softly to me.

"Baby we'll get through this." She said.

"I know." I said back.

Just then a third voice spoke from behind us.

"Oh what lovely flowers."

We turned around and there was Mercedes in the doorway.

"Hello Mr. Gamble. It's nice to see you again."

"Hello Mercedes, how are you?"

"I'm great. Mrs. Gamble? Mr. Reynolds would like to speak with you as soon as possible ma'am."

"You couldn't just call me on the phone to say that?" Deja said sarcastically.

"I'm afraid not. Mr. Reynolds said right away ma'am."

"Then let's go." "Mark, I will see you later."

"Okay Babe."

"Bye Mr. Gamble."

"Goodbye Mercedes."

Deja and Mercedes walked down the hall together. I walked behind them because the elevator was on the way. They walked in front of me and all I could think about was the fact that Melyssa Ford and the model Ki-toy didn't have as much ass as Mercedes and Deja together. Both had a mean walk on them and both of them had ass for days. It was hard for me to keep my composure knowing that I was sleeping with both of them. Some days—both in the same day. It was wrong, but I wondered what a ménage a trois would be like with these two. I knew this would never happen because aside from being the wife and mistress (even though Deja doesn't know) the two of these women hate each other. Deja has hated Mercedes since she was hired, and Mercedes used to talk about Deja like a dog when we would fool around. I stopped that shit and put Mercedes in check about my wife. I think they both hated each other because in some ways they are a lot alike. In many ways they are very different. They are both beautiful black women and well, they are women which, is why I believe that they sometimes can't get along. I watched those asses bounce up and down in those form fitting skirts. It was like watching a subconscious battle royal between the biggest booties. Both women had to have strong thighs and legs and both had to be related to Serena Williams, that is the only way that I can see those legs supporting all that ass.

I got on the elevator and smiled at my wife who smiled back. At the last possible second before the elevators doors closed, Mercedes looked at me and winked really quick. That made my heart almost stop, especially with my wife on the other side of her.

"I need to check that bitch today!" I said out loud.

I took the elevator down.

I then said a silent prayer to myself.

"God, Please don't let Deja have seen that shit."

I went back to work for another two hours.

HOW IT ALL KICKED OFF (A FEW MONTHS AGO).

My wife's bank and my financial firm have to work together from time to time. I work with a guy named JR when we need additional backing or a loan for my firm. When the two companies had to work together, I would show up at their site because it gave me a chance to see Deja and it got me out of my office. Well, one day I was at Deja's office kicking it with her and that same day was when Mercedes had just gotten hired.

"Look at that heifer." Deja said. "She just got hired here and I bet she has no skills. The only reason that they hired her was because she I pretty and has a big behind."

"Is that the policy around here babe?" I asked sarcastically.

"You know what I mean. There are too many men in HR if you asked me, and that's why you have so much eye candy around here."

"Babe, the same could be said for you."

"I have my credentials! I wasn't hired for my looks."

"How do you know?"

"Because my resume is tight and I have worked hard to get where I am."

"That doesn't mean that they didn't hire you for your looks and ass also."

"What do you mean?"

"All I'm saying is, the eyes will see first, before the ear can hear. You were probably looked at for your ass and smile as well as her. You shouldn't be so judgmental."

"Look whose talking?"

I did sound a bit hypocritical. I judge people all day and most of the time, I have something negative to say. Anyway, I stayed with Deja that day and we had lunch. She eventually introduced me to Mercedes even though it was obvious that she couldn't stand her. Women are such interesting creatures. Here Deja was telling me how much she hated Mercedes and when it came time to introduce us, she was so damned polite. I think that is what they used to call being two-faced in grammar school.

I came to visit Deja once a month at work. It was good exercise walking to her job and like I said, it got me out of the office. Every now and then I would see Mercedes and every now and then I would speak. She would always give me a warm smile and some days she would look me up and down as if to inspect my package. I can't front, the girl is fine. I wanted to hit it from the first time that I saw her, but I'm a married man and I don't get down like that—or at least I used to be that way.

My company needed a loan from Deja's bank. We had money. In fact we had mad money, but so much exchanged hands sometimes, we needed what we called "front money" until certain deals went through. Sometimes this money was what was in an account for dummy investors. What we would do is put the money in account A, then tell a second customer that we could not disclose who else was investing but _____ was the amount that another prominent customer invested. That customer wouldn't know it, but they would be the first to invest and we would then use the front money and the second client's money and convince a third, fourth and fifth client to invest, and so on. By the end of the day, we would have so many customers invested, that no one would notice that the initial amount (the front money) would be given back to the bank by the end of the day. This was an illegal but very common practice at my job.

One day, I needed the front money to get a number of investors to back the company of a friend of mine whose company was about to go bankrupt. The problem that I had this one day was that my computer was down and so was the bank's. The electric company knocked out a whole grid by accident, and it was costing a lot of companies in downtown Chicago Millions of dollars. The phone was still working so I called JR to ask him for wire transfer numbers that I could use as well as what I referred to as "dummy files" in order to make everything sound legitimate. Not that I was scamming people, but sometimes with finances you have to work on faith and hunches. JR couldn't email me the file, so he sent it right over ... by Mercedes.

I was in my office on a conference call talking to a number of potential investors. They were all out of town customers that were worried because our black out was being televised and the Chicago market was taking a serious hit. I was on the phone with each on speaker conference, pacing back and forth waiting on this damn dummy file. I paced the room in my Silk Braggi Slacks, Hugo Boss shoes and Kenneth Cole shirt and tie. I looked like I was nervous by the way I kept pacing back and forth, but my voice said that I was cool, calm and collected.

A few minutes later, in walked Mercedes. She had on black 3 inch heels, sheer black stockings, a short form fitting black skirt that hugged the hell out of her ass, and a red silk blouse with a red lace bra underneath. Her breasts were practically spilling out of the top and she was looking stunning as hell. Her hair was long and done nicely and she had on red lipstick that accented her beautiful suckable lips. I was talking to the customers on the phone and the minute that Mercedes came in ... I was speechless.

"I ... um ... have that ... um file, right here ... gentlemen ... and I am confident ... that we ... will ... um ... um."

My eyes were fixed on Mercedes' cleavage. That, and her ass. Her ass was so fat that you could see it from the front like my man Mos Def would say.

Mercedes looked at me and smiled. I was embarrassed. It was obvious that I was looking at her like a flawless diamond. She handed me the file and rather than leave the office, she sat down in the recliner that sits across from my desk. I mouthed the words "thank you" and turned my back to her to gather my composure again. I went back to talking to my clients.

"Like I was saying gentlemen, if you check the following file number, you will see where 4 other investors have put it a significant amount of money. I'm telling you gentlemen, this is a window of opportunity and that window is closing soon. I'm looking to close this deal and make the news by the end of the day."

When I turned back around, Mercedes had undone yet another button on her blouse and she sat with her legs crossed. Her legs were smooth and muscular like Serena Williams. I saw her legs and turned away again to keep from stuttering. Again, Mercedes smiled and I knew then if she went back to her office bragging about my looking at her and Deja found out, I would need a divorce attorney by the end of the day.

"So what is it going to be gentlemen? I need to know now because I have other clients that I need to call."

Apparently Mercedes knew that I was lying. I guess JR told her why I needed the file. She smiled as I convinced each of the investors on the phone to invest a significant amount of cash. One by one they invested and one by one they helped to save the business of a friend of mine. Not only that, but they each stood to make a lot of money at the end of the day. I finished my transactions and when I turned around again to get off the phone, there was Mercedes staring me in the mouth looking devilish (devilish and cute that is).

I looked her up and down as if she were a unique piece of art. This black woman was beautiful from head to toe and I hate to admit it, but I was smitten with her. Her legs were strong and smooth and as I slowly glanced upward, I imagined her strong legs on my shoulders. Her hips were old school, you know, the baby making kind? And her breasts were plump and supple. Her nipples were erect in the light red delicate material. She had gumdrop type nipples. They were hard and pointing at me, almost as if to say, "come here." Mercedes had a smile that could soften a heart and bedroom eyes that immediately made a man think her name was Delilah. I was nervous as hell being in the room with this woman. Like I said, I'm a married man and I didn't get down like that. But there was something about her. There was something within her that called out to me. It was a gentle voice that said "fuck me." I knew that was what the voice was saying because that was the expression that was written all over her face. She looked at me like, *nigga what?* And I looked at her wrought with guilt.

Our eyes met.

It was obvious what we were both thinking.

I turned away.

She looked head on.

I looked back as if to say, *are we really going there?*

She looked at me, raised her eyebrow and licked her lips seductively, she then smiled and spoke like the true seductress that she was.

"You know, I don't like your wife." She said in a smooth voice.

"I'm sorry?" I responded. I was thrown off by her statement.

"I know that she doesn't like me."

"I don't know what you mean."

"It's written all over her face that she doesn't like me."

"I can't comment on that either way."

"I'm not asking you to. I'm just letting you know that it's not like she's a friend of mine or anything."

"And … you are saying all that to say … what?" I asked.

"Come on, we are both grown. We both know how you were just looking at me. Do we really need to play this game?" She said while ever so slightly licking her lips as if I were the last meal on earth.

"I don't know what you are talking about." I said fairly innocently, but not really.

"Okay, so you're married. I guess that means for arguments sake and future reference, you want the right to say that *officially* you didn't kick this thing off."

"Thing? What thing?"

"Our affair."

"What affair?"

"The affair that we are about to have. The affair that I imagine will start tonight at my place."

There was a long silence in the room.

We both knew what was up.

But I still had to follow the script.

For arguments sake.

"I'm married."

"I know."

"I can't give you what you want."

"You can … and you will."

"I won't."

"What you mean to say is this, you can't give me a lot of time but the time you do give me will be quality time. You can't give me birthdays or anniversaries or holidays, but you will try to make time around those dates. You can't give me weekends, because both you and *she* are off. You do want me. You do want to fuck me and you do want us to have an affair, but your wife can never find out. If she comes close to finding out or if one of us becomes attached to the other, you're walking, right?"

There it was, laid out in front of me like a rug on a floor.

She ran the full script. I stood there in silence. I love my wife. I really love my wife. She is good to me. She has my back. She loves me unconditionally. I have no reason to sleep around on her other than greed. I should walk away. I should walk away right now. But this is pussy being offered to me on a silver platter with no strings attached and Mercedes is one fine MF. What do I do? I decided the best course of action to take was to remain silent. Unfortunately, while silent I couldn't help but stare at her breasts, legs and thighs. As far as I was concerned, I was a starving man and she was a 12 piece.

Like my man Lyfe Jennings said, "Everything that shines ain't a dime." But Mercedes was definitely a dime-piece. If there was going to be an affair, I was not going to be the one to initiate it.

As if she heard my thoughts, Mercedes got up from the chair, sashayed across the room to me switching that ass, and she walked up on me and whispered in my ear.

"I tell you what. You get one shot at glory. Your wife gets off work between 11 and midnight tonight. I get off at five. If you want to be sucked, fucked and fed this evening, you will be at my house at six. If not, no harm no foul. We will simply act like you don't want to sleep with me, although we both know the truth. The ball is in your court. Stop by tonight, or wonder what could have been."

She walked over to my desk, bent over and wrote her address down. That ass was round, plump, and primed to be hit. She walked by me and gently caressed my hard dick as she headed toward the door. As quickly as she touched me there, she let go. She smiled to herself before whispering softly.

"I thought so. It would be a shame not to have it in my mouth later."

I became light headed and my knees buckled a little.

I thought to myself, "Damn!"

She left.

I sat in my chair and I didn't do another thing for the rest of the day. I locked my office door and tossed a ball in the air for one hour straight. I sat there and thought over and over again about what I would do to that ass. At 3:00 in the afternoon that day, I went home early and told my boss that I was sick. I did this after, closing a huge deal for my friend's business.

I went home and showered. I then paced my house back and forth as I tried to figure out what to do next. I walked around my house and looked at pictures of me and Deja. I looked at the house that we bought; the house that we made a home. I thought about the fact that I pursued her and when we got married I promised to forsake all others. I was definitely torn. It was a battle going on between my heart and my dick. Believe it or not, it was quite a battle.

I struggled with my emotions and my lust. I tried masturbating in hopes that after getting a quick nut, that I wouldn't want Mercedes anymore. I bust a good one, but I thought about Mercedes the entire time that I was pleasing myself. I thought about hitting that ass from every position. I thought about those juicy lips of hers pleasing me. I pictured that ass in the air as I approached her with savage passion, ready to hit it from the back. I then thought about my wife and what a fulfilling sex life that we shared and how much she meant to me. I took another shower and rubbed down with scented lotion. I then threw on a Roc-a-wear warm-up and some timberlands. I was still struggling about what to do next.

The next thing that I knew, it was 6:00 and I was in front of Mercedes apartment.

I was still struggling with what to do.

Only now I was struggling in my car—outside her place.

I took that long slow walk up her walkway. I thought long and hard about what it was that I was going to do. That walk up her walkway was like a man on a path to the electric chair. I walked slowly toward the door bell but never broke stride. I thought long and hard about what would happen. I thought about the bigger picture and how eventually, no good could come from all this. I walked toward the door and could almost hear the devil whispering in my ear, "Dead man walking." I took a path that many men before me took. It was a path that other men will one day follow. I took that walk knowing that I was gambling with someone else's heart, someone else's emotions and all that I worked hard for in my marriage to Deja. I rang the buzzer expecting to hear her voice on the other end of the intercom asking me who was it at her door.

She knew who it was.

There was no response.

She simply buzzed me in.

Damn, I'm weak.

I walked up to apartment 2E. I knocked on the door and slowly it opened and creaked like something out of an old 50's movie. Inside it was dark, but the room was dimly lit by candles everywhere.

Syleena Johnson's New CD was playing on the stereo. Mercedes was in a black silk teddy looking good as hell. She brought me a platter of fruit. It was about to go down. She put a couple of cold grapes in her mouth and bit into them. She then kissed me deeply on the mouth.

She tasted like fine wine.

I was intoxicated by her passion.

It was on!

I grabbed her firm round bottom and gave it a smack. She smiled at my lack of discipline. I kissed her on the lips and my hands explored her body. I cupped both breasts and tweaked her nipples with my thumbs and index fingers. I lowered my head and kissed her breasts through the material. She let out a moan like a kitten. I removed one of the spaghetti straps and released her left breast. I sucked on her nipple like a newborn. I cupped her ass with the other hand. My lips found her neck, her collarbone and back to her lips. My hands found her special place and I ran circles around her rosebud which was already wet.

"Oooohhhh, right there."

She began breathing hard and whimpering in my ear as I began to finger her slippery clit faster and faster. The room was filled with the sensual sounds of our kissing. Together our tongues danced as if we were in competition with one another. I nuzzled her in her ear and gently sucked and kissed her earlobes. She did the same to me and then whispered sweet nothings in my ear.

"Stick your finger in me."

I obliged her. She was wet—soppy wet. The greatest compliment a woman could give a man.

"Now undress me." She said.

Again, I followed her instruction. I moved the other strap to her teddy and let it drop to the floor. Well, almost. It fell downward, but the material was caught on her ass which was perfectly shaped like the letter C.

"I guess my ass is in the way, "she said innocently with a finger in her mouth like a disobedient child. She smiled as she looked back at her own rear end of which her parents have to be proud (I know I am). I walked over to her and cupped her ass again where the delicate silk material hung. I used the teddy to polish that ass which was shiny like a new penny. I helped the teddy the rest of the way down and bent over while standing to kiss her abs. Mercedes was in good shape. She obviously worked out all the time. I kissed every ripple in her stomach and she let out sighs of thanks with each kiss. I knelt before her. She ran her hands through my dreads as she guided my head to taste her flavor.

I kissed her there, and she let out a gentle sigh. I parted her lips with one hand while on my knees and began to knead her firm round ass with the other. I hated this power that she now had over me. I had every intention on making her keep her word and give me head, yet now, in this moment, I am hers to command. I want her to command me. I want her to use me so I may in turn use her for my own carnal pleasure. I licked her special place. She lets out a gracious moan. I positioned myself beneath her to fully taste her, and I found a pleasant surprise as my tongue penetrated her. She had put some flavoring inside her. A small sin that made me want to taste deeper inside her. A sin that made me want to explore her insides with my tongue.

I French kiss her clit. I treat it not as if we are new, but as if we are age old lovers that are quite familiar with one another. Over and over again I play skillfully with her clit like a cat plays with a mouse that is cornered. I am focused and fascinated at the same time by my own skillful love-play, as well as her responses. I try to stick my finger in her rear. I use my longest digit. I do this for my own carnal pleasure and for control. With my finger inside her, I figure I can guide her and command her as she commands me. I look for resistance as my finger goes deeper into her precious backside. There is none, either that, or because her ass is so big, so round, and so fat, I can only penetrate her, so much. Her ass commanded respect. It had mine. Hell, I was ready to worship it and the rest of her body. I penetrated her with my finger as much as I could and used my thumb to penetrate her vagina as I continued to feast on her clit. My tongue did its thing and my fingers acted like a fleshy rabbit (the sex toy). Mercedes held on tighter to my dreads as she began to grind her sex against my face.

"Shit ... right there ... right there ... right *there* ..."

She held on to my mane as if I was a horse, and my locks were my reigns. She guided me every which way that she wanted me to go, and I offered no resistance.

"Suck my clit ... Suck it ... Lick it ... now *gently* ... bite it. Taste me baby ... make me feel good, yes ... that's it ... Oh baby damn ... that's it ... right ... there.... Oh right there ... Oh right there ... You're the man ... You're my king ... my sire ... my lover ... Oh shit baby ... right there ... right ... motha ... fuckin ... there."

She becomes foul-mouthed. I don't mind. It's turning me on and the more she moans, the deeper my finger and thumb go in her, and the faster I lick her clit. I want her to cum. I need her to cum. I want to be the darkest chapter in her life. I want her to think about me during her day. I want to be able to stick my tongue out at her in a playful type of way, and yet make her wet on command. I want her to remember my tongue and I want to remember her taste.

Her scent was sweet, like strawberry. That must be the flavor she put inside her yet I could almost swear that it was watermelon. I tried to lick her until she no longer had any taste. Over and over and yet over again I licked her clit. Her breathing became rapid like an asthmatic. Her leg began to tremble. She licked her lips, pulled tighter on my mane and her entire vaginal region began to pulse with a life of its own. Her moans went from gentle and sensual to primitive and guttural. Her voice became deeper and raspy. She began to stutter and whisper at the same time. She sounds like Michelle N'Degeocello. Her voice, its pitch and tone were turning me on. I licked her clit faster and faster until I thought I might actually sprain my tongue if that was possible. She became louder and now, she was really foul with it.

"That's it! Oh shit baby that's it. Lick that MF, Suck that MF, make me wanna holler. Oh hell yeah baby, eat me, taste me, do that shit! Fuck yes, do that shit ... Oh damn ... Oh damn ... Oh ... shit yes ... shit ... yes ... shit ... yes, that's it baby, that's it baby ... let me grind on your face ... let me ... right there ... right.... SHIT!"

She started to cum. Her legs buckled and I penetrated her deeply with my thumb and finger and held her tighter as I continued to feast on her. Her vagina pulsed and throbbed around my thumb. Her rear entry pulsed as well. I could feel her heart beat. It was beating rapidly. Mercedes tried to pull away from me but I wouldn't let her.

I had the control now.

I had the power.

Now was the time to really get down.

I tasted her, licked her and penetrated her with my fingers faster and faster. Her legs almost collapsed up under her, and her abs tightened. I moved my mouth from her clit and continued to massage it with my thumb.

"You like that shit?" I said.

"You're playing dirty baby ... I can't take anymore." She whispered seductively.

"You can ... and you will. Say it."

"Say what?"

"Say you will come for me again."

"Baby you have to stop."

"Say you will come for me again."

I moved my thumb around faster and faster and then went back to sucking on her clit while still penetrating her with my digits.

Minutes later, I felt waves of turbulence from within her

"Oh shit."

"Oh shit what?"

"Oh shit."

"Oh shit what?" I asked again in a devilish tone.

"Oh baby ... Oh shit ... I think I'm gonna ... Oh damn I think I'm gonna ... I'm gonna cum. I'm gonna cum ... Oh you MF, I'm gonna ... Ohhhhhhhssshiiiitttttttt!"

She came a second time. As she did, she did in fact slowly make her way to the floor. She bucked like a guppy out of water on the floor, and I slowly pulled my digits out of her. As I did, I gently caressed her body and my touch seemed almost magical because of the response that it evoked from her. I rubbed her gently and she tried to roll away from me. I held her for a time when the shivering subsided and minutes later she rolled on top of me and kissed me.

"So you like to play dirty in the bedroom huh?"

"I don't know what you are talking about." I said with a smile.

She leaned over to kiss me on the lips.

I grabbed that ass.

"Is that your favorite thing about me, my ass?"

"That's all I know about right now." I said.

"Is that so?"

"Yeah."

"I have other skills and assets."

"Do you now, like what?"

"Like my oral skills."

"Really?" I said faking surprise.

"You ever hear of superhead?"

"Yeah, I loved Karrinne Steffans book."

"Well, I have her faded."

"I don't know. I find that hard to believe."

"Believe it."

With that, she went down on me. She began by licking my balls ever so gently while slowly jagging me off. She played with my balls with her tongue and then licked the space between my balls and my anus. She did that shit and I almost jumped. She then massaged the same spot where her tongue once was, and traced her mouth up and down my shaft. She then kissed the head, licked the head and deep throated me. She deep throated me six or seven times before going back to licking my balls, then the head sucking on just it like a charms pop and back down to that space between my anus and my balls.

"Aw shit ... damn where did you learn that shit?"

She didn't respond.

She went back to jagging me off while running her tongue in circles around the head of my penis. She made loud slurping sounds like she enjoyed my manhood like a banana fudge bomb on a hot Chicago day when the heat index feels like 110 degrees. She went from the head to deep-throating me, back to the head again, all the while she was jagging me off.

She then went back down and actually began to toss my salad. She threw my legs up like I was the woman and she feasted on my backside. She did this while jagging me off and I thought that I might explode within minutes.

"Oh shit!" I said loudly.

She began to jag me off faster and faster and my penis was lubed with ounces of pre-cum. My breathing became rapid and my own abdominal muscles began to tighten. My heart began to race, my mind became clouded, and the room began to slowly spin. She licked me faster and faster and no shit … I actually began to not only bitch up with as high as my voice was getting, I actually shed a tear. She then went back to deep throating me over and over and over again. The room was filled with slurping sounds, sucking sounds and music by the artist Kem. While Kem was crooning, I was moaning like a little boy and I actually had to stop Mercedes before I ended up exploding in her mouth.

"Oh shit, stop … stop … baby … shit … stop!"

"I told you that a bitch had skills."

"You ain't never lied. Damn!"

"So now what? You didn't let me finish what I started and I was getting off on it."

"What? Damn … really?"

"No, but I believe in stroking a man's ego when I am with him."

"That's funny because I believe in stroking also."

"Do you?"

"Yeah … I do … come here."

I grabbed her kissed her on the mouth and then bent her over on all fours. I positioned myself behind her and aimed my rod at her womanhood. I slowly entered her from behind and we both let out a gasp.

"OOOOoooooohhhhhh" we said unison.

I was just about to start getting some strokes off when she began to back that ass up. Instead of my fucking her, she began to fuck me. That ass moved back and forth like gelatin on a platter. She backed that ass up and I watched both cheeks clap and bounce up and down on my dick. That ass looked *so good* that just watching it alone was enough to make me excited.

"You like that shit? You like that ass?"

"I love that shit."

"Then speak up nigga, let a sista know."

"Damn that ass is fat. Damn that ass is right. Damn baby this *pussy* is so good."

She backed it up on me and I turned things around and started to get my stroke on with her. I smacked that ass and grabbed her tiny waist and began to get my stroke on with a vengeance. I couldn't believe how small her waist was in comparison to her ass. Pretty soon the room was filled with the sounds of our bodies slamming against one another and the sounds of *Babyface* in the background.

She bent down further exposing more of her beautiful ass in the air. I smacked that ass over and over again and began to hit that ass faster and faster. I grabbed a fist full of her hair and used the other hand to hold on to her shoulder and began to take long deliberate strokes inside of her.

"Oh shit that's my spot." She said.

I hit that ass just a bit harder.

"Oh shit, that's my spot ... that's it ... right there ... just like that ... don't stop ... don't stop ... don't ... stop ... Awwwww Shiiiiiiittttt!"

She came.

I have never dated a woman that came from vaginal sex before.

She came hard.

At *that moment,* I thought I might propose to her. A woman that came from dick? That was the MF jackpot!

I began to stroke her harder. I began to take long slow even strokes and switched it up to long fast pokes. I switched speeds over and over again and now I was beginning to talk shit.

"So whose pussy is this?"

"This is your pussy."

"Whose shit is this?"

"This is your pussy."

"You like that shit?"

"Put your name on that shit baby. Put your MF name on that shit! Hit that shit harder ... Oh shit ... damn that MF is big ... Oh shit ... Oh shit ... That's it, bring it home baby, bring that shit home, FUCK ME!"

I started to hit that ass for old and new. I hit that shit with a vengeance. I grabbed that small waist with both hands and tried to kill her with dick. I hit that ass like there was no tomorrow and pretty soon I was cumming.

"Oh shit, oh shit ... oh.... shhhhhiiiiiiiittttttttt!"

I pulled out and exploded all over her backside. She turned around jagged me off forcing out all the remaining fluid. I came so hard that my head hurt. When she was satisfied that I could come no more ... she then took me in her mouth again.

"Fuck ... Fuck ... Oh Fuck!" I yelled.

"Now, whose dick is this?"

"It's your dick."

"Say that shit louder!"

"It's your dick!" I screamed while pulling on my own damned braids. I thought I was going to fuck around and pull out my own damned hair.

"Say this is Mercedes dick!"

"It's Mercedes dick!"

"Say I got that bomb ass pussy!"

"Oh shit baby, you got that bomb ass pussy!"

"Say that shit!" She commanded.

"Mercedes you are the bomb! You are the one! Dammit girl you are the shit! Damn this is some good pussy, damn this some good head ... I'm gonna ... oh shit ... I'm gonna.... AAAAaaaaarrrrrgggggghhhhh!"

I shot my load—again.

She took in every drop and licked me damn near into unconsciousness.

I collapsed.

We went to sleep. We went to sleep right there on the floor.

When I awoke, an hour had passed. Mercedes hadn't moved. We both lay there on the floor of her place. We laid there in our sin.

It was official.

I had committed adultery.

I watched the ceiling. I counted dots in the stucco.

She spoke first.

"Don't even think about it. It happened, it was good and no matter what you say, you will be back for more. Today was just a sample. Think about that before you start thinking about *her*."

She got up and went to the shower to brush her teeth.

Her? When did my *wife* become *her?*

She was right though. As much as I hated it, Mercedes was right. I sinned yes, but I will definitely be back for more. I felt guilty as I stood up and looked at the mirror in the living room of Mercedes apartment. The candles were still burning and the room was dark. As I looked at the silhouette of my reflection, I didn't recognize myself in the mirror.

"Who is that man in the mirror?" I thought.

The better question might have been, "Who is this man that I have become?"

WASHING AWAY THE GUILT

I looked away from the mirror in shame. I heard the sound of the shower running and I knew that Mercedes was in there probably washing up and waiting on my next move. Do I leave or do I join her? I looked in my wallet and opened it to the pictures of me and Deja together. I felt like shit. What have I done? What am I doing? I put the picture away, got dressed and headed toward the door. I put my hand on the doorknob and paused. I looked back at the bathroom and steam was billowing from it. *Trouble Man* by *Marvin Gaye* was playing on the stereo. I was just as conflicted in my life as Marvin was in the song. I shook my head in disbelief about what it was I was about to do. I got undressed again and made my way to the shower. I stepped into the shower and Mercedes who was washing up, simply looked over her shoulder and smiled. She knew that she had me hooked. I was an addict and she was my drug. She turned to me and began to wash me up. She lathered up a washcloth and some sweet smelling soap that felt extremely good on my body. It smelled like strawberries and lilac. She washed my neck, my back, my pecs and my abs. She cleaned me slowly and meticulously. She then washed my balls, my behind, and knelt down in the shower to do my legs.

She made me feel good. She made me feel like a man. In some regards she worshipped me or at the very least simulated worship. She knelt before me with her long hair being wet and to me, she looked like an exotic bronze goddess. This was a beautiful black woman. All I could think about as she knelt before me was my member in her mouth, my hands in her hair and exploding inside of her. As if she could read my mind, she placed my hands in her hair and made me, make her give me head. The water from the shower washed over our bodies and my whole body relaxed as I had my way with her. I had two pleasures, that of the warm water and that of her warm mouth. I had my way with her until the water became cold. As it became cold I shot my load again. Mercedes took my seed in full spray. I shot her with my soldiers which streamed across her breasts. She rubbed my penis against her nipples and jagged me off until nothing else would come forward. She then washed me up again with the cold water and stepped out of the shower to dry off. She dried that fabulous body of hers everywhere. She then brushed her teeth again, gargled and put on a silk robe that was so short her ass cheeks hung out beneath it. I looked at that ass as I stepped out of the shower and thought to myself, "Damn, I'm a lucky man."

I dried off, got dressed and headed toward the door without speaking. I had my head down as I tried to think about what I would tell my wife. When I looked up at the clock it said 11:30 PM. That meant that both Deja and I would be getting home at the same time on a work night. Normally at this time, I would be sleep. I was too pre-occupied with my own thoughts I didn't even hear Mercedes as she spoke.

"Leave the money on the dresser."

"I'm sorry, what?"

"If you are going to treat me like a whore, leave some money on the dresser."

"What are you talking about?"

"How are you going to suck me, fuck me and let me give you head and then get up and walk out of my spot without a kiss or speaking to me?"

"I didn't mean to offend you."

"Well, I'm offended. I'm not your whore. I'm your mistress and a mistress should be treated with *some respect*."

"Like the respect that we are showing my wife?"

"What?"

"You heard me."

"First of all, you cheated on your wife. I'm single. I can see, date, suck or fuck anyone that I choose. You on the other hand, didn't have to come here but you did. The drama between you and your wife is on ya'll, not me."

She had a point. She didn't cheat, I did. I mean, she knew that I was married so that had to count for something, but she was right—I'm the adulterer.

"I didn't mean to disrespect you in your home."

"Prove it."

"What?"

"Kiss me."

I walked over to her, kissed her on the lips softly and was reminded of my sin as I placed my hand on her ample ass.

"You seem to be pre-occupied with my ass."

"It is a nice distraction."

"Well, it's yours as long as you want it."

"Well, I don't know what to say."

"Why not say that the shit is yours. You sure put your name on the MF today."

I smiled.

She knew how to stroke my ego.

I smiled, kissed her once more and I left.

SWIMMING IN GUILT

That drive home that first night was intense. I raced home from Mercedes apartment to try and beat Deja home. I was driving like a madman and at the same time, thinking to myself *How could I do this to the woman that I love?* I raced home and looked down at my cell phone to see if Deja had called.

My cell phone was off.

I turned it off before I went into Mercedes apartment. That—was a mistake.

I powered up my phone and looked at the screen.

I had two messages.

My heart skipped a beat as I keyed in the password. Perhaps Deja called and asked where I was. What would I tell her? I checked the messages and neither was from Deja. Both were from my sisters, Connie and Deborah.

"Whew." I gasped.

I pulled into the driveway and right behind me was Deja. We both got home at the same time. My heart raced and my head began to pound as I thought long and hard about what I would say to her. I got out of the car and kissed Deja on the cheek.

"Hey You." I said.

"Hey, what are you doing up so late?"

"I just went out to get something to eat."

"Should you be eating this late?"

"Probably not."

"What did you get?"

Oh shit. I don't have any proof that I went to get something to eat. What do I say?

"I got White Castle. I ate there."

"Why did you eat there?"

"I just needed some air and I couldn't sleep and since you weren't home I figured I would just chill there."

"Oh, okay."

She walked in the house and I walked in behind her. I made a B-line for the bathroom to check myself out. Deja started getting dressed in her PJ's and getting ready for bed. Her nightly routine was to watch cable and smoke a joint to unwind from the day. After smoking herb, she usually ended up climbing on top of me for a quickee. I was hoping that she would break her routine this evening.

"So how was your day?" She asked.

From the bathroom I spoke loudly, "What? I mean it was okay … why?"

"Well, you're normally asleep now and we don't get a lot of time other than on the phone, so I was just wondering how your day went."

"It went okay."

"Yeah, you said that. What did you do?"

"Nothing."

"Did you get the mail?"

"Nope, I uh-forgot."

"You forgot to get the mail?"

"Yeah."

"You never forget the mail. What's going on with you?"

"What's going on with you, what's with all the questions?"

"I'm just making conversation. What's with you being so defensive?"

"I'm sorry baby, I'm just sleepy."

"Then go to bed. No, scratch that, just lay down and relax for a while. Let me get a few more hits of this and I will be in there to tuck you in."

Oh Shit.

She wanted sex. I'm tapped out. What the fuck do I do now? I checked myself in the mirror looking for any sign that I had been fucking around. I didn't know what I was looking for, but I was sure searching like hell to make sure that whatever it was wasn't obvious. I reached for my dick and tried to jag off to get myself hard again. I tried, but I had no gas left in the tank. I was thinking that I would take the initiative and sleep with Deja right there in the living room and pretend to be spontaneous. It was no use though, my dick wouldn't get hard to save my life. In fact, my dick was sore as hell. I panicked and then looked at my own reflection in the mirror. *What do I do?* My heart raced as did my thought as I tried to find a way out of this situation. Then it came to me. I went in the bedroom stripped down to my underwear and pretended to be asleep. I prayed that Deja would finish smoking that joint and watch some cable before coming to bed. I hoped she would be too high for sex. The problem was, my wife was actually turned on even more after smoking herb.

Minutes later Deja crawled in the bed. She snuggled up against me and was spooning me in the bed. She reached around for my package and I pretended to be sleep. When my dick wouldn't respond to her touch she figured that I was sleep and under a lot of stress. A few minutes later she gave up entirely.

"Damn, you must be tired." She said.

In our three years of marriage, no matter how tired I was, my body responded to my wife's familiar touch.

Not tonight.

Deja kissed me on the back of the neck and tried to go to sleep.

"Where have I smelled that smell before?" She whispered before dozing off to sleep.

CHAPTER 6

▼

IF I COULD TURN BACK THE HANDS OF TIME

PRESENT DAY-MARK

So I told my wife that we were having financial problems when in fact, things could not be better. I hated lying to her but in the same token, I loved the money that we were saving now that she thought we were busted. Deja had expensive taste. She was a clothes horse and a power shopper. I was glad that we were saving for a rainy day, but mad that the only way for us to save was by substantiating a lie that I told.

I have been sleeping with Mercedes for about six months now. I have been hitting that ass every other day and sometimes stopping by on the weekends to sneak in a quickee. Deja and I lived in Dolton, Illinois. Mercedes lived in the south-west suburbs. Between the geographical locations as well as the fact that the two women hated each other, there was little chance in my mind of them ever meeting. Deja was always cordial to Mercedes and Mercedes was often times cordial back, but these two women wouldn't piss on each other if either of them was on fire.

Deja started working longer hours and making more money. I told her that I was working longer hours and doing more field work and meeting with clients. I told her that if my bosses were considering firing me, they had better take a long look at the work that I was doing. I convinced Deja that my bosses were trying to find some option to keep me. I told her that they loved my work ethic. I told her weekly that I was just *this close to being laid off.*

Then I made partner in the firm.

There was a party held for me.

I brought Mercedes to the party.

I told Deja that I was working late that day.

My lie was beginning to snowball and I didn't know how to stop it.

I joined the softball team because that's what the partners wanted. I hated baseball, but I loved the extra $30,000 that I was making so I joined the team. I forgot how I should have been acting. I forgot that a man losing his job wouldn't play for the employer's team, unless it meant saving his job. A man losing his job wouldn't be working out every other day at the gym. A man losing his job wouldn't suddenly take up competitive swimming. I did these things because they were things that satisfied Mercedes.

I was getting sloppy.

Deja was beginning to notice.

DEJA

I believed my husband when he said that we were in financial straits. The problem that I had with what he said was that he stopped at the 9705 club and my girl Adrienne wasn't there. He said that there was a male bartender and I have never known there to be one there. Finally, I can't believe that any man would be so stressed that he couldn't get it up for me. I mean, I know that money can mess with a man's head. I know that many men equate their manhood with the security of the job that they hold, as well as the money that they are bringing in. In three years, Mark's body has always responded to me. I don't understand why these days he isn't responding to me. Today is Wednesday November 23. Tomorrow is Thanksgiving. I was going to work late today, but the hell with that. I am headed to the 9705 bar to have a drink.

THE 9705 BAR

I walked into the 9705 bar and there was my girl Adrienne. She was pouring drinks, talking mess and looking every bit like she was 26 at 35 years of age. Adrienne was an older girl that lived in my neighborhood back in the day. I'm 29 ½. I have always looked up to Adrienne. When she started tending bar at the 9705 club, I was shocked. I always thought that she should have been a therapist because she was such a good listener. Instead, she opted to be a bartender and she has a Masters Degree in psychology.

"Hey girl!" Adrienne shouted.

"Adrienne, how are you sweetheart?"

We hugged and complimented one another from head to toe.

"So girl what are you doing back in the hood?"

"My husband stopped in here a few days ago and he made me think about you when he mentioned the 9705."

"Really? When did he come in here?"

"Thursday night."

"Thursday, you sure?"

"Yeah, why?"

"I was here all day Thursday and there were no people in here other than my regulars."

"You worked Thursday night?"

"All night."

"By any chance do you guys have male bartenders here now?"

"Oh hell no, the owner ain't going for that. We have male security, but no bartenders."

"By any chance do these security guys pour drinks?"

"Nope, why do you ask?"

I fell silent.

Adrienne looked at me.

We both knew what was up.

"Deja, girl I'm so sorry. Did he tell you he was in here and was probably somewhere else?"

Adrienne was very intuitive. She could tell when a man had been messing around or when a woman was in pain from heartache.

"Adrienne, girl I don't know."

"You know."

"I want to believe him."

"That's your heart talking. What does your mind say?"

I let out a sigh. "My mind says that he is fucking around on me."

"And your woman's intuition?"

"It's confirming that he's fucking around on me."

"And your heart?"

"My heart is trying to hold on to my man."

"There is nothing wrong with that girl. If you love him, hold onto him."

"But what about what he's doing to me?"

"Girl you let him do you wrong, and you keep doing right. Be the best woman that you can be and when he sees what he has in you he will stop."

"And if he doesn't?"

"If he doesn't, then you don't need him to begin with, and there is no need for you to hang on to him because in spite of all he is doing you still gave him your love, the benefit of the doubt, and your absolute best."

Adrienne poured me a drink. She poured me a Hennessey straight up. I told her what Mark told me about our finances and how he couldn't get it up the other night despite all that I did.

"That's some bullshit right there."

"You think so?"

"Girl, I don't give a damn how mad a man is or how stressed he is. Unless he is about to lose his life, a man will take his aggression with the world out on some pussy, unless he has already had some pussy. The only thing that stops a 30 year old man's dick from getting hard is he is on the down low, he has a physical condition, or he has another woman."

Her words stung. She saw the impact that they had on me and smiled. She could have sugarcoated the situation but that's not how Adrienne gets down. We're girls. We're from the same hood. We don't sugar coat shit. *We keep it real.*

"Adrienne, why can't I be woman enough for him? Where did I go wrong that I am no longer his fantasy?"

"It's not you baby-girl, it's the tramp that he's with."

"How can you be so sure?"

"You're a good woman."

"What does that have to do with anything?"

"Men cheat for variety, because they are bored or unsatisfied in their relationship and because they are greedy as hell. A man cheats on a good woman *only if the other woman is a freak in bed, free of inhibition and she is promising him things that are unreasonable and unnatural in the bedroom.*"

"Unreasonable or Unnatural?"

"A straight up freak."

"But I fuck him regularly."

"Do you give head?"

"Yes."

"You swallow?"

"No."

"Anal?"

"Hell no."

"Dress in Lingerie?"

"Sometimes."

"Use Toys?"

"Sometimes."

"And you sleep with him regularly?"

"When time permits."

"When was the last time that you just gave him head and nothing else?"

"You mean not get any love in return? I haven't."

"When was the last time that you catered to him?"

"I don't. I don't have time for all that shit."

"This other bitch does though. Not only is she probably doing all that, she is promising to do it forever. It won't be until he leaves that he realizes that she is on some bullshit."

"If he leaves." I said dejected.

"Yeah, if he leaves."

"So why mess around with this other woman?"

"Because it's new."

"New? We have only been married three years. I would like to think that we are still new."

"Maybe, but she is newer. She is also probably bodied up nice."

"How do you know?"

"Girl, look at you. I would love to have as much T & A as you have. I would kill to have the tiny waist that you have. A man ain't about to leave a fine sister like you for just anybody. This other woman is probably built like you with longer hair and less tummy. You have a nice body, so this other broad must be built like a brickhouse."

"You think?"

"I know."

"So how do I get my man back?"

"You call him on that shit and you tell him that you refuse to be disrespected."

"But what if I'm wrong?"

"You're not and you know you're not. Otherwise you wouldn't be in here today. Yeah your heart says everything is fine, but your head is saying check up on his ass!"

She was right. I knew he had been cheating but my mind was clouded by the pressure coming from my heart to simply let it be.

"I can't just come out and accuse him."

"Then check up on his ass and catch him."

"Where do I begin?"

"Let me pour you a drink and I will tell you where to start."

I drank another shot of Hennessey and listened as Adrienne schooled my ass on men.

"Girl look, there are many ways to find out if your man is cheating. For starters, men change their patterns. Then they get sloppy with their actions. Also if they smell like fresh soap, fresh cologne or fresh pussy, they are messing around. You need to check his phone records, make periodic stops at his job, the gym and surprise his ass with surprise visits wherever he might be when he is not with you."

"He has a softball game this week."

"Then there you go."

"When do I tell him that I am going?"

"About two minutes before he walks out the door."

"Okay, I'm feeling that."

We clicked glasses and shared a laugh between friends although on the inside I was crying. Adrienne brought me up to speed on all of our friends in the hood. She told me everyone's business, and what they were doing to get out of trouble from Derrick and Rose, to Jamie and Mia, to Leon and Erica and everyone else in the neighborhood. All of us on the block had mad drama in our lives.

We drank, laughed and looked at the various men that came in the club and gossiped about whether or not they were good in bed or whether or not they would make good mates. We checked out the clothes on various men, the women they attempted to talk to, and who was in and out of their league as they worked the club. I was scheduled to work that day until two A.M. I went home about midnight.

NOT HOME YET?

I know that Mark was expecting me to be in at 2:30 or a quarter to three. I left the bar feeling quite tipsy and got home at midnight. I walked into the house and all the lights were off. I walked into the bathroom to see if Mark had been there and the shower and sink were both dry. That was a tell-all clue that Mark had not been home. I turned on the plasma TV and the channel was still on the cooking channel that I had been watching last night. Mark hates the cooking channel so I know that he had not been watching that TV. I went in the bedroom where I purposely turned the TV on to the Discovery channel and it was still on that station, so he had not been in the bedroom today either. Finally I checked the caller ID light which had still been flashing which meant that he hadn't checked the phone. The mail was in the mailbox still, so there was no doubt that he had not come home. Wherever he is, he went directly there after work.

I don't know why brothers try to pull it with sisters. The first problem is the fact that they change their patterns. The second thing is they neglect to do certain things. The third thing they do when they fuck up is accuse us of infidelity in order to throw us off. As much as I hated to admit it, my man was fooling around. What's worse is the fact that he is possibly about to lose his job and he has the audacity to be fucking around. I came home tipsy and horny. I wanted to share his embrace. I wanted to talk with him. I wanted to make things right between us. Now, all I want to do is find out who this other bitch is.

I cried for a half hour on the couch.

I then ate chocolates.

Then ... after I was done having pity on myself, I laid my clothes out for tomorrow. He's playing softball at Grant Park tomorrow. Two minutes before he walks out the door, I am going with him.

I wonder what she looks like? I wonder what she is doing that I'm not. I wonder what kind of woman makes a man leave home where everything is secure. I wonder what more I could have done. Am I fault here? Am I the reason that our marriage is failing?

MARK-UNPLEASANT SURPRISE

I hit that ass again tonight. I went to Mercedes house right after work and she and I went at it. I told her on the phone earlier what Deja said about my basically being a closet homosexual by wanting to have anal sex. Mercedes stated that Deja was just scared and didn't know how to please a man. I didn't like her bad mouthing my wife under any circumstances, but on this point we were both in agreement. I wanted Deja to drop some of her inhibitions and to be more sexually free in our relationship. That night, I walked into Mercedes apartment and she had on a leopard skinned teddy, high heels and stockings. As soon as I came to the apartment, she opened the door and had a camcorder in hand. I was surprised and apprehensive at first. She walked backward and beckoned me into her apartment.

"Hey baby, how are you this evening?"

"I'm fine, how about you?"

"I'm horny."

"I'm glad to hear that, but can you turn that thing off?"

"Why, you scared?"

"I don't want to be filmed."

"Why? You don't trust me?"

"No, I don't."

"You worried wifey will find out?"

"I am."

"Then why are you here?"

She kept filming and I was pissed.

"You know why I'm here."

"No I don't ... tell me."

"Put the camera down."

"Make me."

"What?"

"Make me. Punish me. Spank Me."

I was just about to walk out of her apartment. I wasn't in the mood for any games this evening. She could see that I was pissed and before I could protest she handed me the camera.

"Okay scary cat. Here is the camera. Since you don't want to be filmed, maybe you should film me."

She handed me the camera. Before I could grab the DVD out of it, she turned around, pulled her panties off (while I was filming) and she exposed that fat round bottom of hers. In the center of her opening was a butt plug. I was speechless because I had never seen one.

"What ... what is that?"

"What does it look like?"

"Some type of anal toy."

"It's a butt plug."

"And what is it supposed to do?"

"I have been wearing it all day to prepare me for you."

"Really?"

"Really. You said wifey called you a faggot when you suggested anal to her. I'm just showing you that a *real woman,* will do whatever it takes to please her man."

"So you are down with ..."

"... Anything that you decide to do my king."

"King?"

"Sire."

"Hmmnn."

She removed the plug and retreated into her bedroom which, I hadn't been in before. I followed her into the back, the whole time filming that ass sway back and forth. Damn she looked good and damn she had my slacks beginning to stiffen. She climbed up on the bed, bent over on all fours and reached over into her nightstand to retrieve KY and a small dildo. The dildo wasn't as large as me, but I guess the point was to just get her backside ready for me. She took the lubricant, poured some on her fingertips and massaged the warm oil into her backside. The whole time I was mesmerized. The whole time, I was filming. She then took the sex toy and slowly and methodically worked it into her backside. She began to moan as if she were getting off on it.

I watched her for fifteen minutes work the toy in and out of her tight rear. I watched as she supported herself with one hand and penetrated herself fast and slow and fast again from the backside. Her hole seemed tight at first. Then it definitely loosened up. I know, because there were times that she pulled it all the way out and her sphincter just pulsed with a heartbeat all on its own.

"You want me."

"Yes." I said.

"Say it."

"I want you."

"And what do you want to do to me?"

"I want to fuck you."

"Where."

"In the ass."

"Then say that."

"I want to fuck you in the ass."

"I didn't hear you."

"You did."

"I didn't."

"I said, I want to fuck you in the ass."

"Then what are you waiting for? It's here. And you have the opportunity to catch it all on film ... my king."

I don't know what was with the King shit, but it was doing wonders for my ego. I walked over to Mercedes, camera in hand, got undressed and walked over to the edge of the bed. Mercedes balanced herself on her forearms and hiked her ass in the air. Her hole was open and looking very inviting to me. I positioned myself behind her and placed the head of my penis in the small opening.

"Ohhhh, that's it." She said.

I was getting harder with each passing second.

"You like that?" I asked.

"I love that shit. Your dick is so big."

"You like that way it feels in your ass?"

"I love the way that it feels in my ass."

"Then say that shit."

"Oh, I love this shit. Mark handle this shit. This is your pussy and your ass. Have your way with me. Do that shit baby, do that shit!"

I worked the head in slowly and worked myself in and out of her. It had been years since I had last done this. Over ten years in fact. I began to work my manhood in and out of her and to tell the truth, I didn't enjoy it as much as I remember enjoying it years ago. It was tight, uncomfortable and hard to penetrate even with the dildo and lubricant beforehand. I thought this was what I wanted but it wasn't all that people make it out to be. The thing that was turning me on was her talking dirty and telling me how big I was. I hit that ass for about 20 minutes before it started to loosen up.

"Oh, that's it. Open me up baby, open me up. Take this shit. Make me hurt. Oh damn it's so good, your dick is so big, Damn baby I think I'm about to cum."

That shit was turning me on. Mercedes knew what to say. Even if I was ripping her open, which is what the shit felt like, her dirty talk was turning me on. I was loving every minute of it and pretty soon I was hammering her like crazy. My dick hurt. It even burned a little, but her pillow talk kept me going.

"That's it baby, handle that shit! Open me up! Fuck the shit out of me. Oh my God you are so big. That's it baby … hurt me … shit yes, hurt me!"

I was hitting that ass hard as hell now. I was smacking that ass with one hand and the next thing that I knew, I put the camera down to the side grabbed her waist and was driving my manhood into her backside for all glory. Minutes later, I was cumming.

"That's it, bust that nut baby! Bust that nut!"

Without thinking I exploded into her backside and then collapsed on her back.

"Did you like that shit baby?"

"It was good."

"Don't you wish your wife would give herself to you like I do?"

"I do. I wish that Deja would stop being so damned frigid."

I withdrew from inside her and lay on my side. I then made the mistake that all men in my situation make. I began to talk to the mistress about my wife. To make matters worse, I began to bad mouth my wife to my mistress.

"Man, things could be better between us ya know? Deja is so frigid, she doesn't make time for lovemaking, she is not in the same shape that she was in when we met, and sometimes I just get bored with our sex life. I mean, I know that she works and shit. I mean, I know that she works hard … but she isn't putting it down in the bedroom like she used to. She doesn't swallow, she doesn't take it in the ass and she damn sure doesn't want it all the time like you do."

"Why do you think that is?" Mercedes asked.

"You know what? I don't know."

"So why don't you leave her?"

"I love her."

"You have a funny way of showing it."

"What do you mean?"

"You have been fucking me for months. I thought this was just going to be a one time thing. But hell, you have been fucking me every which way there is to be fucked. Shit, Mark baby … you been turning me out."

"Really?"

"Really. Shit I don't think there is anything left that we haven't done."

"We could always have a ménage a trois."

"We could."

"Are you serious, you would do that?"

"I would do anything to please you."

Like I said, she was good as hell at stroking a brother's ego.

"Hey, did you get a new computer?"

"Yeah, now I have one in the living room and here in the bedroom."

"Did you really need two computers?"

"For what I am trying to do, actually I do."

"Oh, what is it that you are trying to do."

"Send a clear message to someone about something."

"Through your computer?"

"Through my computer."

Mercedes and I made love twice again before I left her apartment. I left at 11:30 in order to get home by 12:00. I wanted to get home before Deja and also to have time to shower, de-flower if you will, and get some sleep. I have a softball game with the partners tomorrow at Grant Park. We are going against First National in our fourth game of the year. I kissed Mercedes, which was my ritual when leaving her home now. I got dressed and headed out the door.

"See you tomorrow at the game baby." She said.

"Okay, see you then."

HEART STUCK IN MY THROAT

I was going to wash up at Mercedes' spot, but I figured that I would do so when I got home since Deja is now working later hours. I drove home happy as hell at the prospect of having my cake and eating it too. I listened to V103 the whole time while cruising home on Interstate 294. I listened to Smokey Robinson, Al Green, Ready for the World, the Isleys and a host of other old school joints. I pulled into the driveway at 12:00 on the dot thinking that I had another two hours before Deja got home. I hit the garage remote and almost swallowed my tongue when I saw Deja's car already parked in the driveway.

The side door opened.

Deja was standing there.

She walked back into the house.

I almost pissed my pants.

"What, what the hell is she doing home?" I said to myself as the music played.

Shit, what do I tell her? What excuse will I use? Does she know? Damn, do I smell like sex? Is it written all over my face what happened? What do I do if she wants to be intimate? I am spent after having sex with Mercedes. Jesus Christ, what have I done to our relationship—to our marriage?

I was in a panic. I didn't know what to do. What was worse is after seeing her I *slowly* drove in the garage. All my behaviors were beginning to give me away.

I was scared.

I was repentant.

What should I do?

God please, please don't let her know. Give me some type of excuse to get out of this. I thought that it was pretty fucked up that I was praying to God that my Christian wife believe whatever bullshit lie I was about to tell.

I got out of my car.

That was indeed the longest walk that I had ever taken in my life. I walked in and made a B-line for the bathroom.

DEJA

No this stupid MF didn't come in here and make a B-line for the bathroom. Doesn't he know that is a tell-tell sign that he has been fucking around? And, why the hell did he slow down when he saw me? He is acting guilty as hell so that might as well be an admission of guilt. He must think I am some sort of damned fool! Adrienne was right. He is fucking around on me. I wanted to not see it, but there is no denying it now. The question is, who the fuck is she? I have given this man my heart, my body, my spirit and I have tried hard to be a good woman to him. I bet he is acting this way because he didn't expect me to be home. I guess Adrienne was right about that too. I need to continue to surprise his ass.

I need to play it cool.

I can't let him know how upset I am.

I need to question him but be tactful. I need to inquire, but not interrogate. I need to take note of things and simply add up what doesn't jive. Adrienne suggested that I give this nigga enough rope to hang himself and I plan to do just that.

MARK

Oh shit, oh shit, oh shit! What do I do? Damn, the first place I went was the bathroom. I know damn well that is a sign of cheating. I got scared. I didn't know what else to do. Now what the hell do I do? I ran water in the sink and washed my face, my hands, and my dick. I was going to use a washcloth, but that would be a dead giveaway. I pulled my pants down around my ankles, cupped the water in my hands and *rinsed off my dick as best I could.* I then smelled my hands which were covered by Mercedes scent.

"Shit." I whispered to myself.

"What the fuck is she doing home?"

I dried myself off with a towel, pulled up my pants and tried to play everything off.

THE NON-CONFRONTATION

"Hey babe." I said.

"You're getting in pretty late."

"Yeah, well I had to work late tonight."

"Really?"

"Really. Yeah, we um ... had a lot of things going on at the office and in order to keep my job, I just um, decided to work late this evening."

"Everyone, or just you?"

"Just me."

"Oh, okay ... Hmmnnn."

"Is there something wrong babe?"

"I don't know, is there?"

"Uh-no. Everything is cool. No worries."

"No worries? You Jamaican now?"

"No, why do you say that?"

"I have never heard you use that term before."

"Oh, I use it all the time … at work."

"Really?"

"Yeah, really."

She knows. I bet money that she knows. She is feeling me out. She is too MF calm. Something is wrong. Damn I'm scared. What do I do?

"So, why did you make a B-line for the bathroom?"

"Huh?"

"Huh, Mark you heard me, why did you go straight to the bathroom? Why were you in there for so long?"

"Where is this coming from Deja? I mean damn, I had to take a dump!"

She got up from her seat, walked by me all the while maintaining eye contact with me and then she walked into the bathroom. She came out with a scowl on her face.

"That's funny, it doesn't smell like shit in hear and I didn't hear you use the air-freshener. But wait, yeah … yeah it does smell in here now that I think about it, this story smells like bullshit!"

"Deja if you have something to say, why don't you say it."

I was praying to God that she didn't.

"Mark, you know what? … Nevermind, goodnight."

I leaned in to kiss her. I don't know why, but I did. She moved away from me. She walked into the bedroom and slammed the door.

I went to sleep on the couch—another admission of guilt.

DEJA

I know that Adrienne said to be cool, but it is hard as hell when you know that your man is fooling around on you. It was all I could to not to put a knife under my pillow, offer him oral sex until he got hard (if he got hard) and cut his dick off at the balls. I had envisioned it the entire time that he was away. His slowing down in the driveway was an admission of guilt. His going to the bathroom was an admission of guilt, and his now sleeping on the couch is an admission of guilt. And did he ask himself what am I doing here when he was in the bathroom? I wanted to say, "Motha fucka I live here! I'm your wife asshole, or did you forget that!" I will play this shit cool—for now. But if I catch him—scratch that, *when I catch him*, there is gonna be hell to pay.

I stayed in my bedroom and the room began to spin.

I cried myself to sleep—again.

In my sleep I prayed to the Lord to give me strength.

CHAPTER 7

▼

PLAY BALL!

MARK

I got up early the next morning. Our softball game was at 8:00 in Grant Park and I needed to be dressed and down there at 7:00 A.M. Deja knew that I had the game today and when I looked in on her at 6:00 she was dead sleep. I tipped out of the bedroom after checking on her and went into the bathroom to take a shower, wash away my sin and try and be out the door by 6:30. That was it! The affair was over. I was going to tell Mercedes today that I can't hang and that I was out. I have too much to lose. I love my wife and everything about her. I can't believe how stupid I've been. I owe her better. Deja deserves better. In fact, I'm going to call her and tell her on my way to the game to stay away and that we can't see each other anymore.

I got dressed in my softball uniform in the bathroom. I was careful to be as quiet as a mouse. When I opened the door, Deja was standing in the doorway, fully dressed, makeup on and hair pulled back in a ponytail.

"Hey! Baby, where um … where are you going?"

"I'm going to your game today to support you."

"Huh?"

"I'm going to your game."

"But you hate baseball."

"So did you until a few weeks ago."

"But I um … have to um … play to keep my um … my job. I'm … just … uh, I'm just doing this to … um … you know, help my job … I mean, keep my job."

"Yeah, well that's fine dear. I just want to make sure that I support your every effort. In fact, I think I need to stand by your side now more than ever."

"Oh. Okay … sure."

"You ready to go?"

"Um … yeah."

"Okay, let' go."

Shit! Now what do I do?

10 MILES PER HOUR

I was scared as hell as we drove downtown to Grant Park. That was the longest and most quiet drive that we have taken since I have been married. I drove the speed limit and was in no hurry to get to the Park. Mercedes was never there before me when I had a game. She generally came after the game got started so as she was walking through the park and to the game, all the attention would be on her. I drove to the park pretending that I was all into the music. Nikki Woods from WGCI was working the weekend morning show and she was starting heated conversations this early in the morning between songs.

"Good morning Chicago! This is your girl Nikki Woods. Today's question to our morning readers out there working, hitting the gym, running and doing their thing is, "What makes a man cheat on a good woman? Not just his woman or any woman, what makes a man cheat on a good woman?"

Silence fell between us.

The tension in the air in my Camry was so thick, that you could cut it with a knife.

I didn't look in Deja's direction—I wouldn't dare.

She knew. I knew in my heart that she knew.

I wanted to change the channel but … well, you know.

Nikki Woods went on to make some good points and I was scared that at any second, Deja was going to chop my ass in the throat and we would have had an accident on Lake Shore Drive. Instead of panic, I just kept vibing to the music. I kept acting as if nothing were wrong. I bet money that beads of sweat forming on my forehead were giving me away. I played along like there was no problem. I sang along with songs by *John Legend, Anthony Hamilton and R. Kelly* as I drove slowly through Chicago praying in my head for a miracle. I pulled up along Balboa Drive, parked the car and walked over to open the door for my wife.

"Here we are babe."

"Yeah, here we are."

We walked over to the area where my bosses or partners rather, were warming up. I prayed to God that they didn't congratulate me on making partner in front of Deja. My partners and I didn't get a chance to talk about it, but they all know that I am married. They all have met both Mercedes and Deja. They have seen Mercedes at the three games that preceded this one. Thus far, no one has asked me anything about it, so I didn't volunteer anything. They each had mistresses too. The only thing was, they each had been at this a lot longer than I have and none of them ever brought their mistresses anywhere except for an annual party that they had on the company yacht. This was a party that I was previously looking forward to.

I grabbed a baseball bat and began to warm up. I then tactfully scanned the park to see if I saw Mercedes anywhere. I wasn't sure how to act if I saw her. I wasn't sure what I would do. If Deja saw Mercedes, that alone would give everything away. I started to fake an injury while warming up or at the very least make myself throw up so we could leave. Again I prayed. Again I was blasphemous. I asked God to help me and to be a party to my sin which had to count as a double or triple sin somewhere in heaven.

God please, its Mark. Please help me out of this mess. Please make Mercedes stay home today. Please, maybe even hit her ass with a bus or something [I know, that ain't right] God I really love Deja. I don't want to lose her. Please help me out of this. If you do this, then I promise I will never see Mercedes again. Please God, help a nigga out!

I was tweakin. I was scared as hell that this was it for my ass, and that I would be in divorce court in a matter of weeks. I tried to get my breathing under control and I tried to keep my composure. I looked at my watch and I had been warming up almost an hour. You would have thought that I was Sammy Sosa or something the way that I held on to that bat. I was hitting balls right and left and hitting them each 50-60 yards. I had a lot of aggression in me. So much so, that I thought I might actually destroy some of those softballs. I was upset and terrified. Today might be the day that I lose the most important thing to ever walk into my life.

IF I FIND THIS _____ I'M GOING TO ACT MY COLOR TODAY.
DEJA

I watched Mark warm up. He looked nervous. He looked pale for a black man. I know that this bitch whoever she is, will be here today. All I need to do is watch for eye contact and his reaction when the bitch arrives. I swear if she so much as looks at Mark and then look at me. I'm gonna show my ass today.

Mark stepped up to the plate and was the first one at bat. The opposing team showed no mercy and threw some amazing pitches. Mark thinks that I hate baseball. I just hate watching it on TV. Softball is something all together different. I used to play softball in college. That is what helped me to pay for school. I didn't tell Mark about it because some men think that female athletes are bi or lesbian. I happen to think that men are intimidated by female athletes.

"Strike One!" Is what the umpire yelled as Mark missed the first pitch.

"Strike Two!" He yelled as the second pitch went sailing by.

"Strike Three!" He yelled a minute later after a timeout.

Mark was first up to bat and he struck out in three straight pitches that he swung at. He needs to choke up on the bat some, and change his stance. I wanted to say something, but we had enough drama going on already.

A HALF HOUR OR SO LATER

One by one, I watched as Mark's co-workers walked up to the plate. It seems like everyone is playing well today except him. I know it's because he was worried that his other woman was going to pull up any minute. I didn't want to be here anymore than he wanted me to be here, but this issue needed to be addressed. I needed to know if my marriage was over or if there was no hope. I plan on trying to make things work, but I also plan on checking this bitch that has turned our lives upside down. I love Mark, but if this is a thing, then I'm out!

Just then, one of the senior partners, Mr. Buick, came and sat next to me. He was the oldest of the partners and he was seldom if ever in the office. I liked him. He was a good and kind hearted man. At all of the previous functions that I have been at, he always spoke to me and treated me like a daughter. He was always there with one of his grandchildren at an event rather than walking in with a wife that was 20 years his junior, like the other partners did. Mr. Buick was married to his wife 28 years before she passed. He hasn't remarried since. Let him tell it, he is waiting to be re-united with her. He's a sweet man. I just can't see him firing Mark and not trying to find a way to keep him. He has been like a mentor to Mark these past few years. He has been a treasure to both of us. Mr. Buick was all of 60+ years of age, but he looked 50. He was a handsome man with salt and pepper hair. He reminded me of Stedman Graham. He was an older gentleman with strong features, a voice like James Earl Jones and a hard body. He was a statuesque man that commanded respect even at his age.

"Hello Deja, how have you been?"

"I'm fine Mr. Buick how are you?"

"Oh I can't complain. I'm a little tired and my arthritis has been acting up some, but the good Lord still has me here."

"Well then, Mr. Buick that means you're blessed."

"That I am. Listen, how have you and Mark been getting along?"

"Well, all things considered, I guess we are doing okay. I just started working longer hours so that we can make ends meet."

"What? That raise we gave Mark wasn't enough? Are you guys trying to buy a bigger home or something?"

I had to play it cool. Raise? What fucking raise? Do you mean to tell me that this motherfucker got a raise?

"Yeah, well we are looking to move to a nicer house, get new cars and put away a little more for our retirement." I said calmly, trying to play things off.

"Well, listen you shouldn't have to work longer hours at your job, why don't you just come and work at our firm for more money? In fact, why don't you just take Mark's old position? I think it paid about 65K to start."

Mark's old position? Stay calm, breathe, breathe, girl breathe and say a prayer.Now Speak.

"I don't know if Mark and I can work together." I said almost sarcastically.

"Well, technically you wouldn't work together. You would be in a different department. I mean you would actually be working for Mark in a round about way—with him making partner and all."

*Partner! Did this man just tell me that Mark made partner and I am working longer hours because he told **me** that we were in dire straits?* I was so mad I could spit fire and acid. Exactly what kind of bullshit was Mark on?

"Well, with him making partner, I guess we might be able to work something out." I said calmly.

"So what are you all doing with the extra money?"

"Oh I don't know. Mark handles all those things."

"But you're a financial analyst too right?"

"Yes sir, but I am not the wiz that Mark is."

"Oh I think that you will do fine. Just say the word and I will put in a good word for you."

"Thank you Mr. Buick, I'll think about it."

Just then, Mark walked over and interrupted us.

"Hey babe, you okay?"

"I'm fine." I responded flatly.

"I was just telling your wife here how proud I am that you made partner." Mr. Buick said.

I stared at Mark coldly. I almost looked through him. He was visibly shaken that things had been brought out into the open. He looked at me and then looked at Mr. Buick and tried his best to form a smile and not tip his hand.

"Yeah, well I want to thank you Mr. Buick for the opportunity."

"You are most welcome son."

"I won't let you down." He said while looking at me.

"You already have." I said in a voice just above a whisper.

Mr. Buick looked at me when I said that. He looked at me and could see that I had a tear in my eye that I was holding back. His years of experience told him that there was more going on than what was being told. I played it off though, and spoke to my husband.

"You need to choke up on your bat and change your stance some." I told Mark.

"What?" Mark replied.

"Your stance is all wrong and you need to choke up on your bat."

"And how would you know that young lady?" Mr. Buick asked.

"I used to play softball in college."

"I didn't know that." Mr. Buick said.

"I didn't know that either." Mark said.

"Well dear, we have only been together a few years. There are still a lot of things that you don't know about me."

I stared at him intently.

"Looks like you have a lot to learn about your woman here Mark." Mr. Buick stated.

"I guess I do sir." Mark replied.

"Maybe you should start Mark, with knowing that anything that you can do, I can do. Some things, I might just be able to do better."

That got a rise out of him. He looked like I stabbed him in the chest when I said that.

"With sports I mean." I said sarcastically.

"Yeah, right ... sports." Mark said.

"I mean, you aren't the only one that knows how to play. I haven't played in a long time, but I can get out there if I need to. I still remember the rules to the game."

The remarks were lost on Mr. Buick, but Mark knew exactly what the hell it was that I was talking about.

"Mark, it's your turn up at bat!" One of his co-workers yelled.

"Yeah baby, *it's your turn.*" I chimed in.

Mark walked away from me like he was wounded. He headed to the plate.

He didn't know if I was serious or not, but it was obvious what my message was.

Yeah motherfucker you can cheat but I can cheat too and I bet there are more nig-gas that will come at me than there are women that will come at your ass.

"Change your stance and choke up on that bat!" I yelled.

"Yes dear." He said almost apologetically.

Mark walked up to the plate and looked back at me unsure of what was going to happen next.

"Strike One!" The umpire yelled.

Just choke up on the damned bat.

"Strike Two!" The umpire yelled.

"Choke up on the bat baby! You can take him!" I yelled.

The pitcher yelled, "Hey, you gonna play or listen to your broad? Shouldn't she be at home ironing your shirt or something?"

No this motha fucka didn't.

I got up and walked toward home plate.

"Time Out!" Mr. Buick yelled from the bleachers.

I walked up to my husband, showed him the *correct stance* and showed him how to choke up on the bat and where to watch when the pitcher threw the ball.

"Do it like this. Watch his torso and his stance. Hold the bat, focus and shift your weight this way when the ball comes."

"Okay babe."

"Knock this shit out of the park."

"I will. Babe about ..."

"... Not now."

He looked down. I looked directly at him and that tear fell down my face.

"Handle this shit first."

I walked toward my seat and the pitcher started in on me.

"That's it honey, help your man out because he sure can't hit for shit."

"Shut the fuck up, you pitch like a bitch."

That shut him up.

The pitcher stared at me as I walked back to my seat. He then looked in Mark's direction, stared him down and began his wind up. He pitched the ball, an inside slider.

POW!

Mark hit the ball damn near out of Grant Park. He looked in my direction and I winked at him. He ran the bases and his team was up 3-0. He looked in my direction as he ran in to home plate. I smiled a half a smile and looked away.

We should have celebrated together this small victory.

Instead I am seething inside.

And looking for a woman that I will know when I see her, that she is fucking my husband.

Fucking—my husband.

MERCEDES

It was 9:30 when I pulled up to the corner where the park was. I got out of my car with my hair in a ponytail pulled through a world champion White Sox cap, a black corset and a pair of skin tight blue jeans. I had on high heels and I strutted my stuff as I threw my keys in my Coach purse and headed slowly toward the park. I walked slow of course to demand attention. Yeah, to some I might have looked a little on the sinful side, but when you have got a body like mine, you have to flaunt it. Men love my body and women wish that they had my body. I walked confidently as I headed to see my man play ball. Mark thinks that he is staying with Deja's tired wanna be diva ass, but I got news for him. After I drop these DVD's of us having sex every which way, he is going to have to rethink his whole demo.

I saw Mark's Camry and walked over to it to leave a sexy note on his car. I looked in the driver's side and noticed that there was a small purse in the car.

"Is that a purse in his car?" I said loudly.

I looked at it and it was a small black purse that I often saw Deja carry to work. It was on the floor and beneath the seat not in plain sight, but it was there nonetheless.

"What the hell is her purse doing in his car?"

"I know that bitch ain't here!"

I walked harder toward the playing field. I was ready to snap out on Mark for bringing his goddamn wife to *my event*. It was my idea that he get on the team to impress his partners. It was my idea that he get into shape and play some type of sport. Every other Saturday was *my day*, not his wife's. How dare he bring her here! What type of fucking game is he playing?

I walked harder and faster toward the park. I was so mad that I could spit. There is no way that he should bring her to the game. There is no way he should have done so without calling me. Maybe it's time that she learned about us. I hate Deja's ass. I have hated her since I met her. Bitches like that think that they are special. Bitches like that make me mad with their stuck up, Christian, judgmental asses. Deja acts like she is better than anyone else. She acts like she is above everyone else. I bet she grew up privileged. I bet she got whatever she wanted growing up. I bet she went to a decent school had two parents that lived with her and grew up with a goddamned spoon in her mouth. It's time that somebody took something from her. It's time that someone made her realize that she ain't no better than the rest of us. It's like I said earlier, "Some of us are blessed to be in a monogamous relationship, some of us have to share a man and some of us are going to have to face the fact that some us are going to lose their man to a prettier, better looking and better bodied up woman. That bitch looked at me like I wasn't anything when I first met her. She looks at my clothes, my hair and my style and the bitch has "I'm jealous" written all over her face.

Yeah, I'm taking your man. Yeah bitch he's mine, not yours. I can have your man, your lifestyle and anything that I want just by taking it from you. Trifling bitch, who does she think that she is dealing with? I walked harder and harder toward her until you could practically hear my heels beating on the pavement like a horse on a cobblestone street. I walked closer and closer toward the playing field and then I noticed that the field was getting blurry.

It was then that I realized that I was crying.

I didn't want Deja to see me like this.

Not like this.

MARK

I was in the dugout waiting for my next turn at bat. We had been kicking the other team's ass all morning since I started playing better. We were up 12-8 and we were looking to score at least another two runs. I was next up at bat. I was warming up when I looked across the park and almost 70 yards away, I saw *her*.

I prayed.

I prayed like I have never prayed before.

I prayed like a slave in the back woods hiding in a brush and dogs were sniffing hard on his trail not four feet away.

God—please. If you are there Lord … Please … do … SOMETHING.

I closed my eyes and a tear streamed down my face.

God … If you get me out of this … I will never … fuck around on my wife again … Jesus … Please. I just need one more chance at happiness with my wife. One more. Please.

When I opened my eyes ... Mercedes ... was gone.

DEJA

I was looking at all the women that were now at the game. It was 9:40 and women were everywhere. Mark was up next at bat and I was scanning the bleachers hard as hell to find out who my competition was. I looked at women's faces, body language and eyes to see who was watching Mark and who was watching me as my husband came up to bat. I looked at all the sisters and the six or seven white women in the crowd. I wouldn't put it past Mark to mess around with one of the white women. I stared hard to find out who was the home wrecking bitch messing around with my man. My women's intuition must have been off. I was looking hard to see who was watching Mark with any type of intent. My intuition told me that the woman was not here. My heart told me that she wasn't here.

The Lord told me that she wasn't here—*but she was close.*

So where is she?

MERCEDES

Not yet.

I hate that bitch, but not yet.

I'm going home. I am going home and I am going to try and put this out of my mind. Otherwise there is gonna be a murder in a small town. Deja will get hers. It might not be today, but it will be soon. It's time that I showed this heifer who was the better woman. It's time that I showed her who was the baddest bitch. One way or the other, she had to learn.

Mark is mine—all mine.

If I have to suck him, fuck him, *burn him,* or kill him—he will be mine.

Or he will be no one's man.

MARK

I hit a home run—again. We beat the other team's ass by about 10 points. Ever since Deja showed me the proper way to hit, I knocked every ball thrown at me damn near out of the park. My bosses were on my tip, the co workers were on my tip and the women were definitely feeling me. God answered my prayer. Mercedes walked away. I don't know why and I don't care why, but she is gone and I will never ... sleep with her again. After we won the game, we were all on a high that only comes from playing sports. We went crazy and everyone hugged, cheered and smiled at one another like family.

"Let's go get drinks" one partner said.

"I'm sorry, we have to go home." Deja said.

I looked at my wife. I knew that I was in for a long day. No matter what it took though, I was going to make it work with her.

"I'm sorry, she's right, we have some things to take care of today."

I took my wife by the hand. Her body language suggested that she wanted to pull away. I know the only reason that she didn't, was because it would look bad in front of my co-workers and partners. We walked in silence to the car. I had time as we walked to the car to think, reflect and take the time to figure out what I had done as well as assess how bad the damage was that I had done. We got to the car and there waiting for us was a surprise.

The car window on the passenger side was broken.

Deja looked at me and I looked at her. I put my head down because it was obvious to me what happened. I was just hoping that it wasn't obvious to Deja.

"My purse is gone."

"You left your purse in the car?"

I played it off like that was the reason that the window was broken. I knew better. Deja gave me a look that said, *"Nigga Please."*

Later today, I plan to visit Mercedes at her home.

CHAPTER 8

▼

TIME TO COME CLEAN

MARK

The drive home was long and quiet. We filed a police report and went on about our day. I couldn't think of anything to say. I didn't know how to approach my wife. Many of my lies had been exposed and it was obvious that I had a woman—somewhere.

I walked into the house, threw my keys on the table and sat down on the couch. Deja sat across from me and together, we sat in silence for a few minutes. I could see that she was thinking about her approach and trying to choose her words. I could also see that she was holding back tears. I was afraid and confused all at once. I debated in my head about whether or not I should tell the truth or at least try to come up with a half-way reasonable lie to tell. Then it dawned on me that lying truly would make things worse, so I figured to tyy avoidance instead, if possible.

"So ... partner huh?"

I sighed before saying, "Yes."

"Congratulations."

"And this whole, going broke things was ..."

"... A diversion."

"... You mean bullshit!"

"Yes."

"So, what should I do with all the money that I saved from working all those extra hours?"

"Whatever you want babe."

"Don't call me that."

"What should we do with the extra 30K that you make?"

"Whatever you want."

"Hmmnn."

I remained silent. I wasn't volunteering anything.

"So who is she?"

"Who?"

"Nigga, don't play with me."

More silence.

"Who is she?"

"I don't want to say. All I can say is that it was a mistake and it will never happen again."

"Why should I believe that it will never happen again?"

"Because I love you."

"And you didn't before?"

Again—silence.

"I know what I have at home now."

"And you didn't before?"

"I did, but I guess I forgot ... or maybe took what I had for granted."

"And?"

"And baby, I'm sorry."

"Who is she?"

"I'm not going there."

"Dammit, who is she!"

"No one, she's no one. She means nothing to me."

"Oh that makes me feel a hell of a lot better!" She said before pausing.

"Do I know her?" She asked.

"No."

I lied. I had to lie. How the hell could I tell her not only that I messed around on her, but I messed around on her with a woman that she can't stand? There would be no coming back from that, no reconciliation and probably no way in hell that I would get out of this house alive.

"Is she pretty?"

"D, come on ..."

"... Is she pretty!

"She's A'ight."

"So you messed around on me with a bitch that is just A'ight?"

"It was a mistake."

"Damn right it was."

"It will never happen again."

"The damage is already done."

"So there is no hope for us?"

"Sure there is … after you answer a few more questions."

"D, I don't want to play 20 questions on this."

"Mothafucka if you want this marriage then you will answer 1000 questions if need be!"

I was in no position to argue. I shook my head okay. I began to rub my temples which ached.

"How many times did you sleep with her?"

"D, look …"

"How many MOTHA FUCKIN TIMES … Did YOU SLEEP WITH HER?"

"A few."

"More than ten?"

"Less than twenty."

"Less than …?"

She began pacing the room with her hand over her mouth. She continued to hold her head and pace back and forth. I thought at any minute she was going to leap across the room and beat my ass. I couldn't understand why she was punishing herself like this.

"Do you love her?"

"No, hell no."

"You were just fucking her."

"?"

"What about us Mark, what did I ever do to you?"

"Nothing. You have been wonderful. Baby … I'm sorry."

"I'm sorry too. I'm sorry that you are making me do what I have to do now."

"What is that supposed to mean?"

"It means that maybe I need to take on a lover and sleep with him less than twenty times."

"What?"

"Oh, what … you object? It's a little bit different when the shoe is on the other foot now, isn't it?"

"Deja, you can't mean that."

"Why the hell can't I? If you did it, why can't I do it? Here's a question, why did you do it?"

"I don't know."

"I need something better than I don't know."

"D, all I can say is that it will never happen again."

"All I can say is that it's my turn."

"Deja ..."

"Fuck You Mark!"

"Deja ..."

She left the house, jumped into her car and drove off.

She can't be serious about fooling around on me, can she?

DEJA

Who the fuck does he think he is? Just who in the hell does he think that he is? I can't believe that he did this shit to me. I can't believe that he ruined our marriage. How am I supposed to move on from here? I jumped in my car and when I looked up, it was 12:00 PM. I drove back to the 9705 Bar and Adrienne was unlocking the gates and getting ready to open the bar. She saw me as I pulled up and she smiled. I got out feeling sorry for myself. I walked in the bar and sat at the counter.

"It's a little early to serving drinks isn't it?" I asked Adrienne.

"Girl, no. I have regulars that come in, watch baseball and TV and drink their lives away. Many of the afternoon regulars tip better than the evening guys.

"Well I guess some people can drink any time of the day no matter what."

"It depends on how their day is going. And how is your day going?"

"I didn't catch him, but he admitted to the infidelity."

"Did you pull his phone records?"

"They will be here in a few days."

"So what did he have to say?"

"Girl, a whole bunch of nothing."

"And did you settle for a whole bunch of nothing?"

"Adrienne, I was so tired. I didn't want to know anymore about the affair."

"I think that was a mistake."

"Why?"

"Because you still know virtually nothing. You need to turn this thing inside and out and get to know all there is to know. You need to make this whole ordeal so grueling for him, that he *will never consider pulling this shit again, ever.*"

"You think so."

"I know so."

"You ever been through this yourself?"

"What woman hasn't?"

MARK

I headed toward my car after taking a shower and figuring out my next move. I wanted to follow Deja out of the door, but I needed to let her process all that happened and I needed to give her space. More than that, I needed to shut things down with Mercedes.

I jumped in my car, threw in my Mos Def CD and headed to Mercedes home. My mind raced as I headed toward her house. All I could think about was the sex that we had and how off the chain it was. I also thought about the fact that I was going to miss that pussy. I weighed all my options though, and the shit that I pulled was stupid. I love Deja. She and I worked damn hard to get where we are today. I needed to tell Mercedes goodbye. I needed to end this shit. I needed to do whatever it took to salvage my marriage.

I pulled up in front of her apartment. It took me awhile to get myself together. I walked out of the car, up to the doorbell and rang her bell, 3C. She buzzed me in as usual. I took that long walk up the stairs and the door was already open. A beautiful Puerto Rican woman walked out. She was 5, 5, 120 lbs. She had log black hair, grey eyes, full lips and a body like a sistah's. My mouth dropped as she walked out.

"Hello Papi." She said as she walked down the stairs.

She had a fat ass. I mean she had an ass that rivaled Mercedes' ass, and that was no small feat. She had on tight ass, Levi Blue Jeans, two inch heels, and a *Baby Phat* halter top. I watched that ass as she walked away. I had a quick 30 second fantasy about her. I then walked into Mercedes apartment feeling guilty about checking her friend out like that. Damn that Boricua was fine ass hell though.

"Who was that?"

"My lover."

"Your what?"

"My other lover. What the fuck do you want?"

She had attitude with me? What was this all about?

"I came by to tell you that it's over—we can't see each other anymore."

"Yeah, I figured as much. I saw Deja at the game today, what the fuck was she doing there?"

"She decided at the last minute that she wanted to go."

"And you let her."

"What the fuck was I suppose to do? She's a grown ass woman."

"Saturday was *my day*."

"You don't have a day. What we did was wrong. What I did was wrong. I love my wife. I'm done ... it should have never gone this far. I'm out."

"Just like that?"

"Just like that."

"That's unacceptable."

"I'm sorry?"

"I said, that's unacceptable."

"Yeah, I heard you, are you out of your mind?"

"I love you."

"You don't fucking know me."

"I will treat you better than she does."

"She treats me just fine, thanks."

"Yeah? Then why have you been fucking me all these months?"

"Mercedes, it was a mistake."

"Are you calling me a mistake?"

"I'm calling us ... this ... all this is a mistake."

"And I am just supposed to be okay with you walking out of my life."

"Yeah. I'm sorry that you got hurt. I'm sorry that I got involved, but that's it, I have to walk. Besides, you have someone else already."

"If you are referring to the Boricua, she was for us."

"Us?"

"Us."

That gave me a moment of pause. I have never had a ménage before and ever since I read the one in Darrin Lowery's book, *Still Crazy*, I wanted to have one at least once. That shit was of the chain! I have to admit, I was tempted. I was evry tempted, but I thought about the fact that Deja was my wife. On top of that, she has always had my back. I shook off the thought of me, Mercedes and the Puerto Rican broad in bed and gathered my composure as best I could. I then went back to explaining that this thing with Mercedes, whatever it was, was over.

"Mercedes, I have to go. I just wanted to let you know that we're done."

"She won't fuck you like I will."

I kept walking.

"Can we have sex just once more? Just once more baby, please?"

"No."

"So you are going to turn away this ass, these tits, my suckable lips and your every fantasy for what, Deja's frigid ass?"

I stopped at the door. Mercedes stripped out of her clothes right there where she stood. She was sporting a royal blue bra with black lace, matching panties, a garter and heels. She reached for a pin and retrieved it from her hair letting her hair down and letting it bounce. She then put a hand on both of her hips and rolled her neck like, "Nigga what?"

"So you are going to give all this up? What, she said she would take it in the ass tonight? Or did she promise that she would swallow? Or wait, she said she would wear lingerie and act like a wife is *supposed to act*. I bet she has offered to make no changes. I bet she also doesn't know that the other woman is me."

"No, she doesn't know it's you." I said with my head resting against the door.

"So why are we not fucking anymore? Is it just guilt or stupidity? Mark, you know you want me. You know she will never please you the way that I do. Who are you fooling?"

Damn I'm weak.

"Fuck me Mark."

"No Mercedes."

"Fuck me Mark."

"I can't."

"Then come over here and at the very least let me put your dick in my mouth."

That gave me a moment of pause. I let out a sigh as I turned around and looked at Mercedes ... my mistress.

MERCEDES

Yeah that's right MF bring your ass in here. Make that mistake that all unfaithful niggas make. Hit this one more time so I can really put it on you. You may love your wife but being with me is about to test how strong your relationship truly is. I didn't go through all this to lose. I'm going to make you re-think this goodbye shit.

I walked over to mark and kept things simple by giving him a hug. I then kissed him softly on the lips, kissed his neck, raised his shirt over his head and then kissed his nipples. While I kissed his chest, I reached for his package. I kissed him deeply on the mouth again while jagging him off slowly. He reached for my ass hesitantly. He settled for placing his hands on my waist. I took his hands and put them on my backside as we continued to kiss.

I undid his belt buckle. I then pulled his pants down around his ankles, dropped to my knees and began to please him. I placed his hands in my hair and made him make me give him head. Initially he was hesitant. He was still thinking about *her*. I had to get his mind off *her* so I began to moan as if I was getting off on sucking his dick. Not only did I do that, but I began to gag and make slurping sounds on his dick while jagging him off in my mouth at the same time. Men get off on sound. They get off on the idea of women getting off on their dicks. Men are so stupid. I played the game though and worked him like a porno star giving head to a high school nerd. I blew his mind.

Minutes later, Mark came and came hard. As he came I continued to jag him off and took every drop of his seed. I know that Deja doesn't do this, so I know later when he leaves here he will *at least* think about the head that I gave him. He came and I led him to the bathroom to wash him off. I gargled, bathed *my man,* and went into the kitchen and began to cook. I acted like the conversation that we had never happened. I acted as if I were the top player in this relationship which I think he knows that I am. My motto when it comes to stealing a man is simple, "Suck him, Fuck him and feed him."

MARK-FEELING GUILTY—AGAIN

What have I done? Why did I go there again? Damn, I'm weak. I have to go home. I need to go home. That head was the bomb. That ass on Mercedes is the bomb. But I can't keep doing this shit.

The warm water rinsed the soap off my body. After the blowjob, Mercedes came and washed me up from head to toe. She lathered my whole body and make me feel pampered. I enjoyed a hot shower, but nothing was better than to have a woman lather you up. Deja didn't cater to me like this. Deja didn't swallow, take it from the rear or dress up hardly anymore. Why can't I have this type of life-style? Why can't I have my cake and eat it too? I rinsed the soap off my body and thought about my next move. Do I just go home and never call Mercedes again? Who am I kidding? I'm going to do like most men and stay with both until one of them forces me into a decision.

DEJA—5 MINUTES EARLIER

"I don't know Adrienne, what should I do?"

"Girl, if you want to stay with your man then stay with him. But I would make his ass crawl over hot coals before letting him know that you are taking him back. Also, I wouldn't let his ass out of my sight. When you go to the store, he goes to the store. When you're not home, and he is, call him for no reason. Check the phone records, check that nigga's car and surprise him at work on occasion. In fact, call that nigga now and see if he answers the phone or if it goes to voicemail. Later on, get the password to his phone and check his phone messages periodically. Also check his email on his laptop. In the meanwhile, give that nigga a call.

I dialed the house.

No answer.

I dialed his cell.

No answer on the first ring.

"Adrienne he isn't answering."

"He may be getting closure with the other bitch and telling her goodbye."

He didn't answer the second ring.

"He could be screwing her also." I said.

"He could." Adrienne replied.

The phone rang a third time and the receiver picked up.

"Hello? Hello? Hello?" I asked.

"Yes." A woman's voice responded.

My heart sunk in my chest. I began to tremble. I looked at the phone again at the display to see if I had dialed the right number. My phone clearly said, "Mark."

It was the other woman on the line. I was hurt. I then became angry. The voice almost sounded familiar, but I couldn't quite place it.

"Is Mark there?"

"He's in the shower washing off my sex."

"What did you say?"

"Bitch you heard me."

[click.]

I stared at the phone unable to believe what just happened. I held back the tears and grabbed my coat.

"Adrienne, I have to go. I have to get my house in order."

"Girl, don't let your emotions control you. You control your emotions."

"Adrienne, I just don't know what to do."

"Maybe it's time that you gave him a taste of his own medicine."

"You mean cheat on him? Two wrongs don't make a right."

"You aren't trying to make things right. You want him to feel what you feel right now. You want his world to close in around him like it has for you. You want him to know the *level of pain that you are in*. You don't have to stay with another man, but you need another man."

"Why?"

"Because that bitch answered the phone, didn't she?"

"Yeah, she did."

"Then he has broken one of the cardinal rules."

"Rules?"

"Yeah. Look, if a man is going to cheat, then the other woman needs to be in check. That means under no circumstances should you all meet, talk or should your paths ever cross. If his phone rang then there is no way in hell that bitch should answer it. Where did she say that he was."

"In the shower washing of her sex."

"Then she knows you. She not only knows that he has a wife, she knows you and doesn't like you."

"How do you figure that?"

"If he told her he was single, she wouldn't have thought anything about saying that he is in the shower, which would have put this all on him. To say that he is washing off her sex is personal. Either she knows you, or she wants your man that bad."

"Adrienne, is there any hope of my keeping my marriage?"

"After counseling—and an affair on your part."

"You really think that will help my situation?"

"Oh hell yeah! Men cheat all the time, but they have *very fragile egos*. Let us do to them what they do to us, and they will lose their damned minds."

"So who do I fool around with?"

"Someone younger, better looking, wealthier, and in great shape."

"Why does the other man have to be such a stud?"

"Because when you get caught, he will know that you can not only do the same things that he does, you can do a lot better. If he has a bigger dick, that's a plus all in itself. That will really fuck his head up."

MARK

I walked out of the shower and sitting on the counter was a Porterhouse Steak, baked potato, cheese, sour cream, onion and a glass of wine. I went to the counter, ate the food, and Mercedes went into the bedroom. When I finished eating, I was distracted by a buzzing sound. I checked my phone to see if it had rang because it was on vibrate.

Deja called, about 6 times, but I still heard the buzzing sound. I started to call her back, but I couldn't take a chance on Mercedes making any noise. So I started getting dressed.

Then I heard the moaning.

The buzzing became more intense.

I walked into Mercedes bedroom. She was masturbating with a rabbit. The buzzing was intense and her moans became louder and louder. Her eyes were closed, her hips and ass bucked in the air and she was penetrating herself deeply. She pleased herself with slow, long, methodical strokes. The dildo worked its way in and out of her, and periodically she would stop with the device all the way in her as the tip vibrated on her clit.

I unzipped my pants.

My dick was hard again.

I slowly walked over and I placed it in her mouth.

She accepted me freely.

My pants dropped to the floor. Over and over again I grabbed a fist full of her hair and made her take me in. Over and over again I pulled out of her mouth all the way to the tip and back in again. She slurped and moaned louder and louder until a few minutes later she was beginning to cum.

Few things in the world feel as good as woman giving a man head as she comes. The moaning alone is a turn on. Then there is the fact that the man is most times pretending that the woman is cumming from giving him head. Yeah we know that is impossible, but we think it anyway. She started cumming really hard and minutes later so did I. She came, and I came in her mouth and again she took every drop. My knees buckled and I got in bed beside her. She turned her back to me and spoke.

"Goodbye Mark."

That took me by surprise. I got up, got dressed, looked at her in confusion, and headed toward the door. I hated the fact that it felt like she was leaving me, but the truth was I told her it was over when I first got here. It's over. I guess she's letting me off the hook. That's it, I guess I'm out. I headed toward the door and my mind was racing in many different directions.

MERCEDES

"He'll be back. Two weeks of Deja's accusations and her simple sex life, and he'll be back.

CHAPTER 9

▼

WHAT'S GOOD ENOUGH FOR THE MAN …

DEJA

Mark came home smelling like fruit and lilac. I don't know if that is his woman's soap or her perfume, but it is obvious that he made his choice. When he got home we argued from that night until that morning. I told him that his bitch answered his phone and he insists that he only has the five phone calls that are presently in his phone. When I asked him why he didn't pick up his phone, he said that the music in his car was too loud. My next question was how could he be enjoying himself listening to music, when he should be thinking about saving his marriage? I asked him did he see her. He said he did and he told her that it was over. I asked him who she was and again he declined.

"Why the hell do you need to know who she is? All you need to know is that it's over."

"I need to know because your bullshit has turned our lives upside down."

"Baby … I have no idea how many ways I can tell you that I'm sorry. Can you just let it go?"

"Let it go? Let it go? You fuck someone else quite a few times and you expect me to just let it go?"

"Baby … Please."

"Fuck you Mark! Fuck You!"

I went into the bedroom and slammed the door. I was mad enough to spit acid.

THE NEXT DAY

The next day, I went to work. I called Adrienne on the phone and we talked off and on most of the morning. She then made a suggestion that made a lot of sense.

"Girl, didn't Mr. Buick offer you Mark's old job?"

"Yeah, so?"

"Doesn't it mean a $20,000 raise for you?"

"Yeah, but Mark and I agreed years ago that working together would be bad for our relationship."

"Worse than things are now?"

"Good Point."

"I think you should take that job. This way, you can watch him and at the same time secure your own financial future."

"I think you're right. I'll give Mr. Buick a call."

MARK

I felt like shit when I came home, I did. But things aren't right between me and Deja. Things in fact are pretty bad. Yeah I put us here, but all she needs to do is let the shit go. The relationship between me and Mercedes is over and if anything, she should be glad that it is. Mercedes is better in bed, she has a better body, long hair and she has no sexual hang-ups. Deja, on the other hand, has never given me everything that I have ever wanted in the bedroom. Some things she says are "unnatural." Others, she simply just won't do. Why shouldn't I get what I want? Why shouldn't I be happy? I know that I'm wrong for stepping out on my wife, but I want what I want. I went to sleep that night dreaming about Mercedes and how I can have my every way with her. I also thought about me and Mercedes having a ménage a trois with that fine as Puerto Rican babe.

The next day, I showered and my mind was still filled with lustful thoughts of Mercedes. I thought about what I would be giving up by being with only Deja. I made a decision that day that I would regret the rest of my life. I decided, "Fuck that, I'm going to have my cake and eat it too." I make $95,000 a year now. I'm a nice looking, educated black man. Most women would kill to have a man like me. There are plenty of women out there that wouldn't mind *sharing me*. Hell, there are plenty of women out there that would let me do my thing as long as I don't bring any STD's home and I didn't openly disrespect them. Deja is *lucky to have me.* I have worked hard all my life to have the lifestyle that I want. Hell, I deserve this shit. I will just have to hook up with Mercedes and lay down some ground rules. That way I can *have the best of both worlds.*

LATER, AT WORK.

I sent flowers to Mercedes at her job. I didn't attach a card, but I know she knows damned well who sent them. I then called Deja and tried to salvage our relationship. I told her that I loved her, that I didn't want to lose her and that the infidelity will never happen again. I told her that I was going through some things and that I would do whatever it takes to get her back into my life and to get things back between us the way that they were.

"You will do whatever it takes?" Deja asked.

"Whatever it takes."

"Then I want us to go to counseling."

"Clinical or Pastoral?"

"Both."

I was silent on the phone. I actually hated the idea of counseling. I couldn't fathom sitting down and telling some strange MF my every issue and then having them tell me how to live my life. But, this was my in back into my wife's heart.

"Okay baby, set it up. I'm there. I love you. Bye."

"Bye, I love you too."

THAT EVENING AT MERCEDES HOUSE

I drove to Mercedes house at the same time that I normally met her. I pulled my new car, a BMW into the lot of her complex and I confidently walked up to her bell and rang it. I was going to straighten her ass out this evening. Either that or I was walking away from her for good. The way I saw it, she could either accept my terms or fuck her, I would just go back to my wife. It's time that she learned exactly what her role was as the mistress. The buzzer allowed me entry and I took my time and walked back into our den of sin. She opened the door smiling like a sly cat. She was under the impression that I was back for sex and she had the power. She figured that I was pussy whipped and she had all the control. I was about to flip the script on her ass.

"So, I see that you are back. Why don't you get undressed and wait for me in the bedroom."

"I have a better idea, why don't you have a seat on the couch."

"Oh, you want to do it out here instead of the bed? That's cool."

"Actually, I want to talk."

"Talk? Talk about what?"

"My wife, our situation, and the ground rules."

"Ground rules?"

"Yeah, some shit needs to change."

"Mark, what are you saying?"

"That you need to know your role."

"Excuse me?"

"You heard me. Now listen, you jumped this shit off. Yeah, I wanted you from the first moment that I saw you, but it was you that approached me knowing damned well that I'm a married man. Now, this is how shit is going to be …"

"… Mark I don't know who the hell you think you are talking to but …"

"… Please be quiet."

"What?"

"I'm speaking."

"What?"

"I'm not finished yet. Now like I was saying, we have been disrespecting my wife for months now and that shit is wrong. Now these are the ground rules. You get no holidays, no weekends and no out of town trips. I will help out on the bills around here, but that is it. You are not to call me on the weekends, you are not to call me on holidays, and you are not to ever trip or confront my wife with any bullshit. If you do, I go back to her and only her, and I just might beat yo ass. If you can't hang, tell me now and I will walk out of here and never come back. The pussy is good and you are sexy as hell, but I love my wife."

"You have a funny way of showing it."

"That's another thing. We are not to discuss my wife or my situation. Otherwise, I'm out."

"Why, you feeling guilty?"

"See, that's the shit that I'm talking about. You take it easy, I'm out!"

I headed toward the door. I didn't have anything to lose. The bitch will either accept this shit or I go home to my wife. I got to the door, turned the knob, opened it and Mercedes called out to me.

"Mark! Mark, wait."

"What."

"You win. I will accept you on your terms."

"No drama?"

"No drama."

"Okay."

"Can you promise me one thing?"

"What?"

"If I am a good enough woman to you, will you at least *consider* leaving Deja?"

"I will." *Saying so was a huge mistake, I know but I figured I had to throw her a bone.*

"Then that's all I will ask you for. Are there any more conditions?"

"Just one more."

"What is it?"

"I want you to go in the bedroom, strip and wait there for me."

She looked at me with a confused look on her face.

"What didn't you understand about the instruction?"

"I got it. I'm just surprised at your approach."

"You told me once that you liked it when I took control, right?"

"Yeah."

"Then get your ass in there and get those clothes off ... Now!"

She smiled seductively at me. I began to take off my clothes and she slowly walked to the bedroom and let me see that wonderful backside of hers.

MERCEDES

Yeah, you win right now motherfucker. But you best believe that Ms. Mercedes has something for your ass later. I'll play mistress. I'll be obedient—for now. But I will give this shit six months before I'm the one dictating terms and you are the one begging.

PART II

CHAPTER 10

▼

DEJA'S TURN
(SIX WEEKS LATER)

DEJA

I interviewed with Mr. Buick who was more than happy to take me on as a financial analyst in Mark's company. I had to give two weeks notice at my job, and I didn't tell Mark that I was switching jobs. I figured that he could find out the same way that I found out about his job. Working at his company meant a $15,000 increase for me. I went back to my job after confirming that I got the position, and I began that day to pack my things. People in the office didn't know why I cleared my desk. Everyone was curious, but I felt that it was no one's business other than my supervisor. I cleared my desk and put all my things in my car including my photo of me and Mark. I was just about to call Mark to see how his day was going when the office ho, Mercedes, walked by my desk. I don't know what it is about this sister that I hate her ass so much. She seems like the type to sleep her way to the top and the type that you have to watch around your man. That's why I made sure that Mark only saw her a handful of times and I was there when they did see each other. I bet behind my back, she would be trying to fuck my husband. I bet the bitch that he was messing around with was just like her. I heard that Mercedes slept with an Executive at one of our other branches, and that is why she was transferred here. Other people say that she isn't from another branch of our bank at all. Other people say that she has worked at all the major banks and slept with every financial wizard in the city.

I don't give a damn what her history is. I hated the way that's she dressed, the way that she carried herself, and the way she made black women everywhere look. I bet she has no education, no common sense, and she probably used to strip before she got here. What kind of fucking name is Mercedes anyway? She sounds like she used to be a stripper or a damned call girl.

"Hey girl, how are you?" She asked.

"Fine Mercedes, how are you?"

"Couldn't be better, how is that husband of yours?"

"He's fine. How are things in your department?"

"They're okay. Listen, what's up with your desk? Why is everything all clear?"

I had to think fast on my feet. I didn't want this bitch in my business. I bet she was asking so that she could find my boss, sleep with him and take my position.

"A friend of mine was laid off from her job after 10 years of being there. I decided to take things off my desk to remind me that nothing is permanent."

"Wow, it's funny that you say that."

"Really, why?"

"Oh nothing. Well actually, I was just thinking to myself this morning that very same thought. Things are never quite what they seem and change can come at any minute. Girl, you're right, *nothing is permanent.*"

I don't know what this bitch is talking about, but I will play along.

"Yeah, change is healthy." I said.

"Some people can't handle change though."

Was that a shot? Where is she going with this shit?

"Yeah, well I'm not one of those people. I welcome change if it's for the better."

"For the better, huh?"

"Yeah."

"Hmmnn, okay."

Mercedes walked away from my desk. I guess she already knew that I was leaving. Maybe my boss already told her. Maybe she already knows and she is taking my place. If she is, I don't know what makes her think that she is better than me. I called Mark and made sure that he was going to be on time for our therapy sessions tonight. First we are headed to the church to see my pastor, Reverend Darlene Kelly, and later our counselor, Author and Therapist, Darrin Lowery.

PASTORAL COUNSELING
MARK

We first went to pastoral counseling. Reverend Kelly talked about adultery being one of the commandments, infidelity, the man treating the wife better than he treats himself, and the wife being a help mate to her husband. I listened attentively to Reverend Kelly because I didn't want Deja to leave me, but also because Reverend Kelly was fine as hell. She was light-skinned, she had long black hair, and legs that went on forever. I had a hard time maintaining eye contact with the good reverend because she was just that fine. Deja and I talked with her about an hour as she questioned the both of us. Then at the conclusion of the meeting, the Reverend asked to speak to me alone. Reluctantly, Deja agreed and she waited for me in the hallway.

"Mark, do you love Deja?"

"Of course I do."

"Then why are you still cheating on her?"

"I'm sorry, what?"

"Why are you still cheating on her?"

"Who says that I am?"

That fucked me up. It was like either God was talking to the good reverend or I had a camera strapped to my ass and didn't know it. She continued to talk to me.

"It's written all over your face, plus I just know."

I was stunned. I didn't know what to say. I felt I had no other choice than to lie. It felt bad lying to a minister in church this close to Sunday.

"Reverend, I don't know what you're talking about."

"Don't you?"

I called her bluff

"No, I don't."

"Okay then Mark, you want to lie to me, in my church, in my face? Okay. Do what you feel you have to do. But I am begging you, let that other woman go and keep the vows that you all took in this church before God, your family and friends. Deja is a good woman. I don't have to tell you that. You may have to learn this lesson the hard way. The thing is, once you lose her, you may never get her back. You need to think about that."

"I hear you Reverend, but I don't know what you are talking about."

She frowned at me.

"Okay Mark. Whatever."

"Whatever? That's an odd stance to take as a minister, isn't it? I mean, you're supposed to be supportive and stuff."

"I'm also a woman and I know for a fact that you are lying to me. So what, I'm supposed to just play along and threaten you with fire, brimstone and damnation? Mark you know exactly what it is that you are doing and it is painfully obvious to me that you are going to have to learn a lesson the hard way."

"Is that your position or God's?"

"Both."

"Hmnn well like you said, whatever. I'm not doing anything."

"I hate a liar."

"Damn Rev, how do you really feel?"

"Uh-huh, okay Mark. I tried to talk some sense into you. I guess this situation, is on you."

She got up to open the door. When she stood up, I couldn't help but notice how attractive she was.

"You're going to burn in hell for looking at me like that."

I didn't even realize how I might have been looking at her. I looked away and tried to play things off.

She called Deja into the room and asked me to step out. My heart skipped a beat because I didn't know what it was that she was going to say. I started to protest, but that would just make me look worse. I paced the hall as Reverend Kelly and my wife spoke—privately.

DEJA

The Reverend called me into her office to meet with me alone. I was nervous as hell as well as curious as to what she had to say.

"Deja, pray for your husband."

"He's still cheating on me isn't he?"

"What does your heart tell you?"

"That he is still seeing her."

"And what do you want to do about your marriage?"

"I want to keep my husband."

"Then pray for him."

"If he were your husband, what would you do?"

"I would pray for him. But I would pray for him while we were separated."

"Are you suggesting that I leave him?"

"No, you have to find your own path. I am suggesting that you let God work it out. If I were you, I would ask God to fix his heart. I would ask God to either fix his heart or take him away and send the *right man in your life to be your mate.*"

"Reverend, I'm scared. I love him. We have been together only three years, but it seems like forever. I don't want a failed marriage."

"The only reason that the Bible gives for divorce is adultery. Now, you have grounds to leave. If things don't work out, and I'm not saying that they won't, then your marriage hasn't failed, *your husband has.* You pray and I'll pray too. He needs to see that you're a good woman. The Bible says that a man who finds a wife finds a good thing. He can't know how much he loves you with you going along with his BS. If anything, you are co-signing his behaviors."

"So I should leave him?"

"You should pray about it and follow your heart."

MARK

Our next stop was to see this cat named Darrin. He had a private practice in Lynwood Illinois out of his home. The brother's crib was laid. He seemed like an okay enough brother until his questions became more and more personal. He kept asking how we felt about this, how we felt about that, why I cheated, how it affected Deja and what would stop me from cheating again. The questions became more and more difficult as the session went on. Before I knew it, I was sweating my ass off and mad enough to fight. I hated this therapy shit. If I didn't know any better I would say that this therapist was a straight up hater. At the conclusion of the session, the therapist asked to speak to me in private. I was surprised by his request. He asked Deja to wait in the hall and he asked me to sit down. Here we were, two professional black men sitting across from one another and this cat, Darrin, had a look on his face like he was superior and like I wasn't shit.

"Mark, do you love your woman?"

"Of course I do."

"Then you need to let the other woman go dawg."

"Who says that I have another woman ... dawg?"

He gave me a look that said, "Nigga Please."

"Look, player to player ... you have a good woman here. You need to do right by her. It's obvious that you fucked up. It's obvious that you love her and it's also obvious that she is willing to give you another chance. Do you know what else is obvious?"

"No, what?" I said sarcastically.

"It's obvious that *she knows that you are still seeing the other woman.* I'm telling you man to man, you need to let the mistress go. Deja is giving you enough rope to either save yourself or hang yourself. Make no mistake about it bruh, she knows."

"You can tell all that from one session?"

"I could tell from the first 15 minutes."

"How?"

"Been there, done that."

"So you have cheated too?"

"That's not the point."

"What is the point?"

"The point is, you aren't in need of therapy. Your wife isn't in need of therapy. The two of you need to just get your shit together, specifically, you. The one that needs to be in therapy is the mistress."

"Why?"

"She's fucking around with a married man for starters. Also, you have no idea how stable or unstable this woman is. Didn't you read my book, *Divorce Him, Marry Me?*"

"No."

"Well, the point of the matter is, she might be crazy. Most mistresses are women with some serious self esteem problems. They are looking for love in all the wrong places and many of them are hypersexual."

"So it couldn't just be that I am a handsome MF, huh?"

"No."

"Are you sure?"

"Pretty sure. Women that are mistresses aren't in love with you nor are they infatuated with you. They want what they can't have. They are not in love with you, but the *idea or fantasy* of being in love with you. This woman that you are fooling around with thinks that the grass is greener on the other side. Trust me, once the thrill wears off for both of you, you might find out that she is boring and after all is said and done—just a woman. And then, you might find out that she is not just a woman, but a horrible woman at that. Deja seems like a good girl, like she has your back. Hold on to her brother. If you lose her, the next man, if he is a good man, won't let her go. And then …"

He gave me an odd look.

"… And then what?"

"… And then you are stuck with a fine but crazy ass bitch."

"Who said she was fine?"

"She'd have to be for you to mess around on Deja."

"Have you been checking out my WIFE!"

"Yeah."

"And you are comfortable telling me this shit?"

"Yeah."

"Why!"

"To prove a point. Your wife is fine. Do you see how upset you became at the thought of my just looking at her? Imagine someone else looking at her like that. Then imagine someone else sleeping with you wife and hitting spots that you could never reach. Imagine someone fucking your wife—well! Imagine her in the throws of passion with another man. Now think about how pissed off you are right now. That's just from me *mentioning* another man. Now multiply that shit by 100. That's what your woman is going through right now. What's tripped out is that she is willing to take you back. Bruh, do the right thing. Let this other broad go. You had your fun. You got caught. Now it's time to man up."

I looked at this nigga like he was crazy. I couldn't believe that he was looking at my wife like this. I started to trip, but I figured fuck it, I'll just go.

"You take it easy Doctor."

"Actually, I'm just a Master's level therapist. But okay, you take it easy too. Think about what I said. The next man won't let her slip through his fingers."

"I just don't want the next man to be you." I said hard.

"Careful bruh, you never know."

"What did you say?"

"Deja, can I see you for a minute?" Darrin said.

DEJA

Darrin asked me to come into his office and he handed me a business card.

"You don't need therapy. You may need someone to talk to about the pain that you are experiencing, but you don't need therapy."

"I don't?"

"No."

"What about my husband?"

"He may need a few sessions, but I have a feeling he won't commit to that."

"He won't commit to many things these days."

"I'm sorry to say that you might be right."

"He's still cheating on me isn't he?"

"What does your heart say?"

"My heart is telling me to leave."

"Well ... follow your heart."

"Are you saying leave him?"

"I'm saying, follow your heart. If you need someone to talk to, here's my card."

"Is this for additional counseling or personal?"

"It's for additional support if you need it."

"You said I don't need therapy."

"You don't, but you may need someone to talk to. When that moment comes, I'm here if you need to talk."

I took his card and was unsure if he was hitting on me or really just being there for me as a friend or a counselor. He smiled at me and opened the door. He then told Mark and I goodbye.

A WEEK LATER, DEJA'S LAST DAY AT WORK
DEJA

I was shocked to hear that Mark was still fooling around on me. What did I do wrong? How could I have been a better wife? What the hell does this other woman have that I don't? I felt bad and then it dawned on me, *why do I have to be the one with the damned problem?* This shit is on him. I don't know how much of this he expects me to take, but I will give him either enough time to turn things around, or enough rope to hang himself. For the next few weeks I started calling Mark more frequently. I started asking him where was he, and questioning the hell out of him. I thought that would make him stop fooling around or thinking about what it was that he was doing, but instead, it just caused more arguments. I would ask him where he was, he would say something like, "why?" and I would then curse his ass out my saying, "Nigga you know why, you fucked around on me!" He would say, "Deja, stop fucking bugging out!" He would make me think that everything was in my head and for weeks upon weeks he never took responsibility for his part in this.

I don't know what it was that I wanted from him. He said he was sorry, but he didn't say it with any meaning or any purpose. I mean, I didn't feel his apology. Do you know what I'm saying? Sometimes a woman knows when a man is saying that he is sorry because he genuinely is. Then there are times that a woman knows that the man is saying I'm sorry just to appease us.

I packed the remainder of my things at the office on my last day. I shook my head in disbelief at where my marriage was. Just a few months back, my life was perfect. Well, if not perfect ... I was content. I packed my things and as soon as I got the last box filled up, here comes Mercedes again.

What the hell is up with her? Why is she coming over here again? What is giving her the impression that I even want to be bothered with her ass?

"Hey girl, where are you going?" She asked.

"Today is my last day here."

"Really? Where are you going?"

"I'm going home. I am taking a break and letting Mark work while I get myself together."

Yeah, I lied. Again, what I was doing and why, was none of her damned business. I resented the fact that this nosy bitch was all up in my business all of a sudden.

"So whose idea was it for you to stay home, yours or Mark?"

"Why?"

She was really starting to work my damned nerves

"Oh, I was just asking, you know making conversation."

"Mmm Hmmnn, conversation … right."

"Girl I didn't mean anything by it."

"Why are you so concerned about me all of a sudden Mercedes? I mean don't get me wrong, we are okay, I guess. But we have never been close. We have always just had a type of Hi-and-Goodbye-type of rapport. For the last couple of months you have been talking more and more to me."

"Is that a problem Deja?"

"I don't know, is it? I mean woman to woman, what's up with you?"

"I was just making small talk. Besides, maybe I want to be your replacement."

"You should talk to my boss about that."

"I was thinking maybe I should talk to you."

"Why?"

"I don't know, maybe because you are in the position that I want."

This conversation was getting strange. If I didn't know any better, I would think that she was talking about something else.

"Well I don't know what to tell you other than see my supervisor or talk to HR."

"You don't think that I can replace you, do you?"

I wanted to say to her, "Bitch, hell no." I'm a Christian woman though, so I kept it clean.

"I don't know enough about you Mercedes, can you do my job?"

"No offense girlfriend, but I may just do your job better than you."

This bitch had balls, I will give her that. I could feel the hairs on the back of my neck rise. I felt like I was back in grade school and this was some sort of feminine competition. I hated competing with other girls as a child. I would just resort to whipping their ass. I was looking at this ho like it was 2:45 and we were set to meet in the schoolyard at 3:15.

"You're confident Mercedes, I'll give you that."

"Deja, can I ask you a question?"

"Nothing has stopped you this far."

"Why don't you like me?"

"What makes you think I don't like you?"

"I think you have always hated me. I think that you are judgmental. I think that you can be unfair at times and I think that you think, you are better than me."

"What gives you that impression?" I said coyly.

"Well, woman to woman ... it's the way that you look at me."

"And how do I look at you?" I said with a bit of tension in my voice as the conversation started to get heated.

"You look at me like you hate me, or if I'm a tramp or something."

"Sounds like you are feeling insecure and guilty of being a tramp. I mean no offense ... but woman to woman, you might be reading too much into the way that I look at you. Maybe psychologically you feel like you are less than everyone else and maybe you feel like maybe you are too ... provocative for lack of a better word in the workplace."

"Maybe. Or Maybe you look at me the way you do because you wish that you were me." She said in a harsh tone.

"Excuse me!"

"I'm just saying. I mean you could look like me if you worked at it. You might even be more appealing if you didn't act like such a holy roller. I think that you walk around the office like your shit don't stink and you are better than everyone."

Shit was getting heated quick. I put the box down that was in my hands in case I had to handle some shit.

"Maybe that is just *your perception.*"

"Oh, I'm not the only one that feels this way. I just happen to be the only one that will say so."

"And why are you saying so?"

"Because it's your last day. Because it's obvious that we don't like one another. Because it's how I feel and I think I need to get it off my chest."

"Really?"

"Really."

I started to slap the shit out of her. I really did. But I decided again to be Christian about the situation.

"So why have you been coming over and talking to me so much lately Mercedes?"

"I was trying to be Christian-like. You know, like you."

"MMmm Hmmn, okay. I tell you what, I will pray for you. In the meanwhile … I'm out. If you think that you can replace me—by all means, do so."

"By all means, huh? You know what? I intend to replace you."

I looked at her intently. I was trying to read her and figure out what prompted this conversation. I decided this heifer wasn't worth my getting upset. After all, I don't like her. I never have. I do think she is a tramp and I do judge her. I will pray for God to change that about me. In the meanwhile, I will just leave. Maybe I'm the one that is wrong here. Maybe this is on me. She can obviously read my expressions and body language and who knows? Maybe she is hurt by my judging her. I have no place to judge. God knows I am not perfect. Hell, right now, my marriage is in trouble. I had problems bigger than Ms. Mercedes here.

"Take it easy Mercedes. Good luck in replacing me."

I got my shit and walked out of the office.

She said something as I walked off, but I didn't hear her.

MERCEDES

"I don't need luck bitch, *I've already started to replace you.*"

I started to really tell Deja about herself, but I figured that it could wait. I stopped working out a few weeks back and let my body begin to slip a bit. I hated the idea of getting fat, but I needed to put on a few pounds for Mark's sake. I stopped taking my birth control pills and let my weight increase by 12 pounds. Mark commented one day on my weight gain and I blamed it on *just starting* to take birth control pills. After I made the comment, I decided that I would wait another week or so before I go back to dieting and exercising. In the meanwhile, I have a plan for Mr. Mark. I can't believe that he told Deja that she could stay home. When are we supposed to fuck? Now I needed to put some other things in place. I figured the best way to do that was to limit Mark's options. He was getting a little too comfortable with having his cake and eating it too. He was fucking both of us and thinking that he was a major player. Well, I think I have had enough. It's time that the player got played.

DEJA, THE FOLLOWING MONDAY AT WORK

That Monday, I went to work at my new job. I didn't tell Mark that I was work-ing with him. In fact, he didn't even make note of the fact that I got up and got dressed at the same time that he did, and that we both left the house at the same time. We took different routes to work. He took the Bishop Ford to the Dan Ryan Expressway and got off at Cermack Road. I took Torrence Avenue to Jef-frey Avenue to Lake Shore Drive. Not only was my way faster, but it was more of a scenic route. I knew that Mark listened to ESPN radio on his ride in, and me? I had to have my Tom Joyner show on WGCI.

I got to work in Mark's old office and everyone that was on his staff welcomed me openly. No one knew who was replacing their boss until I arrived.

I knew everyone there from various functions that were held over the past three years at the job. I knew that word of my arrival would get to Mark soon, so I hurried up and set up the office so there would be no argument when he did arrive. I was sure that his woman, whoever she was, was here somewhere. Men generally cheat with women that they meet in the workplace. I figured that word would travel quickly, even to *her*, that I was here. I was here to try and save my marriage and level the playing field.

The first person that I met that I didn't know was a handsome young man with a lot of potential. He was the senior manager on my staff. The guy was a protégé of Mark's. His name was Derryck Hamilton.

Derryck was a handsome 25 year old Christian man. He went to the Univer-sity of Chicago where he was finishing up his Masters degree. He had been with the company for the last eight months, and I heard nothing but glowing things about him when Mark would come home at night. On and on Mark would brag how this kid was, "the shit" and someone that he was actually intimidated by. Mark used to say that the kid was bright, handsome, charming and had a way with numbers. Mark used to say that he was *always worried that one day this kid would replace him.* I used to tell Mark to not teach Derryck everything that he knew. Otherwise he would in fact replace him. Mark said that when he was with Derryck he would try to hold back, but Derryck was always eager to please. He always asked the right questions and Mark said because he saw a lot of himself in Derryck, he wanted to teach the kid everything that was never taught to him. I used to caution Mark against this. I figured one day all this knowledge that he imparted onto Derryck, would one day bite him in the ass.

Derryck was 6, 3. He had a body like Boris Kodjoe and dark brown bedroom eyes. He had a bald head and bushy eyebrows that made him look fierce yet seductive at the same time. He had a bright white smile, rippled stomach (He had on a corporate muscle-t at the time) and arms that made him look like a college linebacker. He had thighs like an Olympic track star and clothes that flowed on him like he was born to model. Today he had on a black muscle-t-shirt made of rayon, black gabardine slacks, Italian leather shoes and a royal blue blazer that laid on him perfectly. I'm a married woman and I'm looking to repair whatever damage has been done to my marriage, but when I first saw Derryck all I could think of was, "Damn, he's fine." I checked him out from head to toe including his package which, from the looks of it, was just—perfect. He came to my door which was open, knocked lightly and smiled a smile that almost made me melt.

"How are you doing Mrs. Gamble? My name is Derryck. I'm glad to be working with you."

I was thinking to myself, "The feeling is very mutual." Instead I spoke cordially.

"Hello Derryck, I've heard a lot about you."

"All good I hope."

"Definitely all good. My husband thinks that you have a world of potential."

"Well please thank him. I hope that I can show you my potential as well. I aim to please."

I was thinking to myself, *"I bet you can."*

"Well Derryck, I am sure that I will be very pleased with you."

Damn, that sounded wrong, all wrong. Damn this man was fine. Shit, I said that already. He's got me all tingling and shit. I would never do anything with him because I'm married but my thoughts—*Oh God, my thoughts.* In a matter of seconds I had already imagined Derryck's hard body against mine, his soft wet kisses, ripped muscles commanding my body every which way, his sweet nothings in my ear, and his tongue dancing with mine. I imagined us walking on a white sand beach, holding hands, making love and sharing everything from thoughts to fruit with one another, while music by Maxwell played in the background and backdrop of my life.

Then … back to reality.

My reality.

Where my husband had been cheating on me.

"I'm going back to my desk now Mrs. Gamble. If you need anything, I'm your man. Just call me."

"Will do."

Derryck turned to leave my office and I checked out his backside. His butt, my God his butt was just mmmnn-mmmnn good. I had to catch myself as I smiled ear to ear. I had some eye candy in my office. A woman needs that from time to time. I felt happy to have him on board and guilty at the same time. In just a matter of seconds I lusted after another man when I should be lusting after my husband.

My husband.

My smile went immediately to a frown when I thought about Mark. This weekend when he came home after what had to be another night out with *her*, I decided to up the ante a little by making love to Mark. Our sex life had been diminishing a little bit more every week since he began his affair. He and I were having less and less sex, and not once did he complain. This is how I knew that he was still messing around. He wasn't tripping about not sexing me because he was sexing her. When I brought it up, he tried to blame his lack of interest on work. Just how fucking dumb did he think I was? I begged him again to stop seeing this other woman. He denied that he was. I asked him about his absence, lack of calling me and inability to account for his whereabouts. He tried telling me, "Deja, I'm a grown ass man and I'm not about to answer a million questions or punch a goddamned clock around here. I'm the one that is a partner in my company, not you. I have way more responsibility than you could ever imagine!"

When he let that BS walk out of his mouth I started to slap him. We have the same degree, the same knowledge, and the only reason that he makes more money than me is because he's a black *man*. I'm a strong black woman which, in the corporate world many times makes my voice *the last to be heard.*

"So because you are partner, that makes you better than me?"

"Not better, just more stressed."

We could have taken this argument further, but I had the feeling that was what he wanted to do in order to not have to sleep with me. I figured he was fucking her so regularly that he probably couldn't even function with me. I walked out of the room, started a shower and tried to relax my mind rather than argue with him. I washed up, let the water wash away my tears and heartache and let the pulsing of the shower relax my sore and tense muscles. I stepped out of the shower, dried myself off and rubbed lotion all over my body. I then threw on a red teddy that I had in the bathroom, heels and makeup. I looked at myself in the mirror and held back tears. Here I was trying to seduce my husband and compete with another woman that I knew … was fucking my husband.

My husband.

I was about to give myself to him. I was about to possibly share bodily fluids with both him and *her*. I was about to lay with my husband in a way that was familiar to not just me, but *her* as well.

Her. I never thought that where there was once just us two, there would be three.

Her.

I deserved better than this. I needed to demand better than this. I needed to give him an ultimatum. I needed to demand that he choose between her or me. I needed to be proud of the woman that I was. I needed to put my foot down. I needed some validation. I needed to know that Mark still loved me.

I was afraid of what his answer might be.

Instead of asking him—I settled.

I just want things back the way that they were.

Before—*her.*

I held back the tears, checked myself out in the mirror and tried to get the courage to sleep with my husband. I don't know why, but the thought of sleeping with him sickened me. It hurt me. It moved me in ways that I didn't think possible. My heart wanted him back. My body ... wanted no part of him. I walked into the bedroom where he was watching TV. I stood in the doorway doing my best to look sexy for my husband.

My husband.

He looked in my direction and made note of my attire. He smiled. I forced myself to smile back. I walked over to him. He sat up on the bed and placed his arms around me. He kissed my stomach through the material. I held his dreads in my hand. I threw my head back with passion as he kissed me. I was light headed. I longed for his touch for months now. He slid his hands slowly up under my teddy and reached out for my ass, my greatest asset. He planted wet kisses all across my front. He then reached for my special place and began to run circles around my clit with his finger as he used the other hand to undress me. My teddy fell to the floor and he began to lick my nipples. His touch electrified me. His tongue once again became familiar to me. I used my imagination and took our foreplay to another place. I went into our past where everything was perfect. I envisioned us locked in an eternal embrace where we acted as we should act, a couple making love in concert. A couple making love for the sake of love, for the sake of existence. Slowly but surely, my body wanted him. Slowly but surely my body began to respond to him. I wanted my husband. I wanted to make love to my husband. I wanted to make love on a higher plane.

"Damn Deja, have you been working out?" He said disturbing my thoughts.

He made note of my now ripped midsection.

"I have been doing it all for you." I said.

"Damn baby, it's working for you."

He thought that I had dropped the weight just from working out. I had been working out, but the weight dropped off because of stress. The stress that he brought to this relationship, the stress that he brought into our life. I wasn't eating like I used to. I spent a lot of days crying and throwing up. I noticed the weight dropping off weeks ago. I figured that I might as well work out since my idle time was no longer being spent with my husband.

My husband.

He kissed my midsection, sucked my nipples and grabbed firmly on to my ass. He kissed down my front and smiled as he noticed my heels were still on. He hiked my left leg onto the bed and I held onto his dreads like a harness. He then began to feast on the ready-made meal I had for him between my legs. I let out a gentle moan as he tasted me. I made sounds to let him know that his tongue was still welcome in my special place. Softly by Maxwell was playing.

He devoured me.

He ravished me with his tongue.

He ate my pussy.

Made me feel like a woman.

Made me feel like his wife.

His … wife.

He placed his longest digit inside me while continuing to satisfy me orally. He worked his digit in and out of me while teasing me with his tongue. His teasing caused a river of juices to flow; a river that I thought had run dry.

Before I could feel him inside me, I wanted to taste him. I wanted him in my mouth I wanted to control him as he controlled me. But first things first … I needed to come. I began to grind my pelvis against his face. His touch once again became familiar to me and his tongue danced inside my club. He sucked on my love button like a Now & Later candy. Right now in this moment, I was his favorite flavor. He licked, sucked and fingered me into a froth. Minutes later I began to feel the muscles twitch in my calves, thighs and vaginal muscles.

The light tremors began.

I felt like a minor quake was about to erupt.

Then came additional tremors.

My leg began to shake.

My heart raced.

My breathing became more pronounced.

The tremors became harder.

A force was moving inside me.

I grabbed onto his dreads with great force.

My pelvis was now grinding against his face.

My juices flooded his skin.

He now had my scent on him.

I didn't even hear the moans, the screaming, the biting or the other involuntary reactions to his oral love that I was experiencing. I didn't even hear the dirty words that spilled from my mouth as he devoured me and ravished me. All I knew was that the dam was about to break and my juices would flow hard and I would later be embarrassed at the fact that his face, my thighs and his tank top would be glistening and soaked with my juices.

It had been too long since he last gave me head.

Too long since I had come.

I came—hard.

My knees buckled, my pelvis was doing its own thing and my vaginal muscles were constricting. Blood flowed to my vagina.

Life flowed to my vagina.

I was a woman again.

I was in that place that all women long to be.

I came and held on for dear life. I came and relished in the passion. I came and was happy that again, some semblance of my life had returned. I held onto Mark's head for a minute or two after I came. I was unable to move and held on for fear of falling. I waited for my balance and equilibrium to return. I waited for common sense and language skills to return. When I was able to catch my breath, I knelt before my husband. I pulled off his tank top, kissed his chest, kissed his stomach, kissed his jewels and took him into my mouth.

His penis remained flaccid.

I thought nothing of it at first and began to work my magic. I took his jewels in one hand and licked up and down his shaft. I then took him in my mouth again.

I took all of him in my mouth.

In three years, I have never been able to do that.

His penis remained flaccid.

I licked, sucked, kissed and even moaned.

I moaned as if I were getting something out of this.

Nothing.

No-thing.

He let out a sigh.

Then came the tears.

She—was back in our lives.

Back in my reality.

I cried in Mark's lap.

He hugged me.

He hugged me in silence.

Enveloped in his guilt—his sin. The next sound was that of my heart breaking. It was broken, by my husband.

My husband.

PRESENT DAY—BACK AT WORK (FIRST DAY)

We hadn't spoken any more over the weekend. It was obvious that we had reached a crossroads. We were someplace that neither of us wanted to be. The question now was, were we at the point of no return? I took my mind off Derryck and shook my head in disbelief at the poor performance or lack thereof of my husband.

It was noon when I looked up from my desk after the thirtieth call to clients I would be serving, that I noticed Mark in the doorway of my office. He had a look of shock and awe on his face. It was a look that he was trying to conceal because any sign of disproval at my being here would increase tension between us; tension that was slowly ebbing into a war.

"So it's true, you do work here."

"Yeah, I do.

"You couldn't tell me?"

"Like you told me about making partner?"

Silence fell between us.

"Deja, what are you doing?"

"What do you mean?"

"Why are you here? When did you ... you know what? Never mind."

"Is there a problem dear?"

"No problem."

"Oh, but there is."

"Deja, don't start—not here."

"Why not here?"

"Deja ..."

"What Mark?"

"Nothing."

"You sure?"

"Yeah ... I'm sure."

Again silence.

"If that's all that you have to say, then I am going to get back to work."

"You do that."

"Excuse me?"

"Look, Deja I don't know what you are trying to prove, but I don't think this is going to work."

"Us, or this position."

"The position."

"And us?"

Silence.

"I'm sorry about this weekend."

"You mean this weekend was sorry."

We exchanged looks.

"Deja … I think …"

"You think what?"

"I think … I want … out."

"Excuse me?"

"I can't keep doing this."

"Doing what?"

"This."

"What!"

"I love you, but we are going through something right now."

"Something that *you started*."

"I'm not arguing that point."

"So you want to be with *her*."

"After this weekend, don't you think that's best?"

So there it was. It was finally in my face. He all but admitted that he had made his choice. All of a sudden, he was in control. Not only was he in control, he was decisive. He sounded confident in his decision to dismiss me, to cast me aside. To choose another woman over me after his dogged pursuit of me.

"Deja … I'm sorry."

I tried hard to hold back the tears. They had a mind all their own. I tried hard not to give in to the emotions, the pain, the heartache. The problem was … it was so overwhelming, so powerful, so … much.

I collapsed in my seat. I looked at Mark and saw that he was hurt that he hurt me. In his eyes I also saw something else. In his eyes I saw relief and that … cut me to the bone.

"You can keep the house. I will make financial provisions for you. I think we can be civil about this."

"Why Mark? Just tell me why?" I said in a tearful voice. "Do you love her?"

"I don't know."

"You don't know?"

"I don't know."

Silence fell again. My hurt was slowly turning to anger. My head and my heart—hurt.

"Get out of my office." I said.

"I'm sorry?"

"Get out."

"Deja, I don't now how to put this, but you work for me. I'll leave, but I need to remind you that you work for me."

I looked at him in an unfamiliar way. I no longer knew this man that stood in front of me. He seemed cold and calculating. But it was him that cheated, and I was the one feeling all the guilt … all the pain.

"Get out of my office." I said again.

Mark walked out of my office. This was the beginning of the end, the end of my marriage and the loss of title. I was soon to no longer be Mark' wife and he would no longer be my husband.

My husband.

CHAPTER 11

▼

STARTING ANEW

MARK

I had to let Deja go.

I loved her.

I love her still.

But *she* deserves more.

I don't know when I fell in love with Mercedes. I don't know when she became my everything, but I do know that my body responds to her and it no longer responds to Deja. I felt like shit when my dick wouldn't get hard with her. I felt impotent. Then it dawned on me that it couldn't be me, it had to be her.

Deja no longer turned me on.

Mercedes, couldn't turn me off.

Instead of going home that night, I spent the first night away from home in three years of marriage to Deja. I went to Mercedes place and told her what happened and how I wanted us to spend more time together.

"You mean we can finally be together?" She asked.

"We can finally be together." I said.

"What sparked all of this?"

"She tried to fuck me this weekend and my body didn't respond to her."

"What do you mean?"

"She tried to give me head, and my dick wouldn't get hard. I've never had that happen before. I took that as a sign that it was no longer meant to be."

"And what makes you think that you want to be with me."

"I don't know, I just do."

"You sure?"

"Pretty sure."

"Pretty Sure? You need to be real sure if you are leaving your wife. Mark what do you want?"

"I want you. Let's do the damn thing."

"Again, are you sure? You know they say to be careful what you wish for."

"I'm sure."

"Okay. We'll see."

And just like that, my relationship—my marriage ... was over.

DEJA

Mark didn't come home last night. That is the first time that has happened since we have been married. I came home, noticed that he wasn't there and broke down crying in bed. The next day, I went to work and I was a hot mess. My makeup was done, but I could have done better. My hair, which was growing, was okay, but I could have done better. My clothes were clean, but I wasn't quite matching. My head was in the game though. I spoke with clients, made financial predictions and played close attention to the market and new trends. I made people money that Tuesday, and anything that I considered knucklehead shit, or things that I didn't want to be bothered with, I passed on to Derryck. Periodically, I closed the door to my office ... to cry.

"You okay Mrs. Gamble?" I heard a voice say.

"Huh? Oh, Derryck ... yes ... I'm fine."

"Can I come in for a minute?"

"You may, what's up?"

"You can't let the partners see you down."

"What? What are you saying? I mean, what are you talking about?"

"May I be candid."

"You are my lead, you should always be candid."

"You're a black woman."

"I'm aware of that."

"No, I mean, you are a black woman in a predominantly white run company with a few strategically placed black people. You are here because you are good at what you do. You are here because you are valued. You are here because you are up to the task. Any sign of weakness ... especially from a black woman, will get you fired."

"Mr. Buick, the senior partner gave me this job."

"And where is he?"

"He doesn't work as much anymore. He does mostly consultation."

"Exactly. He's a figurehead here and nothing more. He hasn't really worked in years. He sits on the board, he makes major decisions, but he is not here for the day to day stuff. He made the decision to hire you, but if you're fired it will be someone else that will let you go."

"Are you serious? I mean is it that obvious that something is bothering me?"

"Not only is it obvious that something is bothering you, everyone here knows exactly what is bothering you."

"Everyone?"

"Everyone."

"And what is bothering me?"

"You are bothered by the fact that your husband, my mentor, wants you out of here and you are upset that he is cheating on you."

"I'm ... I'm sorry, you know he is cheating on me?"

"Everyone knows. I don't want to be out of place, but his mistress sometimes comes here. Sometimes he brings her to events here. I hope I am not out of line with this conversation, but right now your situation is the buzz all around the office."

I was stunned. I didn't think I could be any more hurt by Mark's bullshit. I didn't think that things around here could get any worse.

"What does she look like?" I asked.

"I don't know if I should get into all that Mrs ..."

"You came in here with it, finish it!"

Silence.

"Well, she is just as built as you are, not quite as pretty, and she has long hair."

"What else?"

"She dresses provocatively."

"Which department does she work in?"

"She doesn't work here."

"What does she do for a living?"

"I don't know. I imagine that she is in finances also, but she doesn't strike me as being educated or savvy."

"Is her body better than mine?"

"Not in my opinion."

"But she's black."

"Yeah, she's black."

"And she's beautiful?"

"She's okay."

"And if you had to choose between the two of us?"

"Mrs. Gamble, I'm not comfortable with where this is going. I mean, I don't want to cause additional stress between you and Mark."

I thought about what he was saying. He was right. Where was I going with all this? What had I been reduced to?

"Derryck, you are right. I apologize for bringing this to you. I am sorry for bringing my drama to the workplace."

"No problem Mrs. G."

"Deja, call me Deja."

"Well Deja, remember what I said. Keep your head up. You're better than this. Better than him, no offense. Besides, there is a way around this."

"Really, what is that?"

"Let's outwork him. Let's put our department on the radar. Let's make some money. I bet if you do that, everyone around here will forget about the scandal and respect you for the woman that you are."

"No one respects me now?"

"They don't know you. I mean many people know that you are his wife and that you are a good wife. Many people here know that you are a good woman, a beautiful woman, but that doesn't mean shit in the business world. To get respect here, people need to know that you are in this to make money. People need to know that their jobs are secure. People need to know that the company is doing well and that their kids are going to college. People need to know that our stock is going to rise and split. Everyone knew that you had drama and when they saw you here, many of the women and men here thought that you were brave and stronger than any of them could ever have imagined. People are whispering about your situation, but they are also whispering about how strong you must be and the direction that you are going to take this department. They think you're strong. You shouldn't show them any weakness. You must not show them any weakness. People's lives are affected by your mood."

"You're right. Again, I'm sorry."

"Mrs. Gamble … Deja, you never have to apologize to me."

"Thank You."

"Is there anyone that you can talk to? I mean do you have a sister or a girl-friend that you can confide in?"

"I do."

"Go see her. Take the rest of the day off."

"And what about things here?"

"I got you. Leave it up to me."

"Are you sure you can handle all this?"

"Who do you think handled things before you got here?"

"Mark."

Derryck laughed.

"Mark taught me and then he delegated a lot of the work to me. After he left, he led me to believe your position would be mine."

"He didn't know that I took this job until yesterday. I was hired by Mr. Buick at the softball game."

"Oh."

"You can handle things here?" I asked.

"Deja ... I got it. Get yourself together and start fresh in the morning."

"Okay, thank you Derryck."

He walked toward the door and stopped short of it and turned around to face me.

"You know she was there."

"Who? Where?"

"His other woman, she was at the softball game."

"She was?"

My mind raced to figure out who she was. I didn't see any pretty women there that were built like me at the softball game.

"What happened to her? Was she looking at me? Did she know I was there?"

"She did. She saw you while heading toward the field and she turned around and left."

"Then she knows me."

"I would imagine that she does."

"Son of a bitch."

"Deja, don't trip about this stuff. Use it to fuel your drive. Make this situation work to your advantage."

"You're right."

I gathered my things up and headed toward the door. I was so lucky to have someone in my corner even if he does work for me. I walked out of the door and Derryck stopped me.

"Deja?"

"Yes."

"You asked if I had to choose between the two of you who would I take?"

"Yeah ... Yeah I did."

He walked up to me almost close enough to kiss me, but not quite so much as to invade my personal space. I mean, he was close. He was closer than any man other than my husband should be, but because he was so damned fine, he knew and I knew that he was allowed *just that much more space, because he was fine.* He smiled softly at me and spoke in a voice just above a whisper.

"I would choose you … no contest … no need to think about it … she's mistress material. You … you're wifey." He winked at me when he said it.

I took in his *Black Code Cologne by Armani.* I could smell his soap, smell his cologne, smell his scent and I was intoxicated by it. He was fine and he smelled good and that was a combination that was working my senses. I took his hand in mine, shook it, and walked away.

BACK TO THE 9705 BAR

I went back to the 9705 bat and told Adrienne everything that transpired over the past few months. She told me the same thing that Derryck said.

"Girl, you need to do like that man said at your job and outwork your husband and make the big wigs at that job notice you for the worker that you are."

"Adrienne, I want to, but this heartache is killing me."

"Girl you need to work through that pain and do what you have to do. You need to make that man realize that he fucked up."

"How do I do that?"

"By going on with your life. The best revenge sometimes is simply to live a better life."

Adrienne poured me another white zinfandel and we talked until about 10:00 PM. I poured my heart out to her, and she was there for me. Adrienne was a good friend and a great listener. She consoled me and helped me to get through the pain that I was experiencing.

"Deja, you are a strong, beautiful black woman. That nigga might not know what he has now, but trust me—he will. Most men don't miss their water until the well runs dry and baby, when it's dry … them niggas be thirsty."

"You know what girl? You're right, fuck him!"

"Atta girl! Now you go home, get you some sleep, and give them hell tomorrow. Then this weekend pamper yourself for all the hard work that you put in."

"Adrienne, I'm gonna do that."

THE NEXT DAY

Mark didn't come home the next day or the day after that. I didn't give a damn either. When I came into work that Wednesday, the first thing out of my mouth was, "Let's get to work." Derryck and I came up with a hard core game plan and started making money in our department; lots of money. I met with Derryck who explained his view on the market, aggressive investing and taking chances. I listened to his advice which was great from his *younger point of view,* and tempered it with my years of experience I have to admit, together Derryck and I worked well. After a few weeks, I was wondering what else he and I might be good at. I know it was wrong, but I'm only human.

Weeks went by and Derryck and I started making more money in tandem than Mark had ever made when he held my position. I tell you, God works in mysterious ways and he looks out for his own. Derryck and I started working longer hours, later hours, and started talking more and more on the phone. There were times that he would have an idea in the middle of the night and call me to share it. Generally, there would be a problem with a man calling me at home in the middle of the night, but it wasn't a problem because my man wasn't home. Derryck and I got close very fast. We made so much money at the firm that four months into it, we were starting our own financial firm on the side. We found a little storefront on 94th and Halsted Street in Chicago. We worked our 9-5 jobs and from 6-10 during the week and all day on Saturday's, we opened our own little consulting firm called "The Gamble Corporation." We showed black people in the hood how to make the most out of their 401K plans, stocks, bonds, zero coupons, bank accounts, mortgages, refinancing, auto loans and anything that had to do with money. We took the money that we brought in from the hood and invested it in the company where we worked our 9-5. We took those dividends and put them back into our company. We never told anyone what it was that we were doing. We had a handful of people at our job come work with us after hours. We were making moves that no one else had thought to make.

Various churches, private investor groups and predominantly white investor groups, started buying up a lot of property in the old neighborhood. They were trying to buy every business, every bar, and every space in the hood. Derryck and I started doing the same thing because whenever white owned companies start looking at the hood, that meant that area was about to go white and all the black people were about to take flight. This was an old game that white investment companies have been pulling for years. They did it to the south loop of Chicago, select parts of the affluent subdivision of Bronzeville, and a good portion of the west-side of Chicago. There were many areas that looked impoverished over the years that were later turned into three hundred thousand dollar condos. That is what is happening too many of the projects in Chicago. Of course they have moved all the black people out to the suburbs, and the suburbs are now going down fast because the progressive black people are busy working, and "pookie" and his crew are tearing the suburbs down brick by brick.

Derryck and I started using our profits to reinvest funds into investment properties. People that were in danger of losing their homes to foreclosure due to medical bills, layoffs and inflation, found peace with our new company. We re-financed their homes for a fee with an affordable interest rate. Once we started making homes in the black community *affordable,* banks began to hate us. My professional life was beginning to soar. My personal life was still at a standstill.

LEAVING BUT NOT LEAVING

Mark stated that he wanted a divorce, but he never actually served me with any papers or started moving in that direction. He still paid all the bills in the house, so I imagine that he was going to one day ask me to leave, or stick me with all the bills once he decided to completely move on. I didn't question his behavior, although I was still heartbroken. I just kept on saving my money and preparing for the worst. Mark became more smug as the weeks went on. He would come and go as he pleased and some days, he would actually stay home long enough to eat with me. I never saw him at work. He stayed in his department and I stayed in mine. He didn't even make notice of the fact that I was keeping later hours, or the fact that I was in the best shape of my life. I had been eating differently, hitting the gym and doing yoga.

"I haven't seen you in a while." He said.

"I've been busy."

"Deja, I'm sorry about the way things went down."

"I'm not trippin. Do you."

"What does that mean?"

"It means do whatever you feel you are comfortable with."

"I just feel a little guilty."

"You should. You chased me remember? Then you had the nerve to break my heart."

"I know baby, I'm sorry about this."

"You can't be too sorry. You're still spending nights elsewhere."

There was a silence at the table.

"She must be something special." I said sarcastically

"No comment."

"I bet. You know, on a lighter note, Derryck is truly an asset to the company. I'm surprised you didn't take him with you when you got promoted. He has a lot of ideas."

"He has too many ideas if you ask me."

"What does that mean?"

"Well, that I was always a little intimidated by the kid and whenever he suggested anything, I always thought that he was after my job."

"Do you think he could do your job?"

"No, he has a lot of potential, but he could never replace me."

I smiled to myself. I then thought little sinister thoughts.

"And you don't think any of his financial plans have any merit?"

"Actually, no. He's always talking about helping out the little man and doing stuff in the hood which is admirable, but there is no money in that."

"There might not be any money in it, but what about the idea of helping people and giving back? Everything can't always be about money."

"That's how poor people think."

"We aren't exactly rich, Mark."

"Yeah but we are far away from poor."

"And your new woman ... how is she financially?"

It was a shot. It caused a greater rift between us. Mark just looked at me intently. I guess he figured that things were going okay between us and I had to go ahead and mess things up. He wiped his mouth and got up from the table.

"I'm buying a condo. With your new salary, can you afford the mortgage on your own?"

"Just transfer the title and take your name off the house and I will be fine."

He looked at me and how passive and nonchalant I was about his leaving. I had to act that way. I couldn't show him any sign of weakness. I couldn't show him that his words were tearing me up on the inside. I couldn't let him know that at any second I might either break down crying, or lunge at him and claw his eyes out. No, I had to play this off.

"So you are okay with all this?" He asked.

"What else am I supposed to say?"

He looked at me as if he couldn't understand the words coming out of my mouth. He looked almost wounded as I acted like he never meant anything to me. He decided to change subjects.

"You know, I never see your car in your reserved space."

"I drove the first couple of weeks to work but after I thought about it, I started taking the train in again."

Silence fell between us as Mark remembered that we met on the train. I imagine that he thought back to a time when things were great between us. A time when he wasn't so smug and still trying to make it in the white man's world. I am sure he was thinking about the days when he was still struggling, days when I was by his side, days when we had little to nothing, days before ... *her.*

"You make enough money to cover the gas cost, Deja."

"That's not the point Mark."

"What's the point?"

"The point is, why waste the money?"

"Why not do what is more convenient?"

"Is that your new philosophy?"

"What is that supposed to mean?"

"Are you about taking the easy way out now?"

"When have you known me to take the easy way out of anything?"

"Do you really want an example?"

"Yes, yes I do."

"This marriage."

"What do you mean this marriage?"

"It seems to me that in regard to this marriage you are taking the easy way out."

"As opposed to what?"

"Working on your relationship."

Yeah, I said it. I was hurting. On the inside I was dying. I don't know what happened between my husband and me, but I wanted my life back. I wanted *us* back. I wanted to make things right again. I wanted to be in love again. I wanted that security. I needed that security. I was *this close to begging* but I have my pride. I started to tell him to either leave this bitch alone and work on his marriage, otherwise I would kill them both. I started to say that, I really did. But that would just be an empty threat. Mark and I both knew that I didn't have that in me.

"Mark where did we go wrong? Where did I go wrong?"

"Deja, it's not you … it's me."

"Explain that. What does that mean?"

"It means that I just don't want us anymore. There is no kind way to say this baby, but I think that I have found something better."

"Something … better?"

"Like I said, there is no nice way to say it."

"How did you find something better? Where you out looking?"

"Actually, no. She kind of approached me."

"Does *she* have a name."

"I'm not going there. I won't give a name."

"Which means that I must know her!"

"No, it means that I don't need the name thrown in my face every time that we speak."

"So you are okay with referring to your woman, the person that broke up our happy home and broke my heart, you are comfortable with referring to this woman as *her*?"

"I am."

"That doesn't say very much for **her!**"

"Maybe it doesn't."

"Then why be with *her*?"

"Because she's not *you*."

"What the fuck is that supposed to mean!"

"It means, you are not sexually free in bed, you cut your hair, you don't wear lingerie like you used to, and you have picked up weight over these past few years. It means that I think I have found someone that I am more compatible with! I don't mean to fuss, but I didn't want to go here with you!"

I put my hand on my hip, took a step back, rolled my eyes and my neck a bit and put all my weight on my back foot. I raised my hand and was about to let him have it.

"Excuse me, nigga what did you just say to me?"

"Don't go throwing that word around at me Deja."

"You are lucky that is all that I am throwing at you right now. First of all, you are a nasty mothafucka. If you are referencing my not letting you fuck me in the ass, I will let you fuck me in the ass the minute you let me do the same thing to you. You want to stick your dick in my ass, then I say let me take a dildo and ram you for twenty minutes. If you want to fuck me in the ass, you can. All I'm saying is YOU FIRST! Next, I think niggas that want to fuck a woman in the ass are either closet homosexuals or on the DL. Third, Yeah I have picked up a few pounds, but as your unobservant ass missed, I have lost every pound and then some. I picked up the weight because motha fucka, I work! When the hell do I have time to go to the gym? The only reason that I have time to go now is because I am not working and washing your clothes, cooking your food and taking care of your trifling ass! By the way, you have picked up a pound or two your damned self and that shit affects your sexual performance!"

"She doesn't seem to mind." He shot back sarcastically.

"I don't give a damn about what that bitch likes! Next, so what I cut my fucking hair, it's my goddamned hair! And lingerie? Nigga please! We women dress for you, suck you, fuck you and feed you. What do we get in exchange? We get dick, and baby ... that ain't enough *especially in your case!*"

He looked wounded when I said that. The kid gloves were off. I went from being heartbroken to straight up street on his ass.

"Are you done?" He asked calmly.

"I'm done." I replied.

"Then I'm out."

"What the fuck are you waiting for then, go!"

He shot me a look that said he was surprised at the woman I now was. Hell, I was surprised. I was still hurt, but that didn't mean I had to continue to take this abuse from his ass.

Mark gathered his belongings and that weekend sent a van by the house for the remainder of his things. I cried the day that we fought, but that night I swore that I would never cry over him or any other man again. You know what? I haven't cried again since.

BACK AT WORK

I didn't let my drama at work affect me. Derryck and I started making more money and together we drew up a proposal asking that we be made equal partners in our department. Derryck's working for me just didn't seem fair considering everything that he brought to the table. The senior partners agreed with the exception of course of Mark, and Derryck was given his own office. We were both senior managers, and together we began to take the company in a better direction.

MARK

I was beginning to hate the drama that was going on between me and Deja. I had the divorce papers written up and on my desk. I had them for over two weeks now. For whatever reason, I was having trouble asking Deja to sign them. Mercedes was becoming more and more impatient with my indecision. Not only did she want me to serve Deja with the papers, she wanted me to tell Deja exactly who it was that I was seeing. I refused to do that. I didn't want to hurt Deja like that. In the same token, I was running out of ways to keep Mercedes from coming to the office to see me. Mercedes was becoming more and more insistent. The only reason that she wasn't tripping this week was because she was sick. I am probably going to sleep at the house tonight with Deja because I don't want to catch Mercedes flu. She keeps throwing up and I don't want to catch whatever it is that she has.

I had a departmental meeting today where all the partners and I got together. I tried talking to them about transferring Deja or moving that department to one of our other buildings in the south loop. When I made the suggestion, the other partners including Mr. Buick began to protest heavily.

"Why would you want to move the entire department?" Mr. Buick asked.

"I just figured that we could move the financial department to another building and bring the marketing team here. We have been talking about bringing marketing here for weeks now."

"So move the money people and bring in the marketing crew here?"

"Yes."

"Move the money?"

"Yes sir."

"That's the dumbest thing that I have heard since you made partner."

I felt like shit at being embarrassed in front of the other partners.

"Why don't you just call the situation what it really is?" Mr. Lowery chimed in.

"And what would that be, Mr. Lowery?"

"You want your wife out of the office because you are worried about her running into your mistress."

"What?"

"Oh come on! Everyone knows. Everyone here also knows that you dodged a bullet at the softball game as well."

I was embarrassed. Everyone knew which I was aware of, but I didn't think anyone would actually call me out on it.

"Okay, so I do have an issue with my wife and girlfriend. The thing is, I'm leaving my wife and she doesn't need to be any more hurt than she already is."

"You're leaving your wife?"

"The divorce papers are on my desk."

Each of the partners who were all older than me, began shaking their heads in what appeared to be disappointment and disbelief.

"What? Why are you all looking at me like that?"

"First of all, we are not moving Deja. I didn't like it when Mr. Buick brought her on board, but it was a good move. She's smart, business savvy, professional and humble. She and that kid Derryck are sharing the workload and neither of them has a problem with ego. And, they are making more money for this company than you ever did. Secondly, it was a mistake to leave your wife for that Chicken-head."

"Chicken-head?"

I couldn't believe that one of my partners, Michael Lowery was talking to me this way. Mike was a Harvard Grad, a little over 40 years of age, and a brother that was constantly in magazines like *Upscale, Black Enterprise and People*. He was one of the most articulate brothers that I knew, and he was throwing slang at me like he was straight off of 47th street.

"Look, we made you partner because of your *business sense*, but it is obvious that you don't have a lot of *common sense* or you are new to the whole cheating game."

"What are you talking about?"

"Deja is a good woman."

"How do you know that Mercedes isn't?"

"First of all, her name is Mercedes. She sounds like a stripper. Secondly she is a mistress. She has a role and nothing more. If she is expecting more or you have promised more, in either case, you are the one with the problem."

"Problem? I don't have a problem."

"Oh yeah, you do. You see you never leave the wife for the mistress. The mistress is just someone that you sleep with. She is like a private contractor. Her job by definition, is to meet whatever needs aren't being met at home and nothing more. You make a six figure salary now. She should be in an apartment across town somewhere and you should be putting in a few hundred dollars on her rent, occasionally taking her out of town when we send you out of town, and laying down the law regarding the boundaries of your situation."

"Situation? You mean relationship."

"I mean … situation."

"Mike, no offense, but I like Mercedes a lot. I might even love her."

The other partners broke out laughing, including Mr. Buick.

"The sex must be incredible." Mr. Buick said "He's young, he will figure it out."

I had a puzzled look on my face. Mr. Lowery spoke again.

"You never leave the wife. That's the first rule. Actually, the first rule is that the wife can never find out. The second rule is you never leave the wife. Listen son, you want Deja. She is the type of woman that you can build something with. This other one, is just for passing the time."

I said, "Mike you don't understand."

Mr. Buick said, "No, you're the one that doesn't understand. I hired Deja because I saw something in her. You all have only been married what, three years? I never thought you were cheating on her and I am disappointed that you are, but that is a thing of youth. From the outside looking in, you two look ideal for each other. As I talked with Deja even I came to the conclusion that the two of you could do great things together. The thing is are you man enough to deal with a woman that is not only beautiful, but equally as talented as you? Mark, Deja makes good money now. Between the two of you, you could do wonderous things. She is the type of woman that you *build a future with, have babies with, and do business with.* That other one, well ... she's just a belly warmer."

"She's a nice looking belly warmer." I said.

"Looks fade son. You need a woman that has your back. You need a woman that is your equal. You need someone that can stand in your stead should you ever fall down. That woman is Deja. You need to see that."

I was getting upset that these older brothers were lecturing me. I felt like I was in high school in the principal's office. I mean, what did they know? Mercedes was fine. She was bodied up nice. She had fewer inhibitions. She was quite possibly, *the one.*

"Mark, listen. You like this other woman because she is new. That's all. You like the sex, you like her body and you like her style. But both of you are fooling yourselves. You are in love with a fantasy and she is in love with an ideal."

"An ideal, how can you be so sure?"

"A real mistress is not obvious. A real mistress is doesn't dress so provocative. A real mistress is a real woman trying to get her needs met until the right man for her comes along. A real mistress is a real woman who isn't looking to hurt anyone. A real mistress will understand that holidays and weekends are not hers to have. That time, goes to the wife and kids. A real mistress has your back." Mr. Buick said.

"And Mercedes isn't a real mistress?" I asked.

Mike said, "No, she's a chicken-head."

"Because she dresses provocatively?"

"Because she doesn't know her place."

"But all of you have mistresses."

"And they know their place. Listen, mine has an apartment way across town. I only see her when it is convenient for me. She knows the boundaries that are set and she wouldn't dare cross them. Hell, my mistress was at my wedding."

"Damn, how long have you been with her?"

"15 years."

"You have a woman that is willing to wait around for you and you have had her 15 years. What, is your dick lined with gold or something?"

"It's lined with cocaine." Mike laughed. "No, seriously, there are women out there that will be the other woman for 10,15 or 20 years. They are on love with the fantasy that one day the man will leave the wife for them. My mistress might think that, but it will never happen."

"What if your wife found out about the mistress?"

"Then I would make up with my wife and get another mistress."

"You wouldn't just get with the mistress? I mean what if your wife left you?"

"If my wife left me, then I would get another woman and keep the mistress as a mistress."

"Why?"

"That's her *role*. Look, my mistress is good at bedding me, but that's all. That's why we get the younger ones, the freakier ones and the naïve ones. They are good at what they do, so like most men, I see no reason for the roles to change."

"Have you ever known anyone to leave the wife for the mistress?"

"I have. But none of those stories ever ended well."

"Never?"

"Never."

Mr. Buick said, "Mark strikes me as the type of person that must find that out for himself. Look Mark, all we are trying to say is one, don't bring any drama to the firm and two, please consider all that we are saying."

"Okay gentlemen, I will. Uh, can we get back to the meeting?"

"Sure."

We went on to discuss the future of the company. We also talked about how much money Deja and Derryck were bringing in. I had to admit that I was impressed. Mr. Buick suggested that I go to Deja's department and give her and Derryck praise on a job well done.

SEEING THINGS DIFFERENTLY

I went to Deja's department. It was the second time that I had been there since she arrived. When I walked into the department I was a bit surprised at how things had changed. Deja broke my old staff up into teams and had them competing against one another for various incentives. She also held trainings on the floor to teach each staff member how to act more like a manager. She gave out weekly progress notes and met with each team once per week. She had the storage room on the floor cleaned out and inside she put a cherry oak conference table. There is where she and each team met once per week, and apparently that is where she and her team closed a lot of deals.

I walked toward my wife's office which was open and I had a shudder go through me as I saw Deja sitting in a chair looking at some documents and Derryck leaning over her shoulder looking at the same document. The two of them were talking and laughing. That didn't sit well with me at all. He was close to

Deja, *too close.* I mean, I'm not a jealous man but he is awfully goddamned close to my wife. I cleared my throat to get his ... I mean their, attention.

"Excuse me." I said in a serious tone.

"Hey Mark." Derryck said.

"Hello." Deja said flatly.

"I just came down here to tell you all that you're doing a great job. You are bringing in a lot of money and the clients have had nothing but positive things to say about you."

Deja said, "I give most of the credit to Derryck."

"Derryck said, "This is quite the woman that you have here Mark."

"Yeah, she's something special." I said sarcastically. "Derryck, could you excuse Deja and me for a minute?"

"Yeah, sure."

He walked out of the office and I could feel my heart beating fast in my chest. I could have spit acid at him. That's how mad I was. I don't know why, maybe because he was younger. I might have been tripping because he was a nice looking brother, you know, one of those pretty boy types. I don't know what it was about him that made me insecure, but I was. I didn't want him around my wife.

Damn, where did that come from?

"Deja, what is going on with you and Derryck?"

"What?"

"Derryck, what's up with him all on your shoulder and shit?"

"Well, we were working on the new prospectus. And he was telling me a joke he heard."

"He was awfully close, for a colleague I mean."

"What are you implying?"

"Nothing. I mean ... well ... first you were bragging on him at home and ... well ... he was all up on you and shit and I ..."

"... All up on me? No he wasn't!"

"He was. I mean, it doesn't look professional. He's also younger than you."

"What the fuck is that supposed to mean and what does that have to do with anything?"

"I'm not comfortable with it."

"You're not ... hold up, what?"

"Nothing. I'm going back to my office. I will talk to you later. I might stop by the house later."

"There is something that I need to tell you before you do that."

I didn't even hear her. I was so shocked by my own jealousy that I just walked back to my office. I didn't even hear Derryck say bye as I walked passed him. What was going on with me?

DEJA

What was that all about? I know Mr. unfaithful wasn't tripping on me and Derryck. He has some damned nerve. Derryck is a nice looking young man, but I can't have a thing with him and I am quite sure that he can do a lot better than a woman like me. I bet he has women falling for him everyday. I have to admit, our relationship was changing. He and I were getting closer and becoming good friends. He called me sometimes at night just to talk. In the beginning we kept it professional, but it evolved into something else. I never kissed him, complimented him, or anything like that. But the relationship changed. I found myself confiding in him from time to time. I talked to him until the wee hours of the morning as Mark slept at his other woman's house. Not once did Derryck judge me. Not once during the course of the day did he bring up our conversations from the previous night. He treated me with dignity and respect and as a partner. He treated me the way that Mark used to. If I didn't know any better, I would say that he looked at me the same way that Mark used to. I have had the occasional fantasy about Derryck. I often think in my mind what it would be like to be with him. I wonder is he a tender lover, or a hit it hard type of brother? I wonder what it would be like to taste him and to have him taste me. I wonder what kind of man he will be five years from now and where he might be. I wonder is he as good a partner in bed as he is in business. If he is … Damn!

Just then I heard a knock at my door. I looked up and there was Derryck standing in the doorway looking like Adonis.

"Hey pretty lady, you wanna go and get some lunch?"

"I think that would be nice."

"Then come on, let's go."

Derryck was all smiles and his pearly white and perfect teeth almost made me melt. Damn this man was fine. Too bad he's a few years younger than me and too bad I'm married.

Damn, I'm married, to a man that treats me like shit; a man that once treated me like the queen that I am. Yeah, I'm married, the question is, does my husband see that?

My husband.

KICKING IT AT APPLEBEES

Derryck and I jumped into his new Cadillac Truck and headed out to the south suburbs to the Applebees in Calumet City. On the way there I was surprised at his selection of music. While en route, we listened to Maxwell, MichelleNDeGeOcello, Prince, Goapele and Lyfe Jennings. The mixture of music was perfect. I was equally surprised when he started playing D'Angelo and singing *Brown Sugar* to me as he drove. Derryck was making me hot and bothered when I found out that he could sing. You figure this nigga was fine and he could sing? Shit, I was wondering how many other talents he had.

I smiled as he sang to me in the car. He never put any moves on me or asked me out other than our usual lunch dates, so I figured that today he was just clowning around and was simply more comfortable with me. I saw no reason that he shouldn't be. We had everything that a couple should have including good communication. The only thing is we aren't a couple. We're just friends.

Just ... friends.

Anyway, we walked into Applebees and the place was jumpin to be in the middle of the day. There were lots of couples there, singles, girlfriends and co-workers. The atmosphere was pleasant and inviting. We sat down at the bar until a table was ready. He had a MGD and I had water.

"So why did we come all the way out here?" I asked.

"I wanted a little more time with you than I normally get, so I figured we would drive to the south burbs."

"Time? Time for what?"

"To get to know you better. To get to know you on a more personal level."

"You know everything about me, from my business ideas to my problems. I don't things could get anymore personal."

"Oh, but they could."

Derryck looked deep into my eyes. We were sitting right next to one another and I thought that he might lean in and kiss me. I wasn't expecting him to. Not only that, but I wasn't sure how I might respond. I fingered my wedding ring which I still wear. I kept trying to tell myself over and over again that I'm married. I have a husband. Things might work out between Mark and I. Derryck is fine, but messing around ... right now, would just make things worse.

"Derryck—I'm married."

"Yeah, I know."

"I can't have an affair."

"I'm not asking you to."

"Then what are you asking for, sex?"

"No."

"Then what?"

"You. I want you, all of you. I want the opportunity to make you happy, to make up for the hurt and wrong of the last man. I want you to make space for me in your heart."

My heart started racing fast. I was blown away at how candid he was. He was saying all the right things … but at the wrong time.

"Derryck, I can't."

"You can. I think you want to."

"I may … but I'm married."

"Yeah you are, but is he?"

"What kind of question is that?"

"You know what kind of question it is. I'm just keeping it real. Deja you're a good woman, a fine woman, a smart and classy woman. I'm not asking you to do anything that you are uncomfortable with. I'm not asking you to make a decision today. All I am saying is wherever you are, that's where I wanna be. I'll take you in any capacity that I can have you, but I want you *as my woman.* We make money together, we do good things together, we have communication, honesty and I've been wondering these past few months what else we might be good at together. I'm just saying … I want you. I want you so much that it hurts."

"And what about Mark?"

"What about Mark?"

"This decision or non-decision affects him as well."

"I don't see how."

"He's my husband."

"He's a man with poor judgment."

"You may be right about that."

"I know that I'm right about that. He made a poor choice in not working more with me, he made a poor choice in leaving you, and he made a poor choice in the mistress that he takes to bed at night."

I don't know if it was part of his sales pitch in order to bring me back to reality or if he was just making a point, but his words regarding the other woman hurt. I wanted to ask him her name. I wanted to ask him again what she looked like. I wanted to ask him a million questions, but I knew that nothing that I wanted to ask him was something that he wanted to hear. I knew that he wanted me to answer his question. So I did.

"Derryck, I can't do this … not now."

He looked at me with disappointment in his eyes. He then took a sip of his drink. He shook his head in disbelief and then he smiled.

"Okay Deja." He said disappointed.

"Are we still cool?"

"Always. Whatever capacity, remember?"

The waiter sat us down and we had lunch. He had a steak and baked potato fully loaded, and I had a grilled chicken salad. I was expecting his conversation or affect to be different. He treated me just the same. He didn't judge me. We talked about work, the White Sox, the Chicago Bears and the future.

"Derryck, where do you see yourself in five years?" I had to ask. I was surprised by his answer.

"With you." He replied. He took my hand and walked me back to his truck and we went back to the office to finish the workday.

MARK-HEADED BACK TO HIS FORMER HOME WITH DEJA

I got off work and went to Deja's department to see if she was ready to go. I wanted to let her know that I would be staying at the house with her for a few days. I was hoping that I would be able to maybe get some from Deja since Mercedes was sick. I told Mercedes that I was going to a hotel because she had the flu. What Mercedes told me next blew my mind.

"Flu? Mark I don't have the damned flu."

"Then why are you throwing up so much?"

"Morning sickness."

"Morning ... what?"

"Morning sickness."

"As in, a baby?"

"Yeah, what did you think I was talking about?"

"I don't know ... I mean ... I didn't know ... when ... when did you find out?"

"A few weeks ago."

"And you didn't tell me?"

"I was trying to decide what it was that I was going to do."

"And what are you going to do?"

"Keep it."

It. She called what could potentially be our child *it.* That was an issue for me but not as much as the issue of her being pregnant in the first place. I mean, she is on the pill. She started picking up weight from the pill. She's pregnant? She can't be. Is it mine? Now that I think about it, I have never seen her take a pill since I have been over here. I mean I'm not in the bathroom with her or all up under her 24/7 or anything like that, but pregnant? She must have set me up! I hate it that I'm thinking like this. All men think like this when they get the news. All men have their doubts. Damn, a baby? Am I ready to be a father? Hell, *I barely know this woman.*

"So ... an abortion is out of the question?"

"It is."

"Okay."

"You don't have anything else to say?"

"Huh? Um ... yeah, I um ... need some air."

Without regard for Mercedes feelings, I headed out the door. My heart was racing, my head hurt and a thousand thoughts raced through my head. A baby ... Damn.

I jumped in the car and headed to the only place that I knew to be familiar. After hearing the news, I headed *home.* I went to the place where my wife was. Damn, I am someone's husband. How do I tell Deja? Do I tell Deja? Shit! I'm betting there is no turning back now. I jumped on the cell phone and called Mercedes back.

"Hello?" She said.

"Mercedes are you sure? I mean, you went to the doctor and everything?"

"I am and I did. Are you okay with this?"

"Yeah ... yeah sure, I'm cool. I just ... I just need some air."

I hung up the phone, my heart pounding now in my chest. I started talking to myself in the car.

"No bitch, I'm not okay. Why didn't you tell me? Why didn't you say something? What happened to your being on the pill? I bet you set me up. What the hell do I do now? Babies are expensive as hell! Shit, does that mean I marry you or does that mean I just start cutting you a check for support? Why didn't you discuss this shit with me? I can't have a baby now. I am just starting to get my life together. Fuck, what am I supposed to do?"

I drove a few more miles in silence. I then cut on WGCI to comfort me. It did no good. I then turned to Michael Baisden's show on 106.3 Michael usually pulled me out of whatever funk I was in. Not today.

"Hello Radio listeners, it's your man Mike Baisden on the radio waves. Today's question is, how many of you men out there truly stand on yours and take care of your business when it comes to having a child? Ladies, do you have a real black man by your side or a trifling deadbeat dad? Call in, let me know what's going on with you. This is your boy Mike on the Mic. Holler back at me!"

Callers from all over the nation started calling in. Men called in complaining that support was too high. Women called in saying that it wasn't enough. Men called in saying that women use the money to get their hair and nails done. Women called in saying that they needed to look good for the next man and they went on to say how watching a child is a job 24/7. The radio station phone had to be blowing up with hundreds of calls as this hot issue was burning in the minds of all of Baisden's listeners. I was happy for Mike. He was another brother doing things from the Chi. As far as I was concerned, today he picked the wrong damned topic. Then there was a call that shocked the hell out of me.

"Hello Mike. My name is Dan, from Hinsdale Illinois. I am a stock broker in the downtown Chicago area, and I have to say that Child Support is unfair. I make $100,000 a year and $1600 a month is unfair as hell. I mean, what is a child going to do with $1600. The 20% for the first child thing is totally unfair. I have to pay $20,000 a year which is 20% of my gross salary. My taxes are 35% which is $35,000 a year. That brings my net worth from 100K to 45K. I mean Mike, does that [Bleep] sound fair to you?"

I was like 20% of gross? Are you fucking kidding me? I make about the same amount that this guy makes. $20,000 a year in support, *before taxes*? Are you fucking kidding me? That doesn't include medical, diapers, pre-natal, office visits, medication and day care. What the fuck have I done? The baby isn't even here yet and I think that I am about to have a MF anxiety attack. What fucked me up even more was Michael Baisden's response.

"Well bruh, I guess you have to be responsible with who you lay down with and also use protection. I mean, no disrespect, but that woman didn't make that baby by herself."

[Caller] "I know, but Mike, I think that the [bleep] set me up. I mean, she told me she was on the pill?

"And did you use other precautions also? Did you use a condom?"

"Well, no."

"Then bruh, who's the fool?"

"Mike do you always use condoms?"

"We're not talking about me, we are talking about you. Now, she said that she was on the pill. You trusted that she was, and you chose not to take additional precautions that were available to you. What I am saying brother is you have to be responsible for the part that you play in all this."

Mike was right. I was feeling the other man's pain though. I was sick with the thought of how expensive this shit was going to be. I turned the radio to WNUA to listen to some jazz to try and relax me some. I listened to some Bony James, Al

Jarreau and Lalah Hathaway. It was 7:00 by the time that I pulled up in front of the house. I sat outside looking at the house from the car. Deja and I did okay for two kids that were college poor a few years ago. Together, we accomplished a lot. We each had over $100,000 in student loans. That $1,000 monthly payment was a pain in the butt. But when I look at what we accomplished and where we were in our careers, I was proud. I know that my timing is bad, but I'm sorry for the hurt that I put her through. I wonder is it too late to get things back the way that they were? I can't do this baby thing by myself. I need my woman's help.

I got out of the car and headed to the doorway. Deja's car wasn't in the driveway or the garage, so I figured that she was still out somewhere. I just wanted to pour myself a drink, jump in the Jacuzzi and watch some ESPN on TV. I walked up to the door and put my key in the door.

The lock wouldn't turn.

I looked at the key and couldn't figure out what was wrong. I tried the key again and it wouldn't budge. At first I figured maybe I just used the wrong key. I thought that perhaps I was using one of the office keys rather than the house key. I tried other keys on my ring and the lock would not turn.

"What the hell?"

I went around the back of the house and tried my rear door key and the same thing happened.

My keys don't work.

The locks have been changed.

I sat in my car unsure of what to do next. I was locked out of my home. My girlfriend is pregnant and I don't want to go back there. Where is Deja? Where the hell is my wife?

CHAPTER 12

▼

FRIENDS

DEJA

After we had lunch, Mr. Buick was waiting for Derryck and me in my office. I thought that we were in trouble at first because we took a two hour lunch instead of our usual hour. Mr. Buick didn't seem to be at all concerned about that.

"There you two are, I was waiting on you."

"I'm sorry Mr. B, is there anything that I can help you with?"

"Well for starters, I wanted to come down here and let you know that the two of you are doing a damn good job."

"Thank you sir." I said

"Yes, thanks a lot Mr. Buick" Derryck said.

"I have a project for the two of you to do. It's a pretty big project and I'm wondering if you can handle it."

"What is it sir?" I asked.

"I want you to meet with a new client named Ms. Logan. She has her own company and she is a very wealthy entrepreneur, perfumer and clothier. She has agreed to let us handle some of her smaller accounts and it is my hope that you will be able to persuade her to let this firm handle her larger and more lucrative accounts and investments."

"Wow, Mr. Buick, I don't know what to say. If you get us the file, we will get right on it. We will get started tonight."

"There's no need to start now, it can wait until next week."

"Maybe so, but I think we should start on the preliminary planning today." I said.

"I agree." Derryck stated.

"Fine, well it's settled then. I want a report on my desk by the end of next week on your progress."

"Mr. Buick?"

"Yes Deja."

"Isn't this a job for either you or the partners?"

"It is, but I think that the two of you have proven your worth. I think it's time that we gave you a project with a little more meat. How you do on this project will determine how much more responsibility the other partners and I will give you."

"Mr. Buick, I have one more question."

"Go ahead."

"Do the other partners know about this assignment?"

"Right now, no. They don't need to. I'm the senior partner. I started this company, and what I say still holds some weight around here. I like you Deja, I have always liked you. Derryck, I haven't heard your name since you arrived here, but Deja brought you to my attention and I have to say that I am impressed. I want to see what the two of you are really capable of."

"You have never heard my name before?" Derryck asked in a confused tone.

"No, never. Why, should I have?" Mr. Buick asked.

"Well, I had been working with Mark for over a year before I began working with Deja."

"You were working here, but as far as I know, you haven't done anything substantial."

Derryck looked wounded by Mr. Buick's words and Mark's obvious betrayal. It seems that Mark bragged about Derryck's abilities, but only to me at our home.

"That son of a bitch." Derryck stated.

"I'm sorry?" Mr. Buick responded.

"I'm sorry Mr. Buick. I worked on the Johnson account, the Laurel account, the Dunleavy account, and the Garrison account. I did the research, I decided on the stocks, bonds, t-bills and group consolidation project and I designed the progressive prospectus that each company received."

"You were the co-author of the prospectus?"

"Co-author? I was the sole designer."

"That's a pretty big accusation, do you know what you are implying?"

"I still have the figures in my head and I can tell you that the collective group is estimated to make 115 million at the end of the fiscal year."

"We aren't even a quarter of the way through the fiscal year yet. How can you make that estimate as unstable as the market is?"

"I know numbers sir. I bet my career that those customers will be looking at 115 million by June."

Mr. Buick became quiet. He looked at me for confirmation, but I didn't know if the idea was Mark's or Derryck's. Both men were brilliant. Either could have come up with the idea, but I believe that Mark had become lazy as a manager and simply worked the shit out of the people beneath him. I didn't know what to say. I didn't want Derryck to become distracted either by the task at hand, so I jumped in.

"Derryck, let's stay focused. Mr. Buick, we will get started on this project tonight."

"Thank You Deja. You two don't let me down."

"We won't."

Derryck and I worked until 9:00 that night. We planned, talked, planned some more and did research on Logan Enterprises. The CEO and founder, Nicole Logan was reportedly a tough woman that knew her stuff. This was a huge project and one hell of an opportunity for us. Derryck however still seemed distracted by Mark's betrayal.

"You said when I first arrived that you heard a lot about me, right?"

"I did."

"So Mark told you about me, but didn't tell the partners?"

"It appears that way."

"And he took credit for my ideas."

"Derryck, I don't know what to say."

"Your husband is a son of a bitch."

"I know."

"I think I hate him."

"Hate is a strong word."

"Then I really dislike him right about now."

"So do I."

"How did he land such a good woman like you?"

I told Derryck the story about how Mark and I met. Talking about it brought on some strong emotions, and quite a few tears. I told him how Mark pursued me and how he made all these promises of great things for our future. I told him how I thought what Mark and I had was like a fairy tale, you know, that happily ever after shit. I thought that we would grow old together, have children together and be forever 21 or forever happy. Damn he let me down.

Derryck listened attentively and held my hand as I spoke. When I cried he looked as if he wanted to, but being a man he held it in. He then hugged me and caressed my cheek. He then told me that everything would be all right.

We went from the office of our 9-5 and to our own financial consulting business where we ordered Chinese food and worked until 10:00 on the Logan account. We put all of our other accounts on hold in an effort to show Mr. Buick our earning potential. By 10:15 we had a damned good plan in place. It was then that I started gathering my things so that I could head home to my empty house.

"You know, you don't have to go home. I mean, you could stay the night with me." Derryck said.

"Derryck, I thought we covered this."

"We don't have to do anything. I will be the perfect gentleman, I promise."

"Thank you, but no thank you. I have to get home. I will see you tomorrow."

"Okay."

I headed toward the door and once again Derryck stopped me. He grabbed me by the arm and walked slowly to me.

"Deja?"

"Yes Derryck?"

"I'm a patient man. When the time comes, whenever that is, I'm here."

He kissed me on the forehead like a little sister or something.

"That's sweet." I said.

"I mean it. What did Maxwell say, "Whenever, Wherever, Whatever.""

I smiled a gentle but small smile.

"Goodnight Derryck."

"Goodnight Angel."

"Is that my new nickname or something?"

"It is. I think you are a good woman, a strong woman, a woman that will one day have my children. I think you are good for a man's soul. You're my angel."

"Derryck you barely know me."

"This is true. It's defies logic and all understanding. I don't know you as well as I should. I admit that. But what I do know is I like you a lot. I like the way you make me feel when I'm around you, and I like the fact that just being in your presence makes me want to aspire to be more myself. We work well together, we have good conversation, and I know you feel the chemistry between us. So when you get through playin, baby I'm here."

"So you think I'm playing a game with you?"

"No, that was a figure of speech. I don't think you are the type of woman to play with a man's feelings like that. I think you are hopeful, faithful and prayerful. I also think that you are holding on too tight to what you thought was a sure thing but turned out to be just a stepping stone in your life."

"You mean my marriage to Mark."

"Yeah, your marriage to Mark."

"You believe that it was just a stepping stone."

"I do."

"And what is it a stepping stone to?"

Derryck smiled softly, leaned in and kissed me ever so softly on the lips.

"Me … [kiss] … Us … [kiss] … Happiness."

I closed my eyes and as he kissed me, I kissed him back. For those three brief seconds, I was trapped in time. I was free of drama, free of guilt, free of pain and though it hurt and felt like betrayal, I was free of my marriage. After those three seconds however, I snapped back to reality.

"Derryck, I can't."

"Okay baby."

He kissed me once more, then helped me on with my coat and walked me to my car.

"I'll go lock up. You go home and get some sleep and I will see you tomorrow."

"I'm sorry Derryck. I can't help but to feel that you feel like I am playing with you."

"I don't feel that way at all."

"How do you feel?"

He took a few seconds before answering after giving the question some thought.

"I think you're cheating yourself."

He might be right. He headed back to the office to lock up. I started my car and got ready to pull off.

"Deja?"

I rolled down the window.

"Yes, Derryck?"

"I'm a patient man. Whenever, Wherever, Whatever."

He turned and walked back in the office. I watched his amazing body as it flowed back into the building.

"Damn!" I said to myself

I jumped on the ramp at 99th and Halsted Street and Headed on the Bishop Ford Freeway home. I listened to V103 the whole way and got lost in the beauty of song and emotion. I hated to admit it, but Derryck took me somewhere that I hadn't been in a while. He made me feel again. I had butterflies just thinking about what we might be able to accomplish in the office, in the boardroom, in life, and in the bedroom.

TOO MUCH, TOO LITTLE, TOO LATE

I pulled up in front of my house at about 11:15. I was surprised to see Mark's car in front of the house. Shit, I forgot that he said that he might be stopping by. I was trying to tell him before he walked out of my office that I had the locks changed. I looked in his car and he was asleep behind the wheel. I tapped on the window with my wedding ring.

"What are you doing here?"

"Where the hell have you been?"

"Excuse me?"

"You heard me. I have been here since six something. Where have you been and why doesn't my key work?"

"I tried to tell you before you left that I had the locks changed."

"Why?"

"You said you were out remember? You said that you were giving the house to me. We have been going back and forth for some time now and it appears that you have made your decision about who you wanted, so I had the locks changed."

"And where have you been?"

"That … is none of your business."

"You were with Derryck weren't you?"

"What part of none of your business didn't you understand?"

"Dammit Deja, you are my wife and …"

"Oh now I'm your wife. Tell me Mark, where the fuck is your ho? Why aren't you at the place that you have been spending the night for the past few months? What's wrong, she won't give you any? The bitch is sick? She kick your ass to the curb? Why the hell are you here?"

He just stood there looking stupid.

"I came here because I needed someone to talk to."

"Talk to that bitch that you left me for."

"I needed to talk to you."

"Why the other bitch is retarded or something? Why do you need to talk to me?"

"Because you know me."

"I don't know you. Mark, I don't know you at all, not these days. The man that I knew is gone. I have no idea who the hell you are anymore."

"Deja, I need you. I need to speak with you, to talk to you. I need to know if we can try and get things back to the way that they were."

"What? Why? What the hell happened that you are out of her bed and trying to come back to me? What's really going on Mark?"

He had no answer.

"What's her name?"

He fell silent.

"You got a picture?"

Still nothing.

"Are you going to at least tell me what happened between the two of you that you are over here?"

"I can't."

"Hmmnn, well then, I guess we have nothing to discuss. Goodbye Mark. I hope you are happy with that bitch."

"Deja is there no chance for us?"

"I can't see it. You lied to me, cheated on me, left me, and threatened to divorce me over some pussy. I don't even know who this bitch is, but whoever she is I know that she ain't half the woman that I am. You had me out here wondering what it was that I did wrong. Ain't that a bitch? You had me self conscious about my own self esteem and abilities, like I was the one that cheated on you. These past few months I have put up with your bullshit, the lying, the blatant disrespect and let you come and go around here like you please. I have yelled about you, talked about you and cried about you. You know what? I'm all cried the fuck out. I tried clinical counseling, pastoral counseling, individual therapy and I have even talked with God racking my brains about what the hell I did wrong. Well it finally came to me what I did wrong. I married your trifling ass!"

I let him have it. I was ready to slap the shit out of him but my momma raised me better than that. I never put my hands on a man because I never wanted one to put his hands on me. So with that, I pulled out my house keys and headed toward the door. Mark got out of his car.

"Deja?"

"What Mark?" I said without even turning around, my key was in the door.

"She's pregnant."

Just when I thought my pain couldn't be any deeper, he lays this shit on me. My head leaned forward on the door and those tears that I thought were out of stock began to flow down my face. My husband, was about to have his first child with another woman, his mistress or I guess, his girlfriend.

"Goodnight Mark." I said in a tearful voice.

I went in the house, poured myself a drink and cried. I then ate some *Ghiradelli Milk Chocolate* and took myself to bed. I lay there for two hours praying that sleep would find me. When it didn't, I found myself dialing a familiar number on the phone. A sleepy voice on the other end spoke.

"Hel ... Hello?"

"I'm sorry Derryck, did I wake you?"

"Yeah, but it's cool, what's up D?"

"You have a few minutes to talk?"

"For you ... always."

I talked to Derryck until 4AM. He lifted my spirits and had nothing but kind and encouraging words to say. I then got about two hours of sleep before I woke up to get ready for the next day. When I woke up the next morning I fixed my hair as best as I could and even though I felt heartbroken all over again, I made my face up to the best of my ability. I opened my front door and there waiting in front of the house was a limousine.

"What the hell?"

The driver got out of the car, walked up to me, took my bags and led me to the car. He opened the door and sitting there in a Navy Blue suit, white shirt and red silk tie was Derryck.

"I thought you could use a lift this morning. I hope you don't mind, but I took the liberty of picking you up today."

"What's with the limo?"

"A classy lady like you deserves to roll in style every now and then. Besides, I have it on good authority that you had a rough night last night. So, I have breakfast, some music, and some figures that you need to look at so we can get a jump start on our day today."

I smiled at him. Derryck was so thoughtful. I stepped in the limo and in the car was turkey bacon, eggs, toast and juice on a platter. The TV in the limo was showing this morning's numbers on the stock exchange and NASDAQ. Overhead Maxwell was playing, *Whenever, Wherever, Whatever.* I looked at Derryck and smiled.

"Okay, so where do we begin?"

"That my dear ... is up to you."

I kissed him on the cheek, put a piece of bacon in my mouth and opened the file he wanted me to read. In the file were the papers that he was referring to and a single red rose. I took the rose in my hand, smelled it and smiled.

"You think of everything don't you?"

"A good man is thoughtful and constantly seeking the approval of his woman."

"But I'm not your woman." I said shyly.

"Not yet."

We headed to work to begin our day.

THE BEST MORNING IN A LONG WHILE, BECAME THE WORST DAY OF MY LIFE.

We arrived at work in the limousine 90 minutes later. The traffic on the Dan Ryan Expressway was crowded as hell and there were a number of accidents on the road. It didn't matter to us though, because we had plenty of food, plenty of juice and our laptops. I thought today was going to be rough at first, but Derryck saw to it that my day started off right. In the back of my mind I thought about what it would be like to wake up to this man each morning. Would he always be this thoughtful, or would he only be this way in the beginning like all men? You know the type, roses, candy and lots of compliments and sex in the beginning. Later on though, they usually become boring, speechless Neanderthals with huge stomachs.

We got out of the limo at 7:30, both of us tired and dragging ass, but we made our way up to the office and called the rest of the staff into the large conference room to discuss our plans for the Logan account. Together, Derryck and I presented what we felt was the perfect plan to reel in Ms. Logan. I was three-quarters of the way through the presentation when Mark walked into the conference room.

"Can I help you Mr. Gamble?" I said to my husband in a professional tone.

"No, I was just wondering what you all were doing in here today. I wasn't aware that you were working on anything major, but by the looks of the presentation you are working on something huge, what is it?"

I started to say *None of your motha fuckin business*. But again, my momma didn't raise me to be that way.

"We are working on a project for Mr. Buick."

"What is the project?" Mark asked.

"All due respect Mr. Gamble, you will have to inquire with Mr. Buick."

Mark was thrown off by my response. He looked across the room at Derryck.

"Is that your response as well Derryck?"

"It is." Derryck said.

"Deja, can I see you in my office?"

"Now?"

"Right Now."

I started to say go to hell, but he is still one of the partners in the firm. I couldn't decide what to do. I started to tell him no, but that could be seen as a sign of weakness. I started to simply say yes, but I didn't want him to think that I was at his beckon call either. I thought about my response which only took a few seconds, but those seconds seemed to take forever.

"Derryck, take over for me please."

"Okay Ms. Gamble."

"Mrs. Gamble." Mark said.

"Yeah, that's what I meant." Derryck said.

"Yeah, I'll bet." Mark responded.

Mark headed toward his office and I followed. Derryck continued with the presentation. Mark and I got on the elevators and rode them up to the 30th floor in silence. I followed him off the elevator into a grand hall with bleached and waxed hardwood floors that had red carpet leading to each of the offices. Psychologically, these men, the partners, were telling themselves that they were better than everyone else and that they were celebrities or something. Mark walked ahead of me into his office and without turning around spoke to me.

"Close the door behind us."

I closed the grand oak door and stood there in front of my boss who also happened to me my husband.

"Deja, what are you working on for Mr. Buick?"

"Why Mark?"

"Because I want to know. I was expecting him to assign a huge account to me this morning and I just have a feeling that he might have done something stupid like give it to you and the pool boy."

"You mean Derryck?"

"Yeah, I mean Derryck. Now this account, it wouldn't happen to be the Logan account would it?"

"Ask Mr. Buick."

"I'm asking you."

"I have nothing to say to you."

"Is this about last night? I mean if it is, I'm sorry about all that. I was just hurting and I needed to reach out to someone and I thought the woman that I married would be the one that I should speak to."

"No, this is not about last night. In fact, I don't even want to re-live last night. I have nothing to say about the account that I am working on because I am under instruction from Mr. Buick to keep it confidential from everyone."

"Everyone? Including his partners?"

"Yes."

"He can't do that. We are supposed to know everything that is going on in this building."

"Well, that doesn't appear to be the case now, does it?"

"Dammit Deja, what the hell is up with you?"

"Me? What's up with you Mark? Why the hell did you call me up here?"

"I wanted to talk to you?"

"About this Logan Account that you keep referring to?"

"Yes … No … I mean, I do want to know about the account, but even more I want to know what's up with us. I mean, is there a chance for us Deja?"

"You mean after leaving me, lying to me and playing with my heart strings will I take you back even though you have been fucking another woman for months and now expecting a child with that woman? Is that what you are asking me?"

Silence fell between us and it was not golden. I looked into the eyes of my husband and tears were streaming down his face.

"Deja … I fucked up. I fucked up and I know that I fucked up. I need another chance. I'm sorry. If you give me another chance, just one more chance, I swear … this will never happen again. I will never hurt you again."

"Mark you can't hurt me anymore. Oh wait … each time that I say that shit, something more creative happens and you somehow sink to a new low and find a new way to fuck me over. Last night I thought I was all cried out and then you spring your baby mamma drama on me. How the fuck do you think I am supposed to feel? How the hell am I supposed to take you back after you tell me that another woman is having your child? Do you have any fucking idea how hurtful that is to a woman? Every woman that wants children deep down wants to have her man's first child. How am I supposed to accept a child that was born to *another woman during the course of our marriage?* Do you even realize that we are still married? Do you have any fucking idea, how much you have hurt me? How much you have betrayed me? You haven't just hurt me emotionally Mark, you have hurt me spiritually. Do you understand what the fuck I'm saying? Mark, *my soul hurts.*"

"All I can say is … Baby, I'm sorry. I'm willing to go back to counseling, I'm willing to go see Pastor Kelly again, and I am willing to do whatever it takes to get us back. Deja please, you have always been there for me. You have always had my back. I am just asking you to have my back *just one more time.* You hear me baby, just one more time. Can we try again?"

Just then, I heard a woman's voice in the hallway. First I heard the voice of Mark's secretary then I heard another familiar voice.

"I'm sorry he's in a meeting, you can't go in right now."

"I need to see him, right now." The voice said.

"No. I mean ma'am, Mr. Gamble is busy right now."

"Then he will just have to get un-busy for a minute." The voice said again from the outside of the door. I looked at Mark and he looked to be a whiter shade of pale. He recognized the voice and knew it well. I recognized the voice from the quick telephone conversation.

He's in the shower washing off my sex. I remembered her saying.

The door opens.

My senses are bombarded with the smell of lilac and strawberries.

My heart beats rapidly and I became light headed. Mark started speaking to me, but I could not understand his words.

I could hear my own heartbeat inside my chest.

I could taste the acid forming in my stomach.

I could feel the tremors in my legs as they shook as if they were going to give out from under me.

In my mind I called out to God.

Again came the tears.

Then came the heartache.

I now knew who *she* was.

I had smelled this scent that was burning in my nostrils before.

I looked at *Mercedes with pure and absolute hate.*

CHAPTER 13

▼

HE, ME AND NOW ...
SHE

DEJA

"So what the fuck is going on here?" Mercedes demanded.

I was sick, sick to my stomach. My legs became weak and I sat down in the chair closest to Mark's desk. Mark ran close to me when he saw that I might pass out.

"Oh I see, someone is just now getting the news about who her replacement is" Mercedes said in a cold voice.

I looked up at Mark who couldn't even look me in the face. The betrayal and the pain, had reached an all new low.

"So what is *she* doing here Baby?"

Baby? Baby? Who the hell is she to be calling him baby?

In a tearful voice I spoke, bottom lip trembling "So this is who is having your baby?"

"Yep." Mercedes said triumphantly.

"I wasn't talking to you." I snapped.

"Well, I was talking to you."

"Mercedes, stop." Mark said.

"Stop what? I think as the mother of your child, I'm entitled to say whatever I want to your soon to be ex-wife. Has she signed the papers yet?"

"Papers?" I said

"Yeah bitch, the papers, did you sign them?"

"Bitch?"

"Bitch."

"Mercedes, that's enough!" Mark yelled.

"I looked at the two of them in disbelief. I was ready to beat the hell out of Mercedes, but I realized that she was pregnant. I just looked back at Mark and he could see on my face that I was more than through with his ass.

"Mercedes will you excuse us for a moment?"

"What?"

"Step out into the hallway."

"Mark, you can't be ..."

"... I said step the fuck into the hall!" He said in a voice with more bass than I have ever heard him use since I have known him.

Mercedes cut Mark a look that only another woman would recognize. It was a look of hate, anger and payback. It was the same look that I was giving him. I imagine that Mark thought I might be the lesser of two evils. Mercedes backed down from Mark. She stepped into the hallway and looked back at me. I got up, I walked in her direction not sure of what I might do. Mercedes smiled smugly at me as if she knew that I could not touch her since I knew that she was expecting. Still, I walked slowly and confidently in her direction.

"I just have one question, Deja. Why are you here?"

"I work here."

I grabbed the door and slammed it in her face. I then turned around slowly. The tears were gone. My heartache was replaced by rage. I walked over to Mark who now had fear in his eyes.

"Deja, baby I ..."

[SLAP!]

I slapped him with all that was in me. I reached back from New York to Georgia to hit his ass. I slapped him so fast and so hard, my grandmother, God rest her soul, had to crack a smile. It was one of those slaps that stung. You know the type, the proverbial *slap the taste out yo mouth*. After I slapped Mark, I grabbed him by both shoulders and looked him dead in his eyes. I then looked past him, through him and in him, I saw nothing, nothing that I wanted any longer. He could see it in my eyes. He looked dejected. I—I looked triumphant. Today was the day. This was the day that I would Exhale. With my breath went away my troubled soul. My body however, needed rest. I opened the door and silently made my way into the hall.

Mercedes was no longer there.

The partners, a few of my co-workers and Derryck were in the hallway. I walked up to Mr. Buick and casually spoke to him.

"Mr. Buick, I am feeling slightly under the weather. Can I have the rest of the day off? I will be back tomorrow and I will be ready to go right back to work."

Mr. Buick could read my face like a proud father. I could tell that he liked the way that I carried myself in spite of the obvious which happened.

"You most certainly may." He said.

Derryck gave me a look that said that he wanted to speak. I gave him a look that said that he shouldn't. Instead, he got on his cell phone. By the time that I reached the elevators, he told me that the ride that brought me here would be waiting for me downstairs. I went back to my office to gather my things. When I got to my desk, I noticed a white card sitting on top. I picked it up and was surprised that it was my driver's license. Across the front in red ink was the word Bitch.

I put my old license in my purse and laughed to myself at the reality that it was Mercedes who I had missed at the softball game. It was she that bust the window on the car and took my purse. I then thought back to the conversation that we had on my last day of work. When she spoke of replacing me, she meant in my husband's bed, not at my job.

"She's good, I'll give her that."

I walked confidently to the elevators on my floor so I could go home. Derryck was waiting for me on the first floor in the lobby.

"Do you want me to go with you?"

"No, thank you."

"Do you want me to call you later?"

"That's sweet, but not today."

"Do you want me to kick Mark's ass?"

"No, I'll take care of that. I want you to ask Ms. Logan to come to the office tomorrow and I want us to make the presentation."

"But we're not ready yet."

"I am."

"What about me?"

"Baby, I got plans for you."

"Will I like these plans?"

"I think you will."

"Are you sure that you are okay?"

"Derryck, I could never have been better."

I walked out of the sky-rise and headed to the limo. I stepped inside, fixed my hair and makeup and took a few deep breaths.

"Where to ma'am?" The driver asked.

"Oh, quite a few places."

I gave the driver his instructions and we went several places before I had him take me home.

LATER THAT EVENING

When I got home, there were several messages on the machine. Most of them were from Mark. The others were from Derryck. I had the Limo driver take me shopping for a brand new business suit by Donna Karen and I had him take me to see my attorney, my broker, my real estate agent, my pastor, my therapist and my girl Adrienne at the 9705 bar. All six were women and they all had ideas about how I needed to deal with Mark. They each quoted the same bible verse to me. "Hell hath no fury like a woman scorned."

I booted up my PC to work on my proposal for tomorrow. I typed until my hands were raw. I had a few sips of Hennessey and 7up. As I typed, the phone rang and rang and rang. I started to get it in the hopes that it was Derryck. I knew at least one of the calls had to be from him. The others I'm sure were from Mark.

"Not now baby, I have to get myself together." That's what I said to the ringing phone. I played music from Kem's second album. I then lit a few candles, smoked a joint that I had hidden in my top dresser, and I went back to typing. In the middle of the last paragraph of the last page of my presentation, I received a ring tone on my computer.

"You have mail!" The booming monotone voice said.

"Great, Mark can't get me on the phone so he is trying to get me on the PC." I was tired and almost done typing. I was shocked when I saw what was on the computer screen next. The subject in the email was titled, "The beginning of the end." My voice left me, and my stomach which had been in knots for months, finally rebelled. I vomited right into the trash can by the desk where I keep the PC. I then lay on the floor, motionless for what seemed like eternity. When my panic attack/stress attack was over, I said a prayer to God.

"Lord Please, give me the strength, stop this pain, stop this heartache. Father God please ... end this."

I lay there on the floor another twenty minutes. I then got up, reviewed the items on my screen, played the audio, grabbed a blank CD and copied the material. I then send out emails to everyone in my que. I then showered, went to bed and prayed again to God that sleep would find me. I called Derryck on the phone and asked him to meet me at my home at 4:30 AM. He agreed. I got three hours of sleep which was one hour more than I got the night before. At 4:30 on the dot, Derryck was at my house looking GQ and very fatigued.

"I was worried about you."

"Don't be."

"Are you sure you are okay?"

"I'm fine."

"You look like you need to sleep."

"There will be time enough for sleeping when this is over."

"Are you ready for the presentation?"

"I am."

"Can I see it?"

"Here you go."

I walked over to the desk as he read the presentation that I prepared. I paced back and forth as he read the 15 page report.

"This is brilliant. It encompasses all the things that we talked about the other night." He said.

"Did you get a chance to check your email this morning?"

"No, I came straight here."

"Sit down and check your email here from my PC."

Derryck had a puzzled look on his face. He walked over to my PC and checked his email account.

"Is this?"

"It is."

"And these are all the people that you sent it to?"

"Yep."

"Deja, are you sure about this?"

"I am."

"Okay."

"If I lose my job, we are still partners, right?"

"I got your back."

"Okay then, let's go to work."

"Wait, you have more mail."

"Oh I don't care."

"You might want to see this."

MERCEDES, THE NIGHT BEFORE WHEN MARK CAME HOME

I don't know who the fuck Mark thinks that he is dismissing me like that, especially for Deja. But I got news for his ass. He will respect me up in here. When he got home we had the mother of all arguments. He walked in with an attitude but I had him match for match with anger. Whatever he thought he was feeling, I was ten times as upset as he was. We both cut each other dirty looks. He broke the silence first.

"What the fuck was that shit at the office?"

"What the fuck was she doing there?"

"Obviously talking to me."

"And what the fuck were you so tearful about?"

"I was hurt that I hurt her."

"And what? You now want her back?"

"She won't take me back."

"So you do want her back?"

"I don't know what I want anymore."

"What about me? What about our baby?"

"I don't know."

"What kind of fucking answer is that?"

"Mercedes, I don't know. I just don't know."

"You knew a few months ago."

"No, no I didn't. You staged all this shit."

"So this is my fault?"

"You approached me, remember?"

"You didn't have to accept!"

"You're right, but you didn't have to open your legs either."

[SLAP!]

I hit him with all my might.

"Bitch!" [SLAP]

He hit me back and I fell to the floor.

"You would hit a pregnant woman?"

"How do I know that you are pregnant? How do I know if you are, that the baby is mine? Bitch you ruined my life!"

"Motha fucka you ruined your life!"

I reached for my lip and saw that Mark had drawn blood. Now I was really pissed. First he rejects me for this ho, Deja, now he is defending her in my house and then this MF has the nerve to tell me that I am not good enough for him anymore? Who the fuck does he think he's dealing with? I jumped up and slapped him again and then bit him on the ear. I bit him so hard that Mike Tyson would have been proud. He slapped me back and I scratched him up as much as I could, being sure to get his skin under my nails. He slapped me again to the floor and this time I fought back less and less.

"You ignorant bitch! I can't believe that I gave up everything that I worked hard for by messing with your crazy ass. I hate you!"

"Not as much as I hate you and no where near as much as I hate Deja's ass!"

"What the hell do you have against my wife?"

"I hate bitches like that! I hate bitches that think that they are better than everyone else. I don't like her or anything that she stands for. Worst of all, I can't believe that she was in love with a weak pathetic ass man like you!"

"I can't be too pathetic. You have been messing around with me for how long?"

"Fuck You Mark!"

"No, Fuck You!"

I slapped him again as he bent over yelling at me. He slapped me back and I went back to the floor. He got himself together and tried to calm down and then quietly walked away from me. He took a few steps back, put his head in his hands and wept. Then he gathered himself again, walked toward me and then decided to walk away again, this time in the direction of the bathroom.

He walked to the bathroom to shower. I walked to the living room mirror to assess the damage that was done. I then walked over to my PC and pulled out a stack of CD's. I then booted up my PC and send Deja a series of emails.

"I need a little insurance that this nigga ain't about to go running back to wifey. I bet she is crazy enough to take his ass back. Most women do. I also think it's time that Mr. Mark Gamble had a time out also to think about what side his bread is buttered on."

I compiled a number of large emails and hit the send button. Every email went to the same address—Deja's.

MARK

What have I done? I can't believe that Mercedes would take me there. I can't believe that I could hurt another individual as much as I hurt Deja. I mean, Mercedes is pretty. Sexually she is off the chain, but my partners were right. Now that it's no longer new, the thrill is starting to wear off. I showered and prayed that the water would wash away my sin. I felt bad for what I did to Deja. I also felt bad for what I did to Mercedes. I never put my hands on a woman before. I guess tonight was just a combination of everything that I went through. I guess it was the buildup of anger, the fact that I have a failed marriage and the fact that I hurt the one person that was closest to me, the one person that always had my back.

I examined my face in the mirror after getting out of the shower. Mercedes scratched me up pretty good. Those slaps stung. Deja slapped the shit out of me earlier. I didn't think that she had it in her. I was just beginning to shave when there was a knock at the bathroom door. It was a loud an insistent knock.

"Come in Mercedes, I'm not sitting down, I'm just fixing my face. Damn baby, you messed me up pretty good. I'm sorry about all that. I never put my hands on a woman before. It's just that I was mad and I have been through so much at work and with you. I hope you can forgive me."

I heard Mercedes speak from behind me as the door opened.

"I forgive you baby, but I think you and I need a timeout."

"A timeout? What the fuck are you talking about?"

I turned around and there were four police officers standing next to Mercedes in the bathroom doorway.

"Aw shit."

"Sir, you knew that she was expecting with child?" One officer said.

I was stunned. I didn't know what to say and my whole body was frozen with fear. I had a few scratches on me and any other damage was washed away by the hot water from the shower. Mercedes on the other hand, looked pretty bad and had bruises on her face where I slapped her.

"Sir, did you or did you not know that this woman was expecting?" He repeated.

"We live together and ..."

"According to her, the lease is in her name. You however, live across town."

"What?"

"Is your name on the lease?"

"No."

"And she is expecting a child." Another officer said.

"I think she is lying about that." I said.

Mercedes held up a form from the doctor confirming her 9 week pregnancy.

I didn't know what to say or do.

"Mercedes, don't do this. My career is on the line."

"You should have thought about that before you put your hands on her." A female officer said.

I said, "I think I need an attorney."

Another officer said, "Yeah, I think you do."

CHAPTER 14

▼

THE BIG PAYBACK

DEJA

I went to work with Derryck. We drove in his truck and went over all the material in the packet with a fine tooth comb. Ms. Logan was due to meet us at the office at 8:00. We went into the office building feeling confident. I was tired as hell, but the potential that the day had kept me going. Today I was a new woman. Today I would be both emancipated and redeemed. I walked into the office and greeted people as if yesterday hadn't happened. Everyone in the building knew what happened and everyone in the building and then some were about to learn a hell of a lot more. When I got to my office, there were flowers on my desk. I was just about to throw them away thinking that they were from Mark. When I looked at the card however, they were from Mr. Buick. I looked up and in the doorway was Mr. Buick smiling.

"I was wondering if you were going to come in today."

"I wouldn't let something like what happened to me yesterday get me down."

"The average woman would." He said.

"I'm not the average woman."

"No, no my dear you are not. Are you sure that you are ready to try and close the Logan account?"

"I am."

"So why today, why now?"

"You said that you wanted to see what Derryck and I are made of. You said you wanted to see how much potential we possess. Well, after yesterday I think our team took quite the blow. But I am here to tell you that we are prepared and we are ready and we are going to make you some serious money. Today I intend to show you exactly what we are made of."

"Is that right Derryck?"

"Yes sir, it is."

"Deja, you are truly a woman of class. They don't make them like you anymore. I thought my wife, God rest her soul, was the last one but then there is you."

"Thank you sir."

"Make me proud."

"I will."

"Deja, one more thing."

"Yes sir?"

"I got the strangest email today from an anonymous yahoo account. Do you know anything about that?"

"Why no, no sir I don't."

Derryck and I glanced at one another.

"Well okay then. You know, we can trace emails. If I were the person that sent the email, I would delete the anonymous account this morning before the tech support people get here in the next half hour."

"You know what Mr. Buick, if it were me that sent the email, I would probably have deleted the account shortly after confirming that all the parties received it."

"Hmmnn, I guess you would prove to be a bit more savvy than I would."

"You're too kind."

"So I have been told."

Mr. Buick left and Derryck and I headed to the conference room where the meeting was set up. My entire staff was ready and waiting for the arrival of Ms. Logan. At 8:00 on the dot, she was there. At 8:30 our presentation was finished. Ms. Logan asked question after question of Derryck and me until 9:00. Then, her advisors started in with their questions. One by one, we answered them. One by one, her advisors nodded in agreement and approval as they too wrote notes. Mr. Buick walked by the conference room a few times and was surprised at how long the meeting went. Generally, meetings with Ms. Logan took a half hour. At least that was the rumor that I heard. When we finally got up from the conference table, it was 11:30. Ms. Logan, a beautiful black and Asian looking woman in her mid thirties, asked to meet with Mr. Buick. Minutes later our CEO was in the conference room.

"Mr. Buick, your people are very thorough."

"But did they impress you?" He asked.

"They did."

"So we can handle all of your accounts?"

"Not all, but more than we originally discussed."

"Fine, we will send the contracts to you by the end of the week."

"I'd really like them by the end of business day today."

"Why so soon?"

"I'm going on vacation next week and I will be out of the country for the next thirty days or so. I am anxious to work with this team however. I want to close the deal today, so when I get back we can hit the ground running."

"Okay Ms. Logan, then you will have everything that you need by EOD."

"Thank you Mr. Buick."

"No ma'am, thank you."

And just like that, she left. Derryck and I closed the biggest deal of our lives. Mr. Buick was all smiles.

"You all did a good job."

"Thank you sir."

"I have something for each of you, stay here."

Mr. Buick left and came back with envelopes for me, Derryck and our entire staff. I was just about to open my envelope when Mr. Buick asked me to refrain from opening it. My staff each opened their envelopes and they each had a bonus check of $2,000. They were all smiles.

"For all your hard work." Mr. Buick told the staff.

"He then excused my staff and asked that Derryck and I wait."

"Now open your envelopes." He said.

"I opened mine and in it was a check for $15,000 and a ticket to Jamaica."

Derryck was about to open his envelope when Mr. Buick spoke to him.

"I checked the stats with accounting. I had them check the numbers twice. You were right. The projected earnings by the end of fiscal year may be at or exceed 115 million dollars. I'm sorry that I didn't know your name before the day we spoke. You can rest assured that I know your name now?"

Derryck opened up his envelope and in it was $15,000 and a second ticket to Jamaica.

"You all have two weeks off. Enjoy yourselves on the company's dime and in two weeks and one day, get your butts back here and be ready to work."

We both chimed in, "Yes Sir!"

I will have someone watch over your department.

"Sir no disrespect, but I have no idea who to leave in charge of our department while we are away." I said.

"I do."

Mr. Buick smiled and walked away. I hugged Derryck and tried to hold in my happiness. God knows that I need to get away for awhile with all the drama that I have been through. I took the rest of the day off, went home and began to pack. It was an open ticket and both Derryck and I decided that we needed to leave within the next 48 hours.

MARK

I spent the night in jail. I was processed, thrown in a cage and told to wait there until I could either make bail or could be seen by the judge. I sat there on a hard wooden bench with my head in my hands. I now had a record. The minute that my job finds out, that's it for me and that's it for my partnership. I wept with my head in my hands. I stayed in the cell for six hours until Mercedes came to visit me. She met with me on the outside of my cell and decided that we were due for a talk.

"You and I need to talk about what happened."

"Mercedes, you might have ruined me with this bullshit."

"You should never have put your hands on me."

"You hit me first."

"So? Look where hitting me back got you."

"Are you going to bail me out?"

"I'm thinking about it."

"What's stopping you?"

"I don't want you to put your hands on me again."

"I will *never* do that again, I swear."

"Okay."

"Is there anything else?"

"Yes, there is."

"Okay, what?"

"You're done with Deja."

"What?"

"You heard me. I sent her photos of us."

"You did what?"

"I sent her photos of us."

"I never took any photos."

"You did, only you didn't know it. I sent her photos, video footage and audio footage. I have you on tape dogging her out, talking about how bad she is in bed, your dissatisfaction with her cutting her hair, how she is so frigid in bed, and how she won't let you take her from behind. I have footage of us giving one another head, and even the conversations that you had with her that time that you answered her on your cell phone at my house."

"What … How?"

"I had cameras on the laptops. The video feed that you thought came from the camcorder or DVD player was actually coming from a very expensive but very tiny camera on top of my PC's. I have cameras in the bedroom and the living room. Every time that we kissed or had sex is immortalized on film."

"Mercedes, why?"

"Because I get what I want and I want what I get."

"So my shit is all fucked up."

"Yeah, your shit is all fucked up."

"Why?"

"You said that you loved me. This is just a little insurance that you will never go back to her, never cross me, and never put your motha-fuckin hands on me again."

"Mercedes you are sick."

"Sick or not, Nigga I'm all that you got."

She was right. There was no going back to Deja now. I was stuck. Things could be worse, Mercedes could be ugly, but she's not. She's pretty, she's sexual and she's right. She's all that I have left. There is no way in hell that Deja will take me back now.

"Okay baby. You win. Can we get out of here now? I am going to be late for work."

Mercedes bailed me out of jail and took me home. My court date was set for three months from now. I drove home with Mercedes in silence. I took the time and thought about all that happened and how much trouble my dick got me in. When we pulled up in front of the apartment, Mercedes went inside and got dressed for work. Surprisingly, she already pulled a suit and tie out for me that was clean and pressed. She went off to her job and before she left, she kissed me on the mouth.

"I love you." She said.

"Love you too." I didn't sound very convincing, but at the time, it seemed wise to at least mimic her words.

I got dressed and went to work. I was late as hell. There was an accident on the expressway and I was tired as hell from the night before. I called in to the other partners who told me that it was fine that I was late, but I could not miss a team meeting that we were having today at 2:00. I told them I would be there and at 12:15, I was walking in the office door.

Generally when I walk in the office I am hit with a barrage of good mornings and other salutations. Today people just kind of stared at me and it looked as if some were bold enough to whisper behind my back. I walked down the hallway to my office where I was met by one of the partners, Mike Lowery.

"Mark, please come in to the large conference room."

"But the meeting doesn't start until 2:00."

"Actually, the meeting starts when you get here."

I followed Mike into the large conference room. Inside, there were the other partners seated at the conference table. All of them had somber looks on their faces. Mr. Buick didn't look pleased at all. He spoke first after asking me to take a seat.

"Mark what was the last thing that I told you when we last met?"

"Um, I believe you told me not to bring any drama to the firm."

"Do you think you have kept your word in that regard?"

I was wondering if they had already heard about the domestic battery that Mercedes hit me with. I was hoping she hadn't called my job as well as the police.

"Well Mark?"

"I think I may have made a mistake or two Sir."

"A mistake or two?"

"Yes Sir."

"What would you say if I told you that you have embarrassed the hell out of our company and cost us millions of dollars in endorsements?"

"Millions Sir? I don't think that's possible."

"What is apparent young man is that you don't think."

"I'm sorry, what exactly are we talking about?"

Mr. Buick nodded and his secretary brought in a laptop. She then booted it up and told me to check my email. I booted up the PC and was shocked at various photos, audio feeds and video footage of me and Mercedes having sex. I was at a loss for words.

"Sir, I ... I don't know what to say, I mean ... I don't know what to say. I'm sorry that this came across your desk and ..."

"Not just my desk." He interrupted. "This footage and audio was sent to every employee in the company. Not just this department or this branch, but the entire company."

"Oh my God."

"Not only that, it was sent to every *customer* that we have; every client that we have including Ms. Logan. Fortunately, she was here for a presentation and she has already been given a contract to sign. I have a feeling though that as soon as her contract with us is up, she will go to another agency. Other clients of ours are bailing right and left, especially clients that you have worked with in the past. Not only do they have copies of this footage, so do our competitors and our partners, subsidiaries and affiliates. You literally cost us millions of dollars."

"Mr. Buick … I'm sorry."

"Son, I'm afraid that you are no longer partner. On top of that you are being sent back to your old office to run that staff. Two weeks after that, we will decide whether or not to keep you on with the company. After the scandal that you have caused, it would not surprise me if you were blacklisted."

"That would mean that I could never find work again in finance unless I started my own company."

"I don't think that you would even be able to start your own company."

I collapsed in the chair. My mind was racing. In just a day's time, my life was taking a turn for the worst. I hurt my wife, I went to jail, my mistress is pregnant and I might be losing my job.

"How is it that I can work in my old position, did Deja quit or are you suggesting that I work for her?"

"Deja closed the Logan account. She's going on vacation."

"Isn't Derryck going to resent my being in the department over him?"

"You wouldn't be over him if he were here. He is going on vacation too."

"They are going together?"

Mike said, "Why? You didn't want her?"

I hated what he was implying. I looked at Mr. Buick for some sense of understanding.

"They have been sent by the company on a vacation for a job well done."

"Where are you sending them?"

"Jamaica."

My heart sunk deep in my chest. My mind raced with images of Derryck and my wife in a passionate embrace. Jealousy not only reared its ugly head, it possessed me like Linda Blair.

"You sent my wife and another man to Jamaica?"

Just then, there was a knock on the conference room door. In walked Sincer-era' [pronounced Sin-seer-ee-yea] Douglas, my wife's attorney.

"Mark, I am here to place you on notice that you have been served. My client, Deja Gamble is seeking a dissolution of marriage based in infidelity, mental cru-elty, emotional abuse, economic abuse, defamation of character, fraud and a number of other incidentals. We will both see you in court where we are seeking alimony and damages herein."

Mike Lowery became a smart ass and said, "Well, it looks like we are sending your *ex-wife* and another man to Jamaica."

Mr. Buick said, "Mark please report back to your department. We will let you know about the status of your job in two weeks."

I finished out the day and when it was over, I raced home to find out why Mercedes did this to me. I stormed into the house ready to beat her ass. Then I remembered that she had me over a barrel with the domestic battery from earlier. Had I gone and touched her once, that would be it for my ass. I would be looking at some serious time.

"Mercedes please come here."

She walked over to me.

"Please … sit down. I have to ask, why did you do this to me?"

"I told you that you should never have put your hands on me, that's why I signed the complaint."

"I'm not talking about the complaint. I'm talking about the photos of you and me."

"I sent them to Deja for insurance, I told you that."

"Not the pics to Deja, the pics that you sent to my job."

"Your job?"

"Yeah, my job. Photos of you and me were sent to every employee in my com-pany, our partners, subsidiaries and our customers."

"Damn! Baby, I didn't do that."

"You told me that you sent the pictures. You told me that while I was locked up."

"I told you that I sent them to Deja. That is the *only person that I sent them to.*"

Then it sunk in.

Deja sent the pictures.

I didn't think that she had it in her. I didn't think she would set out to ruin me like that. I can't believe what she did to me.

"I … I don't believe it."

"Why not?"

"What do you mean why not? These pictures ruined me!"

"Can you blame her?"

"You of all people, are taking her side?"

"I'm not taking sides. All I'm saying is that as a woman, I understand."

"But you started all this shit!"

"No dear, you did."

"I need some air."

I got up and walked out of the apartment. I headed to my car and drove to the only place that I knew to go—home. Or what was formerly my home.

JUST WALK AWAY

I drove like a madman to my old house. I was crying, praying and thinking about all that had happened. I could hear my mother's voice in my head saying, "God don't like ugly!" Then I thought back to how hard I prayed that day during the softball game. I prayed fast and I prayed hard. Then it dawned on me that I asked God for a favor and lied in the same breath. I said, "If you get me out of this, I won't cheat anymore and I will leave Mercedes alone." Just think, a few hours after God sent her away and a few hours after that prayer, I was already sleeping with her again. I lied. What's worse is that I lied *directly to God.*

I felt bad. I felt like I was getting my just due. I also came to the realization today that God is a woman with an ironic sense of humor. She was punishing me for hurting one of her own. I raced to the house, pulled up in the driveway, and noticed that there was a Cadillac Truck in the driveway.

"Whose truck is that?"

I got out and started fumbling with my keys. Then I remembered that they didn't work. I rang the bell and there was now a camera trained on me. I also noticed that a house alarm had been installed. I looked into the camera and started to appeal to it.

"Deja, Deja please, baby I need to see you. Let me in."

The door opened.

Without hesitation, I walked in. As I turned around, there in the doorway was Derryck.

"What are you doing here?"

"I was just about to ask you the same thing."

"I live here."

"Once upon a time you did. Now, you're just visiting."

I stared at him intently, did he think his young ass was about to take me on?

"Derryck, I don't have time to deal with your shit. It's obvious that you have a thing for my wife, but you need to step off. I need to speak with her."

"She asked me to ask you to leave. As far as I know, she is divorcing you. You should have been served with papers today."

I was beginning to wonder just how involved Derryck and Deja were. It made no sense for the two of them to be fooling around. Deja wasn't the type of woman to fool around. I would like to think that she wouldn't see anyone else until our divorce was final. I wanted one more chance at convincing her that I could change. I walked over to the stairs and yelled up for my wife.

"Deja? Deja I need to speak with you. Deja! Baby please, come down here."

Nothing. Not a sound.

"She doesn't want to speak to you. Don't you get that? You turned her world upside down. She doesn't need your lies, your drama or your bullshit!" Derryck said.

"And what would you know about it? What do you know about me? You need to stay the fuck out of grown folks business!"

"Grown? Nigga you ain't grown. You're trifling. And as far as what I know about your business, I know everything. I know everything that she told me and anything else I need to know is all over the Internet."

That hurt. Even my new rival knew about my drama with Mercedes.

"Deja! Deja Please come down!"

"She's got your ass on ignore. Look, you don't deserve her. If you love her, really love her, step aside and give someone else the opportunity to make her happy."

"So you are telling me that you love her?"

"I do."

"And you are better for her that I am?"

"I am now."

"I should kick your young pretty boy ass."

"Mark, don't play yourself. Just walk away."

I balled up my fist as if to prepare to fight. Derryck looked at my balled up fists and smiled before he spoke.

"All I'm gonna say bruh, is be sure."

That scared me a little. I didn't know what Derryck was capable of and I wasn't sure that I was ready to find out. I wanted to hit him. I needed to hit him. After all, this was about my wife, the woman that I love. I swung wildly at Derryck. He blocked the punch and countered with one of his own. He put all his weight behind a right cross and down I went. My pride was hurt more than the blow, although I have to admit that the blow hurt. I felt like Ali after Frazier took his title. As I lay on the floor trying to clear my vision, I looked at my surroundings. I looked at the wonderful home that Deja and I shared. I thought to myself how the mighty have fallen. I failed. I failed my wife, I failed God and I failed in my marriage. I stood up and balled my fists again.

"Mark—walk away." Derryck said.

Tears streamed down my face. My life had imploded on me in the past few days.

"I just want to see her." I said.

"Your very presence bothers her. I love her. I can't let you hurt her any more. Now leave or I am not going to be held responsible for my actions."

Derryck walked over to the door, opened it and motioned for me to leave. He was right. I didn't want to hurt Deja any more than I already had. I got back in my car and I went back home—to Mercedes, my soon to be baby's mother. As I pulled off with tears in my eyes, I didn't even notice Deja passing me in her new car headed back in the direction of my former home.

DEJA

I promised Derryck that I would be at my house by 7:00. It was 7:15. We had an 8:45 flight out of Midway. I knew that Derryck was always on time and that I would probably be running a little late, so I gave him the code to my house alarm. It was the first time that a man other than my husband would be in my home and I not be present. I will of course change the alarm code when I get in. I like Derryck but I don't trust any man like that, at least not yet. I was running late because a sister needed to pick up a bathing suit for Jamaica. As I raced home, I swear I thought I saw Mark pass me in his car crying. It couldn't have been though. Anyway, I headed up the driveway, parked my car and ran in the house to get my bags which I packed earlier.

"Sorry I'm late, did you find everything okay?"

"Oh, yeah. Cable and sandwiches in the fridge, that's all any man needs. Hell, if I had some Ghetto Kool-Aid, I would be perfect."

"Ghetto Kool-Aid?"

"Extra Sweet."

"Oh."

"Deja, listen, Mark was just here."

"That was Mark? I thought that was him that I passed but I didn't picture him crying, what was that all about?"

"I told him that I cared for you and that he needed to walk away."

"You did what?"

"I told him that I cared for you, and that he needed to walk away."

"How did he take you saying that?"

"He took it pretty hard."

"You had no right to do that."

"I know."

"He is still my husband."

"I know."

"I'm not trying to lead you on or hurt him, that's not what I'm about."

"Deja—I know."

"Then why …"

"… Because I love you."

"You don't know me."

"We covered this, remember?"

"This is not what it looks like Derryck. We are two colleagues and friends that are going away on a mutual vacation set up by our employer. Just because they are sending us together doesn't mean that we are together, got it?"

"Yes Dear."

"Don't call me dear."

"Yes, sexy?"

"Don't do that either. This is not a date, it's a retreat."

"Okay, I got it. But you know what the thing is about retreats, right?"

"No, what?"

He walked over to me moved my hair from my face, took my chin in his hand and talked softly to me. I took in his Lagerfeld cologne and his adorable smile and I hate to admit it, but I hung on his every word. This man had me under his spell. It was a spell I had been fighting all too long.

"A retreat is supposed to be so relaxing and so refreshing, that when it's over, you are ready to come back to work and do what needs to be done. When *this retreat is over, I guarantee you will feel relaxed and refreshed and like a new woman. Baby, that's my word.*"

"Uh—Oh—kay."

"Now Let's go."

"Okay."

Damn this man was fine.

CHAPTER 15

▼

COME BACK TO JAMAICA

DEJA

We went to the airport and left the hustle and bustle of the windy city for the warm sun, white sand beaches, gentle breeze and cultural delight of Jamaica. The company put us up in the Franklin D Resort in a three bedroom suite. Derryck had the suite that was on the far right and I had the one on the far left. We used the suite in the middle as a common area where we would eat, receive room service and if need be, entertain. We were here in Jamaica for 10 days. We both planned to make the most of it. I of course re-iterated to Derryck that although we shared a three bedroom suite, he would sleep in his suite and I would sleep in mine. He smiled at the suggestion.

"You keep reminding me that we aren't having sex, does that mean that sex is on your mind?"

I blushed, was I that transparent? Yeah, sex was on my mind and in my body and yes, there was one hell of a fire burning between my thighs, but I was here to relax and that's all.

"No, no sex isn't on my mind, but because you are a man, I figured that I would just remind you again."

"Uh-huh, yeah ... right. Okay D, whatever you say. I'm going to get in the shower."

"We just arrived here."

"I know, but I'm feeling a little ... dirty."

He smiled at me and walked from the middle suite where we were talking back to his suite. I watched him as he walked away. Derryck had a nice ass. I looked. I had to look. It was just so … out there. I wanted to run up behind him and have a squeeze, but that wouldn't be lady like. The little devil on my shoulder started speaking to me.

"Lady like? Bitch who are you foolin. You better go jump on that shit!"

"But I'm a married woman."

"Married my ass, you better handle that man and handle your needs … give him some!"

"I like him, but I don't love him, at least not yet."

Love? What's love got to do with it? You can love him later, right now, fuck him. Besides, what is there not to love, just get you some. You know he wants you and we both know that you want to fuck the hell out of his young fine ass!"

"It's wrong to just sleep with a man. I can't just use him like that. What if I get with him and discover that he isn't the one?"

"Wrong? Bitch please. Men do the shit all the time. Our new motto should be, if he ain't the one, fuck him and then move the fuck on. Get your needs met. Get that ass slapped, get your hair pulled, get crunk with that shit! And who knows? While you are playin, he just might be the one."

"We work together, sex might complicate things."

"Ain't nothing complicated about an orgasm. Girl, put that man between your legs and ride his ass like a jockey at the races. He's fine! And we ain't gettin no younger."

"Amen to that shit."

I stopped talking to myself in my head and headed back to my suite where I took a shower also. I let the water wash all over my body and tried to lose myself in the warm gentle stream of water. The water was so warm and so relaxing that it felt like I was being massaged everywhere all at once. It felt like my body was being touched in 1000 ways and that every pore was open, every toxin was being cleansed, and every pain was slowly beginning to slip away. My body had been so tense that I had no idea how much stress I had been under these past few months. This bullshit with Mark, this job and my mental state had taken a serious toll on my body. I stood in the shower for twenty minutes. The next thing that I knew, I heard music playing overhead in my suite. Sade's *No Ordinary Love* was playing on a loudspeaker in the ceiling. The soft music was hypnotic. Apparently, we had surround sound in all three suites where music of our choice could be played. Initially I was worried that Derryck might come in the shower with me. My heart raced as I was frightened with anticipation of his possibly walking in on me. That little voice in my head started talking again.

"Girl, what are you scared of? Relax. You are in Jamaica. If Derryck walks in here, he walks in here. He's a grown man and you are a grown woman. Let him bring his ass in here if he wants. I say let nature take its course. You are in one of the most romantic places on the globe. All the pain, the drama and the bullshit ... girl, let it go. Let God, let love."

My whole body relaxed. I let the water wash away the fear. I let the warm air of Jamaica have its way. I let the pain go, and I decided that today, this day, I would let go of the pain.

I dried my body off, rubbed scented lotion all over my body and put on a two piece purple bikini that I bought yesterday. My stomach was tight, my breasts were swollen and my ass was looking damn good if I must say so myself. I then took a white sheer wrap and tied it around my waist. My hair was starting to grow back some, but it was still cropped short. The wet look worked for me and I was hoping in the back of my mind that it might work for Derryck as well. I made up in my mind that I'm not going to throw my sex at him, but I am no longer going to decline his advances either.

I walked out into my suite, put on some sandals, grabbed my DKNY glasses and my small purse and headed to the middle suite to see if Derryck wanted to get a bite to eat. I was stunned at how fine he looked when I walked in the middle suite.

Derryck had on white linen pants, brown Hugo Vittelli Sandals and that was it. He had on no shirt, and his abs were tight and ripped, his pecs looked like that of a male supermodel and his bald head was glistening. He smiled at me and his pearly white teeth were so bright, had the sun hit them I might go blind. He had a remote in his hand and he changed the music to Maxwell's *The Hush* from the debut album. He was wearing *Chrome* cologne and smelling good as hell. I tried to keep my composure, but I couldn't stop looking at his ripped body.

Is all that for me? I thought.

"So ... no shirt?" I asked

"Naw, I'm cool. We're in Jamaica, remember? It gets quite hot here. I figured I would just walk around like this."

"You need to put on a top."

"Why?"

"Well, cause your stuff is all out. And, I was going to suggest that you eat me ... I mean, that we get something to eat. You uh ... up for that?"

He smiled. I had to turn beet red at my mistake. He didn't call me on it and he didn't embarrass me any more than I had already embarrassed myself. I closed my eyes and just wished that I could disappear. When I opened them again, he was standing right in front of me. He took my hands in his and we began to dance. With each beat and each lyric that Maxwell sang, my anxiety, fear and embarrassment began to disappear.

"I want to get something to eat. I would love to dine with you."

"Okay."

He held me close and I took in his scent. He then kissed my earlobe and whispered in my ear.

"I would love to do the other thing as well. But we will do things at your pace, at your convenience. Remember what I said D, I'm a patient man."

He held me closer as *Purple Rain* began to play overhead. I held on to this man and danced with him like he was my man. I felt safe in his muscular arms. Not only did I feel safe. I felt wanted. I felt ... loved. We danced without speaking, my heart was racing. Derryck must have felt it, because he held me just a bit tighter and whispered again in my ear.

"It's okay. I'm here, no worries, just let go. Baby ... relax."

I held him closer and a single tear streamed down my face. Do I dare trust again? Do I simply let down my guard and allow myself to be fooled by a man again? What do I do? That voice spoke again.

"You don't have to let your guard all the way down, but let him in ... just a little and remember girl, he's a man ... but he's not that man. He's not the one that hurt you. You can't punish that man for what the last man did. That's how many good, strong black women lose so many good black men. He may not be the best, I'm sure that he's not the worst, but one thing I do know, he's your friend and with all that you have been through, he's here."

I held on to Derryck until the final rifts of Prince's guitar went off. At the end of the song he took me by the hand, led me to his suite where he put on a white shirt that matched his pants. We then took me by the hand and we walked to the lobby. I walked with him and placed my head on his shoulder. He held me as we walked and he held me like I was his woman; like I have always been his woman.

I didn't trust him. Nor did I let down my guard. But I let him in, just a little.

We could have eaten in our room. The suite that we were in had private air conditioned bedrooms, full showers, tubs, Jacuzzis, separate living and dining room areas, satellite TV, a kitchen with a refrigerator and stove, and a spacious patio that overlooked the beach. It was so nice that we quite honestly never had to leave the room. As we walked passed various rooms toward the elevator, we heard over and over again various couples that were in the throws of passion. Couples were either making love or fucking. The couples making love were speaking in hushed tones beneath the music playing in their rooms. The sounds of squeaking beds were heard in the background of the rooms and the sweet sound of pleasure unmasked reverberated off the walls.

Couples that were fucking were more vocal, more verbal and more primitive with their acts of passion. As we walked down the hall, in some rooms we heard the sounds of headboards knocking against walls, music that had no hope of drowning out the sounds of activity going on in the room, and dirty pillow talk along with the sounds of bodies slapping against one another and hands slapping asses. I knew many of the women getting fucked were black women, strong black women. I knew because in many of these rooms men were putting it down. I mean Jamaican men who were used to fucking visiting women with a vengeance. That grudge fucking as I call it, worked well on the white women that came down here. They would be dick whipped and spending all types of money as they tried to mimic Angela Bassett in Terry McMillan's *How Stella Got her Groove Back*. The sisters however came down here for the sole purpose of getting fucked. For them, the Jamaican men were a challenge. For them, fucking like this was their therapy. For many, the session had begun, for many more, they might have been the patients, but halfway into the acts, the sisters were the one's taking over the session. One sister in particular in room 501, was in her room breaking her man damn near in half. We knew because she was the most vocal. From the hallway she was so loud and so vocal, that both Derryck and I had to stop and listen. We smiled at each other as the sister dropped verse on her lover.

"That' right hit that shit! Don't be shy! Hit that! That's right baby, that's right baby, right there! Oh shit! That's my spot! That's my mothafuckin spot! Hit that shit! Fuck me! That's it, fuck me! Put your name on that shit! Fuck me like you mean it! Fuck me like you want it! Put your back in that shit! Put your ass in that shit! That's right, out to the tip, now drive that shit it. That's it! All they way in … all the … way … in. Aw shit, Oh shit, that's it … Oh shit … shiiiittttt! I'm cumming! Oh Fuck! I'm Cumming!"

I was thinking to myself "Damn." I looked at Derryck who winked at me and was all smiles.

"Come on let's go." I said.

"Shit, I don't know. From the sounds of things in there, that brother might need a wheelchair or some oxygen."

"You're funny."

"I try."

We went to the Verandah Restaurant. Derryck held my chair out for me and we sat down at the table and ate. We talked about work, the future, favorite music and other interests.

Derryck likes R & B, Jazz, some Rock and even a little country which I found to be a bit weird. Me? I like Jazz, R& B, Blues and Neo-Soul. Our favorite authors are Eric Jerome Dickey, Wahida Clark, Brenda Hampton, Michael Baisden, Sistah Souljah, C. Kelly Robinson and Travis Hunter. His favorite travel spots include Vermont, Brazil, New Jersey and Florida. I like hitting Vegas, Texas, The Cayman Islands and Mexico. We talked about where we traveled, why we chose the schools that we chose, and where we each saw ourselves in the years to come. I felt bad and old because Derryck was still in school. He pointed out that he was only four years younger than me and when you think about it, that's nothing.

"So, what do you want to do today?" I asked him.

"You." He said slyly.

I smiled. "That's cute, and it' also obvious. What else would you like to do today?"

"Well, we got here late, let's go back to the room, nap a little and then go dancing."

"Why don't we do a few activities first, then take a nap and then go dancing."

"Oh, so the old woman thinks she can hang with burning the candle at both ends?"

"Old? Who are you calling old?"

"You. You bring up our slight age difference all the time. I just thought that maybe you were feeling a little self conscious, that's all." He said smiling.

"Oh it's on now."

"Okay, well we'll see. We can do whatever activity you want and I am anxious to see if you can hang with me Ms. Lady."

"I'm anxious to see if you can hang too."

That came out all wrong.

We looked at each other and broke out smiling and laughing. Again I was embarrassed.

"Derryck listen, about these little Freudian slips of mine …"

"… Shhh. No excuses, no explanations, let's just let things run their course."

"But I think I need to explain and …"

"… Nope, don't want to hear it. Eventually you are going to have to stop running from me."

"I'm not running, it's just bad timing that's all."

"No it's not. This is a good time. This is a great place and you … are a beautiful woman that needs to be shown that there are brothers out there that appreciate you for the person that you are on the inside and out."

I smiled a bright smile showing all my teeth.

"There it is."

"There is what?"

"That smile that I have been looking for, the thing that keeps me going."

"You're crazy. Let's go."

We went horse back riding on a quiet trail in the wilderness. Then we went kayaking on the water. From there we rode a glass-bottom-boat where we watched the underwater world do its day to day thing. I was so amazed at the different hues of blue and green the water gave off, as well as how clear the water was. It was like God's own painting on the surface of the planet. The blue was so peaceful and inviting, that watching life beneath the sea was almost hypnotic. We went back on land and played pool, golfed a little and then went back to the room to change clothes. I switched into another bathing suit and Derryck changed into a tan linen suit.

For dinner we returned to the Verandah, where we ate Jamaican specialties along with Mango, Pineapple and other exotic fruits. We ate dinner by torchlight and a gentle cooling breeze washed over our bodies gently caressing us like an age old lover. A live band made its way out onto the deck and as the wait staff took away the food. Derryck and I made note of the beautiful purple horizon as the sun finally went down ending its struggle with the inevitable night. The sky was lit with a tapestry of stars and the heavens themselves seemed to shine down on this wondrous place.

A Jamaican brother walked in from of the band and asked Derryck was there anything special that he wanted to hear. He whispered in his ear and the next thing I knew, *Sweet Lady* by Maxwell was being played. It was a song that moved me but scared me at the same time.

It's been so long since I've seen you,
And your chocolate legs wrapped around me,
Your sexy smell drives me crazy,
Let's get married.
Sweet lady, will you marry me?
Sweet lady will you marry me?,
I never thought I would ever,
Want matrimony forever,
But you brought that sweet, sweet familiar,
Let's get married,

I know that he was not serious. I prayed that he wasn't serious. Hell, I wasn't even divorced yet. I tried to play things off.

"So what is it with you and Maxwell anyway?"

"That's my guy. He knows a lot about love."

"So is that all that you listen to?"

"No. You know I listen to other types of music."

"Well then …"

"… Shhh, listen to the lyrics."

"Why?"

"Why do you think?"

"Derryck you can't be asking me to marry you."

"Maybe not today, especially since your divorce to what's his name isn't final. But I do want you to warm up to the idea."

"Really?"

"Really."

"And how do I know that you are serious?"

"Because I want you to hold on to something for me."

"Really, what?"

"This."

He reached into his pants pocket and pulled out a two and a half carat ring from Rogers & Holland. I knew this ring. I had been admiring it for months now. It was a ring called *Carmen.*

"You can't be asking me to marry you." I said.

"No, you're right. I'm asking you to think about marrying me."

"Derryck we don't know each other well enough."

"That stops now. Today, and each day that follows, I want to get to know everything that there is to know about you."

"But …"

"No butts. Let's dance."

The band played *Chante's got a man.* A beautiful Jamaican sister came out and sang and she blew so tough, that you would have thought Chante Moore herself was there singing along the beachfront. Derryck held me, kissed me and although I thought about resisting him, by body responded to his every touch. I became alive with his touch, fire burned within me with his every kiss and his scent … my God his scent was captivating. His hands wrapped around my waist and his lips found my neck like a vampire in the thick of the night. I wrapped my arms around him, threw my head back and enjoyed the spoils of being held by a man, a real man, a strong man, a fine-ass-show-nuff black man!

We danced for twenty minutes and soon after, Derryck led me up to my room. He kissed me goodnight at my door, and let me in to my suite. He smiled at me, kissed me once more on the lips and headed back to his suite.

I slowly got undressed.

I waited patiently in the bedroom.

My bedroom door was open.

I thought tonight that Derryck might come in.

I hoped that he might come in.

He was respecting my wishes.

He remained in his room.

The only thing separating us was one of us getting up and turning two door knobs. He decided to respect my wishes, and I was damning myself for making those foolish wishes known. I wanted him. My body was aching for him. I never wanted this night to end, but it did. I took pleasure in knowing that he respected me. I had pity on myself for protesting his advances so much. Sleep found me twenty minutes later, and it was a good restful sleep.

THE NEXT DAY

I awoke to the smell of turkey bacon, toast, eggs and fruit. Juice was chilling on the countertop, and in the kitchen was Derryck. Again he was topless and his pecs looked as if they had been carved out of granite. He prepared my plate and welcomed me with a smile and a kiss.

"Good morning beautiful, did you sleep well?"

"I slept okay." I said sarcastically.

"That's no one's fault but your own." He said smiling.

"And what is that supposed to mean?"

"You know what it means."

"Do I?'

"Yeah."

"Explain" I demanded.

"You might have slept better had you called me into your room last night. You might have slept better and still awakened to breakfast in bed and well, a half our or so, we might be having each other for an early dessert of seconds. But you want to deny yourself happiness and hey, I'm cool with that."

He sounded confident and sure of himself. I liked this about him, but I hated it also.

"So this is some sort of game to you?"

"No, this is a courtship."

"Like Eddie's Father"

"Like the prelude to a marriage."

I looked at my hand and eyed the ring that he gave me. I thought that part of last night was a dream, but here this ring was blinging on my finger. Right now it was on my right hand. In the back of my mind I was hoping that it might one day be on my left. I don't know why, but I was finally beginning to see Derryck in a whole new light.

"So you are serious about all this?"

"Deja, how many men do you know would spend a vacation with a woman, not try and get in her pants and give her a rock like that? I know you doubt my sincerity and with all you have been through, I understand that. But I want to make something clear to you while we are down here. This will either be the best time of your life, or the one time in your life that you regret for the rest of your life."

"What does that mean?"

"It means, when people ask us after we are married when was the first time that we made love, you will either smile to yourself and say, **Jamaica.** Or, you will laugh and be kicking yourself in the butt for not taking advantage of the romantic time that we had here in Jamaica."

He laughed and continued to make his own plate after serving me mine.

"Oh really?"

"Yep."

"You know, you talk a lotta trash."

"I know, but unlike a lot of other men, I can back that shit up."

"Can you?"

"Shit yeah, you better check that right hand woman."

I looked at the ring again, damn it was nice. I tried to give it back last night but Derryck was insistent that I hold on to it until I made a concrete decision about him. He said whether I chose to marry him or walk away, until I chose a specific side of the fence, he wanted that ring to remain on my hand.

"So, what do you want to do today?" I asked.

"You."

I smiled again and looked at him sarcastically.

"What? You keep setting yourself up for that one."

I smiled because he was right.

"What … on this agenda … would you like to do today?"

"Anything I want?" He asked.

"Within reason."

"Well, eat and get dressed and today I will take the lead on our activities."

"Okay."

We ate while Kem played overhead on the speakers. We listened to the song *I think about us*. My head bobbed up and down as I ate. Derryck just looked at me and smiled as he saw how into the music I was. I looked at him and knew what he was thinking. He was thinking if I could get this much into the music, I should have no problem getting that much into him.

DATE TWO

Today we played golf, we went snorkeling, windsurfing and danced in the disco studio. We visited the Dolphin Cove in Ochos Rios, went shopping and purchased some fine art that we had shipped back to the states. That night we went to Karaoke where Derryck got up, placed a chair in front of the stage and sang yet another joint that *Maxwell* made famous. I think the song was originally done by *Kate Bush*. Today he blew *This Woman's Work*. He sang so soft and so beautifully, that tears streamed down my face. Especially when he sang, "I know you've got a little life in you left; I know you've got a lot of strength left." Only the two of us knew what he meant. I knew exactly what it was that he was saying. He was saying in spite of the hurt, in spite of the pain, in spite of the betrayal, there has to be a little room left. Just a little room left—for love. He was asking me to trust him, to be with him, to take his hand and be his lady. As he sang, my spirit was lifted. I teared up a little, and he teared up a little, but his focus was never taken off me. It was in that moment, that single moment, that I knew this man—this man … was meant for me. He serenaded me and at the end of the song I kissed him passionately, and the entire crowd applauded.

The next singer got up and sang *I see you in a different light*. As the sister sang, I was blown away. Her timing could not have been better, It was a like a veil had been lifted from my eyes as I saw Derryck for who he was … a man in love. More importantly, he was a man in love with me. We danced as the sister sang and I held on to him like he was my man. I then whispered in his ear.

"If you are serious, my divorce will be final when we get home."

He looked me in the eyes and spoke. "I have never been more serious about anything in my life."

I kissed Derryck.

Scratch that. I kissed my man.

My—man.

THE NIGHT THAT THE EARTH MOVED

We made our way up to the room and Derryck led me to the couch in the middle suite. He set the mood by lighting candles everywhere, turning down the lights, drawing me a bubble bath and pouring me a glass of Chardonnay. He also handed me a small cigarette of Maui Gold. It was specially cultivated herb that was all natural and sweet to the taste. I hadn't smoked in a while, but tonight was different. Tonight was the first night of the rest of my life. I lit the joint, took two puffs and sipped on my drink. I then smiled at Derryck as I retreated into my suite and slipped into the bath. Derryck retreated into his suite and did the same. He took a few hits of the joint and sipped on wine himself.

I changed into a silk red teddy that I bought from Fredrick's. I know I said that I hadn't planned on sleeping with Derryck but every sister brings at least one teddy when she travels, *just in case.* I know, I know, just in case we happen to *fall on top of some dick.* I knew what time this was and Derryck did also. As I caught my breath and prepared to walk back into the middle suite, Prince's song *Adore* played overhead. I was surprised that it wasn't another Maxwell song. I walked into the suite and there in the doorway to his suite was Derryck. He was again topless and standing there in the doorway in red silk pajama pants that perfectly matched the teddy that I was wearing. He took a hit of the joint and put it out. He then sipped on his wine. His bedroom eyes found mine from across the room and his eyes and sexy dark bushy eyebrows locked in on me. He gave me a look of both passion and lust that beckoned me to come to him.

He smiled.

I smiled.

I then walked over to him and tilted my head up to kiss him. Our tongues danced and the room was filled with the erotic sounds of Prince in his heyday and our kisses all over one another. *Smile* by Angela Winbush began to play overhead and as Angela sang, I kissed Derryck deeply on the mouth and ran my fingertips across his rock hard chest and down his rippled midsection. He let out a gentle sigh as he welcomed my touch. I moaned as his large firm hands found my tender backside. He kissed my lips and then my neck. His talented tongue reached my inner ear and he softly nibbled on my earlobes. My leg raised along his side and his strong hands rubbed along the side of my body. His touch was welcome. His body was welcome. His love was welcome. I would have him this day and every day to follow as my soul mate, my heart, my man.

I rubbed his bald head and as I did, his hands explored my body. He fondled my breasts and I shivered with anticipation. My nipples hardened and began to protrude through the delicate material letting him know that his touch was accepted. My mind, body and soul ached for more. *How Soon* by Joe came on and as it did, Derryck picked me up, took me in his arms, kissed me on the lips and carried me back into his suite. His new scent was that of Mesmerize, the cologne by Avon. He gently laid me down on the bed and bathed my body in kisses. He kissed my lips, my neck, my collarbone and back to my lips again. He took his time with me. He carefully and meticulously explored my body. He kissed every inch, every fiber, and with each kiss my body welcomed him and the many walls that I put up emotionally, and spiritually began to slowly fall. He kissed the pain away. I began to cry and as the tears streamed down my face his strong hands ever so gently wiped the tears away.

"Its okay baby, let it go, let it out. I'm here—and I'm not going anywhere."

He continued to kiss me. His made his way down to my breasts. He bit them gently through the material. He then took the straps off my shoulders and then kissed my shoulders. My body quivered in anticipation as no other man had seen me naked since my husband. He peeled my top off of me and stared. I felt self conscious. I felt afraid as if my top were my shield. With slight anxiety I spoke to him.

"What are you looking at?" I whispered.

"I just can't get over how beautiful you are."

Sade's *Kiss of Life was now playing.* We had gone through so many songs that I was beginning to lose track of time. I didn't want this night to end and at the rate we were going, it looked as if it might never end. Derryck tossed my teddy to the floor and lay on top of me in a push up position. He kissed my breasts, licked my nipples, gently bit my nipples and ran circles around them. He kissed in between my breasts, down my stomach and tongue-kissed my naval. He then kissed my outer thighs, my inner thighs and gave one gentle kiss to my special place. He then kissed my manicured toes, licked them, sucked them and took me some-place different. He turned me over on my stomach and gently licked the back of my calves, my thighs, my apple-bottom, and then licked ever so gently up my spine. My back arched as his tongue send waves of ecstasy through my body. Just when I thought we were done with Maxwell, *Whenever, Wherever, Whatever came on.* As I lay on my stomach with my eyes closed as I experienced the pleasure of a gentle lover's touch, I smiled to myself as Maxwell played. Without looking, I knew that Derryck was most likely smiling also.

He bathed my back with kisses. He kissed my shoulder blades, the back of my neck and behind my ear. I let out gentle moans and sighs to let my lover know of my satisfaction with his progress. His hands ran up the side of my body as he arched his back and kissed my backside.

"You are so beautiful." I heard him say.

My body relaxed. As he turned me over, he kissed up the front of my body again as his tongue reunited with my nipples and soon after danced again with my tongue. Our kisses seemed to go on forever as the next song played overhead. The next song was *How come you don't call me anymore* by Prince. I loved the song. I smiled to myself as I listened to the lyrics. If the lovemaking will always be like this, Derryck will never have to worry about my not calling. Hell at this rate, I might put a low-jack on his ass and keep him on speed-dial.

He kissed my stomach and slowly and methodically made his way between my legs. I opened my legs inviting him to feast on my flesh. I was embarrassed at how wet I was. It was as if my vagina was a dam and my juices flowed like the Euphrates River. I was *so wet,* that I was worried he might not be able to stay inside of me once the foreplay was over and we finally experienced one another. *Now that you're gone* by Martha Wash played next and I thought to myself whoever programmed this music had to be seriously in love.

Derryck parted my legs and placed a finger inside of me. My body shuddered and I let out a gracious sigh as he began to finger me. When his tongue found my clit, that sigh evolved into a welcome moan. He tongue kissed my vagina like a familiar lover. He made love to me with his tongue. It danced in and out of me and explored the entire region. There was no stone left unturned as he explored my special place. The vaginal area is small. It's very small. But somehow, someway, Derryck licked places that *had never been licked before.* Vaginal muscles that I didn't know I had … flexed. He didn't do like a lot of men and concentrate on just my clit. He explored me, he feasted upon me. He did tricks with his tongue that I thought no other man knew.

My breasts heaved up and down in the air. My nipples pointed north and I was beside myself with passion. My stomach floated up and down and my stomach muscles began to tighten as well as my vaginal muscles and my legs slowly began to shake. *Love Calls* by Kem was now playing. My breathing became more and more pronounced as the tremors of orgasm slowly began. The fire between my legs was slowly being quenched with passion. Something inside me that had been dormant for so long was re-awakened. My breathing became more rapid, my breaths were deeper, my heart raced like a champion sprinter in the final leg of a race. My pulse was ticking like a passionate yet primitive clock that alerted the world of the passing of time. With each second that passed I felt an eternity of passion. The longing and yearning that my body had was being put to rest. As my eyes rolled in the back of my head and I began to bite my bottom lip and pull hard on the sheets beneath me, the tremors began. The launch of waves of passion started. My river began to flow heavy and my ass hiked in the air giving more of me to Derryck. I opened my legs and allowed him to taste more of me, to feast on me, to have all of me and to eat me as if he were a dying man on death row and this was his last meal.

I tried to restrain myself. I tied to savor this feeling forever. I loved an orgasm. I loved a good hard—nut. But more than that, I enjoyed the seconds, those few precious seconds, that moment of anticipation, that moment of primitive uncontrollable lust, those few seconds where a woman can't think, when a woman can't speak, those moments where the mind takes a needed vacation and the body takes control of every body part. I long for those precious and erotic moments seconds *before orgasm;* the time where the only function that the body knows is pleasure and breathing. I love that time that the only thing that we want is this moment to never end, and for us to continue to take in oxygen.

"I'm cumming. Oh shit, Oh shit … Oh … shit … baby I'm … shit baby … I'm … shit … oh my God … oh my … God yes … Oh shit yes … I'm cumming, I'm cumming ohhhhhhhh shhhhhiiiiiitttt!"

My legs locked around him. I screamed. I began to grind against his face. I reached out to him. I held onto his head. I never wanted this moment to end. I didn't want to stop cumming. I began to grind harder and harder against Derryck's face and he held firmly on to my thighs trying to penetrate me with his tongue. He continued to lick my clit, tongue my clit and explore every millimeter of my pleasure principal.

"Baby stop! Baby stop! Derryck! Oh baby please stop! Baby I can't take any more! I can't … Oh shit! Oh shit! OH SHIT! SHIT! STOP! OH FUCK! THAT'S IT! THAT'S IT … THAT'S … IT!"

I pulled away from him barely able to breathe. I gasped for air and turned over in the fetal position trying to grasp the concept of breathing and remembering how to do it on my own without sounding asthmatic. *Cherish the Day* by Sade was going off and I don't even remember it coming on.

It took me ten minutes to get myself together. My vagina was still throbbing with anticipation. Derryck was spooning me and caressing the side of my body. With each stroke of his hand, my body shivered. He loved the way that my body responded to him.

"Get up." I said.

He got up.

"Stand over there."

He smiled and stood against the wall where I told him to stand.

"Anything else?" He said as I sat up.

"Yeah, one more thing."

"What's that?'

"Strip."

He smiled at me and pulled off his pants. As they hit the floor. He stood there in naked glory wearing nothing but a smile.

"Oh my!"

I got my first look at his manhood and baby, a sister was pleased. A little intimidated, but pleased. I looked at 10 beautiful inches of man. Ten inches that I planned to have my every way with.

"Come here." I told him.

He walked over to me and smiled. I took him in my hands, began to masturbate his rock hard member and slowly took him into my mouth. I hadn't had another man in my mouth in years since my husband.

Those were wasted years.

I made up for lost time.

Derryck threw his head back as I licked his shaft, jagged him off, licked his balls, the tip of his penis and gave him head. He began to breathe hard and his pecks rose up and down as I had my way with him. 15 minutes into it, he stopped me and lay me on the bed. I opened my legs and invited him in. I was somewhat anxious at looking at his girth, but just as he was gentle with me before, he was gentle with me again. He put the head in and I let out a moan. My pussy was still wet. This was good because I think it would take all my juices and a lot of will power to accommodate him. He entered me ¾ of the way and we both let out a moan. He worked his way in and out of me slowly. He pulled out all the way to the tip and never went more in me than ¾ of the way. His penis glistened with my juices. Never before had I been so satisfied by a man. Never before had I felt so *full*. With every stroke, with every touch and every kiss, I threatened Derryck again with orgasm. I had never come before from vaginal sex. I didn't know that it was even possible—for me. Derryck put all those doubts to rest. He made love to me over and over and over again. *Lonely Christmas* by Prince was playing now and we made love missionary style, doggy style, woman superior, in the bed, on the couch, in the chair and all over all three suites,

I came three times that night.

Once orally, the other two vaginally.

I came—from dick.

Now you know that had to be some good dick.

When the last song, *God Shiva* by Michelle N Dege' Ocello came on, Derryck came. When I looked at the clock, it was 5:00 AM. The sun was just beginning to come up. He came, and we both went to sleep in each other's arms.

We slept until 6PM.

Then, we started all over again and by 8:00 we ordered room service.

Our first meal of the day bedsides one another.

We ate our meal on the patio balcony of our three bedroom suite.

And we watched the sun go down.

With the passing of the sun, went the last of my inhibition.

I gave Derryck head on the balcony.

He gave me head as well.

He then took my doggy style on the balcony as the winds of Jamaica washed over our bodies.

Isn't reciprocity beautiful?

We bathed each other in the whirlpool bath and then we stepped into the Jacuzzi. I straddled Derryck in the water and he grabbed my ample ass and we made love again well into the night.

We didn't leave the room again for the rest of our stay.

We didn't need to.

I thought that we would tire of each other.

His hunger for me was never satisfied.

My lust for him never waned.

Once again—I found love.

CHAPTER 16

▼

A LIFETIME OF REGRET

MARK

Derryck and Deja returned from Jamaica and something about Deja had changed. She had a glow about her that I hadn't seen since we were first married. She also was sporting a hell of a rock on her right hand. I looked at her left hand to see where our wedding ring was, I was saddened to see that it was gone. While she was away, she somehow expedited our divorce. I was in court trying to explain myself to the judge and her lawyer and good friend presented the court with photos of my infidelity, audio of my dogging Deja out and video footage of my sexual escapades with Mercedes. I was ordered to pay $1100 a month in alimony for mental cruelty and I was also told to give away a portion of my assets.

The company released me upon Derryck and Deja's return. I thought they might keep me, but I was released for violating the company's code of conduct that I helped to write. I was blacklisted from every major financial company in the nation. I was able to get a job with a bank as a broker, but my six figure salary was gone. I tried to go see Deja at the house when she returned, but when I pulled up to the house, there was a sign in the front yard that said, "SOLD." Another of her girlfriend's sold the house that we once lived in. I imagine that she was not only getting closure, she was moving on with her life. Within a year's time, she and Derryck were married. They also had a child. They had a little boy that they named Jaylin.

Mercedes and I had a daughter a few months earlier than Deja and Derryck had their son. I named my daughter Evelyn. I asked Mercedes to marry me and she said no. She took Deja's position at the bank that she worked at although I'm not sure how she got the position, because she wasn't qualified. I would later find out the hard way as to how she moved so far up the ladder in the bank.

One day while at work I became violently ill. I was a broker for Chicago National Bank. I asked my boss could I go home early because I wasn't feeling well. He gave me shit about leaving and I can't believe that I had to work for such an asshole. Just over 15 months ago I made twice what he made, and if he were in the financial firm that I used to work for, he wouldn't even be a manager. He would be working in the mailroom. I only put up with his bullshit because he was willing to overlook the domestic battery on my record.

At any rate, I left work early and drove back to the apartment I now shared with Mercedes. I was shocked when I walked up the stairs to the apartment and heard music outside the apartment door. Mercedes should have been at work. I used my key and opened the door. Music was blaring from the stereo. *Mr. Do Right* by *Jade* was playing, and from our bedroom I heard familiar moans. I felt like *Ron Isley* in an *R. Kelly* and Mr. Big video. I walked up to the doorway and riding on top of a man that I would later find out was her boss, was Mercedes. Our daughter was at the sitters and here she was in our house, in our bed, fucking her boss's brains out. I stood there in awe, tears streaming down my face. I grabbed the radio remote and changed the CD that was playing to track six, *I hate you* by Prince.

Switching songs alerted them both of my presence. Mercedes got up casually. The man however was in a panic not sure of my next move. I went to the closet and retrieved a gun. I came back into the room and pointed the barrel at them both.

Mercedes appeared to be unmoved by the threat of the gun.

The man, her boss, was about to soil the sheets.

With tears streaming down my face I spoke.

"What's going on here?"

"What does it look like?" Mercedes said coldly.

"It looks like you are fucking another man in our bed!"

"My bed."

"What?"

"My bed. Nigga ain't nothing in here in your name."

She was right.

"Mercedes, why?"

"Listen man, I didn't know that she was married and …" Her boss said.

"Shut Up!" I screamed at him.

"I'm not married." Mercedes said to the man underneath her.

"Then who is this?" He asked.

"My crazy *ex-boyfriend, that used to live here.* He's also my baby's daddy."

"Ex boyfriend?" I said.

"Now Mark, I have been telling you that it's over and you need to get your shit and get out of here. Do I need to call the police on you again?"

This was a cold bitch. If she called the police I was looking at time. If he called the police, I was looking at time. I had reached an all time low. I had a choice, kill her or kill myself. My hand trembled with fear. The man, her boss turned a whiter shade of pale. He just knew that today was the day that he might die. I cried. My mind snapped. I had a mental breakdown and I could barely think or speak. Never in a million years would I have guessed that cheating on my wife would bring me so much pain. I heard the front door open and to my surprise there was Reverend Kelly, Deja's Pastor. She walked in the apartment as if God himself commanded her to be here in this specific moment in time.

"Mark, put the gun down."

"Reverend Kelly? What are you doing here?"

"Saving you. Put the gun down brother … please."

"How did you know? I mean why are you here?"

"I'll explain all that after you put the gun down."

"But she … she …"

"… I know baby, I know. Put the gun down."

I lowered the gun and put it on the stereo. I walked into the bathroom and put water on my face. I walked back into the bedroom crying.

"Mercedes … Why?"

"Why what?"

"Why would you cheat on me? Why would you do this to me … to us?"

"You cheated on your wife. What makes you think that I would want to be with you?"

"What?"

"What don't you understand Mark? What else can I say other than, the thrill is gone?"

"So you ruined my life … for nothing?"

"It's like I have been telling you all along Mark, I didn't ruin your life. You did."

"You never loved me?"

"I did, once."

"And now?"

"Now … I'm done with you. Didn't anyone ever tell you that you never leave the wife for the mistress?"

She laughed at me. It was a laugh that burned in my mind for the months to come. The Reverend took my hand and walked me out of the apartment. I looked at her with a puzzled look on my face.

"Reverend Kelly, how did you know?"

"I live across the hall."

"That's how you knew that I was still seeing Mercedes behind Deja's back?"

"I told you to leave her alone."

"How did you know she was no good for me?"

"You're not the first man that she has done this to."

"There were others?"

"Many others. She's a sick woman. She's a beautiful woman, but she's sick."

I was arrested again. I lost my job at the bank. I ended up going back to school and getting a second degree in education. Reverend Kelly appeared with me in court and acted as a character witness. I received three years probation. I taught English at an alternative high school. They were the only place that would hire me. I had $2,000 in student loans, a month, $1100 in alimony to Deja in spite of her re-marrying and another $680.00 in child support that went to Mercedes. I found God that year and began to go to church. I paid my dues, paid my support and eventually got full custody of my daughter. We live in a tiny two bedroom apartment in Alsip Illinois.

When I first started attending church, Reverend Kelly preached a sermon on *A Woman Scorned.* It was a moving sermon about doing right by your woman. It was almost as if she were preaching to me that day. There was no need to however. I think I learned my lesson. I had a damn good woman, and I fucked up. It was hard going to Reverend Kelly's church because this was the same church that Deja and Derryck attended with their son, Jaylin. There were times that I looked at the two of them on Sundays and wondered what could have been. I had the world at my fingertips once upon a time and infidelity took it all away in a heartbeat.

Deja and Derryck left the firm. They have a booming financial business in the hood. Deja and I never spoke again. She did however stop the alimony payments. I guess she had all that she needed now that she had Derryck.

DEJA

I married a wonderful man in Derryck. We made a beautiful life together and we are raising a beautiful boy named Jaylin. He was conceived in Jamaica. He was conceived in love. I have made love to Derryck hundreds of times since that night in Jamaica and I don't know if it's because I am so in love, but every night that we make love is better than the last night that we made love. We built a business in the hood that gave back to the community and I learned a lot about myself from my man. I learned with regard to pain to *Let Go and Let God.*

Peace to you all.

This was my story.

—Mrs. Deja Hamilton.

THE END.

ACKNOWLEDGMENTS

First thanks goes to God for allowing me to complete yet another project.

To my readers, I am nothing without your support!

My fellow authors and friends: Brenda Hampton who has been a sister to me through this whole trip, Author and radio personality Nikki Woods, Lissa Woodson who is the leader of my author's group, Cindi at Waldenbooks in Calumet City, J.L. Woodson, Trista Russell, Leblanc and Earl Sewell I had a blast kicking it with you guys at the Cavalcade of Authors in my hometown of Chicago! Wahida Clark, who has also been an inspiration to me. Marc Gerald, Marc Anthony at Q-Boro Books, Eric Jerome Dickey, Michael Baisden, Travis Hunter, C. Kelly Robinson, Sistah Souljah, Voices Publishing which has been like a second family, WGCI, V-103, Power 92, Melanie Palmer, Knowing Books and Café in Saint Louis, Tracy L. Foster, Devonshe Pearson and all the authors I met at the Saint Louis Event in February 2007.

My people at work: Nicole Logan, Tonona Robinson, Kelly Williams, Susan Cullen, Emerge, Daryl Gaulding, Alexia Leday, Drennon Jones, Wendy Pack, Simona Haqq, Janene Barrett, Wanda Smith, Monique Bodley, Drennon Jones, Will Ellis, Mike Janicki, Ricardo "Rico" Prosper, My union brothers NOLSW Local 2320, Tim Yeager, John Bowman, My NTN Crew: Justus, BB, Adrienne, Geneva, Ms. Bessie, Trina, Mandy, Amy, Timel, My little sister Farrah Ellison, Andrea Johnson, Andrew, Terrell, Larry Gill, Barry Reed, Cortaiga "Country" Johnson, Adrienne Thomas, and all the other staff at NTN.

Friends and Family: My bartender, Adrienne "AB" Banks, Lisa Thomas, David Allen, David Wilson, The Gandy Family, The Blakemores, Melanie

Griffen, The Lowery Family, The Smith Family, R.I.P. Keith Lloyd Jackson, Jeffrey Lamont Allen, Mark Groves.

Hugs and kisses to: Leslie Swanson, you were there when I was in the valley of death. R.I.P. to my grandmother Virginia D. Clay "Ginger" also to my extended peeps, Carmen MacIntyre, Kyle Underwood, Noonie, Robin, Dimples, Wootie, Tanisha Underwood, Dani, Yvette, Yvonne, Kevin, Ant, Two Fingers Entertainment, Sean G-My brother and my ship/flight "863". Jo Oliver, Korie Kellog, Dionne Johnson, Genia Bishop, Stephanie Drayton, Michelle Alexander, Nancy Rodriguez, Joy Johnson, Loretta Carter and my extended family and friends like Davetta Collins, Rose Marie Speed & Nurse Sonja.

I want to say hello to some young adults whose lives I have touched and whose lives have touched me. They are: Kirby, Porcha, Ebony, Denise, Erica B, Eric, Myra, Andrew, Tyris, Izabella, Mike, Rico, Xneia, Keisha, and Keneshia. To all the kids in the Emerge Program, although I am no longer your caseworker, I am now your friend and still your mentor.

Rest in Peace once again to Virgina D. Clay-My Grams, "I love you."
To anyone else that I have forgotten, charge it to my head and not my heart. If you truly know me, then you know that I stay busy and time is a luxury that I very seldom have.

AUTHOR'S NOTES

What's up! I just stopped in to say hi to you readers and to ask that you check out my website at www.dlsmith.net and feel free to email me at chicagoauthor@yahoo.com

So, another one down, huh? I want to thank each of you that have stayed with me on this journey. It has indeed been a journey. 2005 was a rough year for me and 2007 should prove to be a prosperous year. Many of you know that I had a P.E. that took me out for most of the year. I thank you all for the prayers and support. The cards, letters and prayers were felt even when I was unconscious. It felt like a half million people prayed for me.

This book was written in about three weeks. Actually, I did the first 100 pages in two weeks and in a fit of anger, I finished the last 190 in a day (no joke). At any rate I hope you enjoy this book as much as I enjoyed writing it. I started to end it with Mark getting back on a train one day and seeing Deja and Derryck on the train and Mark getting off saying, "That's okay, I'll get the next one" meaning that the next good woman that comes along, he will get her and do right by her. I didn't think anyone would get what I meant by that, so I left it out.

So what's next? One more book and then I am retiring the pen for a while. I mean, I will write, but publishing, who knows? I plan to go back to school, finish that Masters Program (that being sick stole from me) and getting back to God. I am working on stage plays, doing some acting, consulting work and looking into investments. I also plan to get married again although I have no idea when. I welcome your feedback on this book and if you want me to do a signing, check out my website and call me.

(The above were the original notes left back in 2005)

Author's Notes (written November 24, 2006)

What's up readers? I finished this book in November of 2005 and decided to release it in Spring 2007. I proofed it to the best of my ability and it is my hope that this book has fewer errors than my previous ones. This is a work of fiction. This is not my story although I have to admit that various events influenced it. Each time that I release a book a get emails at chicagoauthor@yahoo.com where women write in and say, "A real woman would never do _____." I know the emails are coming, but I tested this book out on a test audience and I talked with women who have been mistresses to men and many say that this book is on point.

I got the idea about the hidden cameras from a guy that I know and have little respect for. The guy was at a previous job showing pictures and footage of unsuspecting women that he had bedded in the workplace. This guy was in upper management and did not seem like "the type" that would do something foul like this. I decided that was something that I could incorporate in a book.

I know a lot of men that have indeed left their wives for their mistresses just to be burned by them later with either a child, STD's or simply lifelong heartache. One of my friends is a master player that did his wife *so wrong,* she did indeed go out and begin seeing another man, who approached my boy and asked him to leave the woman alone and allow someone else to love her. So that is where the concept of Derryck comes in.

I wasn't going to release this book. It was just sitting around and one day I decided to do something with it. I am trying to incorporate a number of different styles in my writing. I remember while writing this that Stephen King has characters that you love to hate and characters that you really root for in his books. I wanted Mark to be someone that the readers hated and Deja to be triumphant.

Each time that Deja thought things could not be worse, they were. Each time that she tried to forgive Mark, he reached a new low. I know women that have been burned by men like this. I know women whom have had men go through their credit, sleep with their sisters, cheat, abuse them and do the whole nine yards. Many of these women are good women, but they will never trust a man again and who can blame them? I know a lot of good men that are madly in love with good women, but those women have been *so burned,* that they don't allow anyone else in their hearts.

I would like to invite you to continue to visit my website at www.dlsmith.net. In 2007, I am going to try to keep the website updated and have new pictures posted monthly as well as what is going on with me. I am still in school and I finally left social services in May 2006. Many of you know that I have been talking about doing that for years. I am still working, I will be done with school sometime in 2007 and in the meanwhile, writing will still be my outlet. My hope is that one day a major publisher will come and sign me and re-release all of my previous books with no errors in them (Damn that would be cool).

I have written other books that are just lying around the house and to minimize errors, I will proof them two or three times and continue to pay other people to edit them as well. Many of you have commented on amazon.com that you want me to put a better product out there and I am working on it. That's all for now. I love you guys and you each keep me going. Peace from Chicago!

BOOK CLUB QUESTIONS

1. Do women really know when a man is cheating? Deja seemed to know from the start. Is there really a such thing as women's intuition?

2. Do you believe that women that are mistresses will go as far as Mercedes did with regard to oral and anal sex?

3. Was Mercedes mentally ill in your opinion or just a bitch?

4. The way that Mark and Deja met, is that realistic? Have you ever met a man and was looking "a hot mess?"

5. If a man cheats on a woman, should the woman cheat back and get even or do the right thing?

6. Why do some men start off romantic in the beginning and later fall off?

7. How can you tell if a man is cheating?

8. Derryck is younger than Deja. How much younger would you be willing to date a man?

9. What is the difference between younger men and older men in and out of the bedroom?

10. Would you ever (or have you ever) let someone film you?

11. Mercedes brings up a threesome, do you think there are mistresses willing to go there? What about wives? Have you?

12. At one point, Deja tries to win her man back by sleeping with Mark *even though she knows he is sleeping with someone else.* Could you do this?

13. Would you try and win your man back if there was another woman?

14. Would you forgive your significant other for cheating if you thought it was a one time thing?

15. Is it true that more successful black men have mistresses in apartments and are paying their bills?

16. Do you have other women in the office that you hate for no reason? Why?

17. Why do women let men abuse them and ruin them to the point that they may be no good for the next man?

18. Would you consider counseling if your relationship was in trouble?

19. What would you change about this book?

20. How were the sex scenes in the book?

21. Have you ever been the other woman? Why?

- Write down questions that you have about this book or the author. Want to see Darrin Lowery in person or invite him to your book club outing? Send him an email at chicagoauthor@yahoo.com

978-0-595-43687-3
0-595-43687-0

CPSIA information can be obtained at www.ICGtesting.com
Printed in the USA
LVOW041717030812

292843LV00008B/49/A